When would-be diamond miner, Andrew Burns, disappears with Lizzy Lawson's life savings, she's determined to track him down. With the help of local man, Henry Morgan, she locates Burns at his clapped-out mine in Western Australia's Kimberley, but it looks like he has been murdered. Lizzy has motive and opportunity, so the police lay charges.

For Lizzy to prove her innocence, she must navigate a dark web of outback betrayal, littered with fake diamonds, real diamonds and odd characters who aren't always who they seem to be. Along the way, with the help of Henry's mother, Rosie, Lizzy becomes a student of the Dreamtime, encountering hangovers from a dark past of white occupation and the establishment of one of the world's largest diamond mines.

Most of all, in her Season of the River, Lizzy will find out who she really is, and the person she wants to be.

First Edition Stories of Oz Publishing 2023

storiesofoz.com

ozbookstore.com

admin@ozbookstore.com

© 2023 Chris Muir

ISBN: 978-0-6453511-7-0

Cover design: Angus Crowley

Cover Artwork: Angus Crowley

Proofreading: Brad Connors

Typeset in 12/16 Bembo

SEASON OF THE RIVER

CHRIS MUIR

Also by Chris Muir

Random House

A Savage Garden

For my wonderful sons, Luca, and Liam. Be curious.

CHAPTER 1

Most of the passengers panicked and crossed themselves as their plane was swallowed whole by mountains of swirling, black thunderheads that looked more like a greasy bouillabaisse of street brawlers' black eyes, but not Lizzy Lawson. While QF1652 shuddered and flashes of lightning jagged her face, she sat calmly, staring at an invisible spot a million miles in front of her. All she could think about was Andrew Burns; how savagely he had betrayed her, and what she had to do if she ever wanted to feel whole again.

She had tried passing the time reading, but a novel lay neglected on the seat next to her. On top of it was a pen and a well-thumbed document with a cover sheet that read Adamas Mine, Tenement #12967/99 Summary of Geological Findings and scrawled under it, a love-heart with the initials LL AB; Burns' handiwork in a moment of pretend tenderness. She brushed her hand over the page, stalled on the love-heart, and viciously scribbled it out until it was a mess of ink and paper shreds, then shook her head in disgust just as the plane emerged from endless black into a clear blue sky.

Below, kilometre upon kilometre of orange and black-striped mountain-sized beehive mounds seemed to ebb and flow as if they were an ocean of terracotta waves. Among the domes, an ancient world of vertical gorges was lined with sky-high palm trees and all manner of Jurassic ferns. Lizzy could make out a wide plateau of time-smoothed sandstone and beyond that, scraggly woodlands of eucalyptus and acacia. Past the trees, straw spinifex grass wilted in the sun. Then there was a hodgepodge of Mitchell grasslands, samphire shrubland and tropical savannah broken by the occasional herd of galloping wild camels throwing up dust clouds.

'Ladies and gentlemen, the worst of the storm is behind us, but please keep your seatbelts securely fastened,' crackled the pilot, through a speaker above Lizzy's head. 'We will be landing at Kununurra in about twenty minutes. The local time is 12.35pm, and the temperature on the ground is thirty-nine degrees Celsius. For our overseas visitors, that's one hundred-and two-degrees Fahrenheit, so it's another warm day here in sunny Western Australia.'

Lizzy didn't hear the pilot, or if she did, she didn't react. She just kept staring out the window at those odd-shaped mountains. For some reason, they entranced and confused her in equal measure. What were they? Why did she feel like they were pulling her towards them? Where had she seen them before? What did they have to do with finding Andrew Burns? She had no idea.

The plane levelled out, rocketed past Lake Argyle, then headed north-north-west. She could make out a large river draining into Joseph Bonaparte Gulf where the Indian Ocean and the Timor Sea meet, and back to the south, smaller dry riverbeds wound their way across the landscape like a thousand stillborn snakes. Soon after, the jet bounced onto a remote runway with its flaps on full and its engines' reverse thrust groaning. Then, just when it looked as though it might run out of bitumen, and career off into a field, it stopped, turned and taxied to a halt outside the terminal building. Along with a dozen or so other relieved passengers, Lizzy stepped out of the plane only to be pummelled by a blast of hot, dry wind and the feeling she was stepping into a world beyond her comprehension. It was a feeling made all-the-more ominous by a cocoon of purple-black sky, the distant rumbling of thunder and the empty *arrk, arrk* of a single crow circling overhead. She hesitated at the top of the stairs, wiped her brow, bit her lip, and took her first step towards revenge.

CHAPTER 2

Inside the terminal Lizzy asked about the car she had hired but was met with a lazy shrug from a woman too busy with a crossword puzzle to reply. The woman licked her pencil, filled in some squares, then looked over the top of her glasses.

'You must be Lizzy Lawson then?'

'Yes, that's right. I am.'

'Well I've got some bad news for ya love. Ronny, he's our mechanic, he called about half-an-hour ago, he said ta tell ya that ya car is rooted; blew a head-gasket, so ya can't rent it no more.'

'You're kidding me, right?'

'Suit ya self, love.'

'Is there anyone else I can hire a car from?'

'This ain't the big smoke love. Everyone is booked out this week. There is some big miners do downtown. We ain't got a million cars on tap or nothin' like that.'

'But ...'

'Can't help ya.'

'But ...'

'Do ya know a six-letter word that means possible?'

Standing on the curb outside the terminal, Lizzy looked like a Dorothy who had come all the way to Oz only to find no one home. A **tear** wound its way down her cheek.

'Are ya waitin' for someone?' asked a man, loading a utility **truck** nearby.

'Excuse me?' she replied, wiping dust out of her eyes with the **back** of her hand.

'I said, are ya waitin' for someone?'

'No, no I'm just, well I'm, I'm just wondering how I'm going to **get** to a place called Mistake Creek. Adamas Mine. Do you know it?'

'Mistake Creek ya say?'

'Yes. Do you know it?'

'Well I'll be stuffed. It's ya lucky day love. I'm goin' sort of that **way** meself, well near to it anyway, that's if I can beat this bloody storm **that** is. I've gotta deliver this stuff to that old bastard Jimmy Orion,' explained the man, indicating ten beer kegs he had just finished securing **with** ropes. 'He owns a pub, at least that's what he calls it. It's not too far **from** Mistake Creek, just a hundred or so kilometres further on. I've **driven** further for a loaf of bloody bread.'

'Thank you but I ...'

'Don't thank me love, there's not very bloody much there.'

'Is there anything, anything at all?'

'Haven't been out that far in a while. As far as I remember there's **just** a coupla cattle stations and few old shacks, but there's plenty of **them** drongo half-wit miners lost out there somewhere though. Bloody **idiots.**'

'Is there another way to get there?'

'Nah love. It's me or nothin',' he lied. 'Hop in. We'll getcha a **ride** to Mistake Creek at Orion's. A good lookin' sheila like you **shouldn't** have no problems; no problems at all. Jimmy has a few rooms so ya **can** even stay there if ya want. They're not much, but it's a place to **put ya** head down at night. The only trouble is ya might have to stay for a **while** if those bloody clouds up there drop their load.'

'Can I hire a car somewhere, a taxi? Maybe there's a bus?'

'Ya gotta be kiddin' love. A lady like you shouldn't be out in that by yaself. Ya never knows what could happen to ya. Do ya?'

'What do you mean?'

'Never mind love, best we don't talk about that kind of stuff. Strange things happen out there, especially in a storm. Ya don't want that do ya? Hop in.'

Lizzy swallowed hard and looked the man up and down. She didn't have to look very far. Rising only five feet from the road, he was more like an animated garden gnome than a truck driver. She hesitated for a moment, but the man's toothy grin made him look harmless enough; if maybe a little half-witted.

'Your truck looks like it knows the way all by itself.'

'She's not much, but she's as faithful as a blind man's dog. Do ya want a ride or don't ya?'

Lizzy looked up at the sky and grimaced. 'That would be very kind of you Mister ah?'

'Miles, Shorty Miles. Pleased ta meet ya.'

'Elizabeth, Elizabeth Lawson. People call me Lizzy.'

Shorty wiped his hands on his filthy shorts, shook her hand, blushed, and made a show of running around to open her door.

'Let me just get rid of some of this bloody junk before ya get in. Hang on a tick.'

Shorty grabbed mouldy sandwiches, old newspapers and long overdue crumpled bills and threw them into the back of his truck along with the beer kegs and a blue-grey cattle dog.

'This is me mate, Lucky,' said the gnome, patting the dog.

'Lucky?'

'That's his name. He's deaf in one ear, blind in one eye and as ya can see, he's only got three bloody legs. He likes ta chase them road trains. Sometimes he gets a bit too bloody close for comfort.'

'Lucky huh?'

'It's what they call irony, love. Don't they teach ya that where ya come from?'

Lizzy felt the smart of the gentle rebuke but bit her tongue. 'It's very kind of you to offer me a ride.'

'No problem love, no problem at all. What brings ya to this neck of the woods anyway?' replied Shorty, as they drove off.

'I'm looking for a man.' she replied, trying to find a place for her feet among the remaining rubbish on the floor.

Shorty looked at her strangely. There was an odd glimmer of hope in his eye; hope that *the man* might be him.

'A man?'

'No not like that. I'm looking for a man who owns a mine. At least that's what he says.'

'Well bugger me love, you've just described every second bloke for a thousand bloody miles. They've either got a mine that does bugger all, or they're gonna get one … one of these days.'

'His name is Andrew Burns. Do you know him?'

'Nope. Never heard of him.'

'He's a geologist.'

'I thought that ya said he was a miner?'

'He is.'

'I knew it.'

'What?'

'I never met a geologist who didn't want to be a miner. They get sick of finding all that shit for other people ta make a fortune. Sometimes they even find good stuff but tell people there's nothin' there so they can go back and get it for themselves. They just wait until the lease runs out or the owner stuffs up and don't pay their rent because they think it's worthless. Government says ya gotta use it or lose it. People forget.'

Shorty was normally a man of few words but by the time they turned south onto the thin needle of highway connecting the south of the Kimberley with the north, he was loosening up. Four hours later, when they bounced off the Great Northern Highway onto the rut-riddled excuse for a road to Orion's, Shorty was still jabbering ten to the dozen. As his confidence grew, he entertained Lizzy with grim tales of outback survival and his glory days as a carnival boxer when he had taken on ten drunks at a time; two shows a day and never been beaten. The wife, who had left him for a truck driver, got a snarly dissection and the shortcomings of every government, no matter which political persuasion, also got a good going over. Lizzy didn't mind though; it helped to pass the time and took her mind off the ugly reason she had come to the Kimberley.

CHAPTER 3

Eventually, Orion's pub appeared on a lonesome road with only a shawl of bustling rain clouds for company, and if not for a couple of dusty motor homes and 4WDs parked outside it and Shorty's local knowledge, Lizzy would have continued straight past it, excusing it as just another of the rundown, deserted buildings along the way.

'This is it? Are you sure?'

'It's not much, but that's what passes for a pub in the back of beyond. Be careful when ya get out. It ain't air-conditioned out there. Ya might get a bit of a bloody surprise. It'll be hot enough to cook a goanna on a tin roof.'

To prove Shorty's point, half-a-dozen mongrel dogs lay on the pub's wide wooden veranda, panting with their tongues dangling somewhere between their knees and paws.

'It's better inside.' encouraged Shorty, noticing Lizzy's hesitation. 'But not much.'

Orion's was the outpost of outposts, and if not for a smattering of low-grade iron ore found by a lunatic Englishman in the 1920s, it wouldn't exist. It's a place where small-time, would-be miners have a drink or twenty; reprovision; tell lies to gullible backpackers and grey nomads about the riches they've discovered then breast the bar asking for credit. Orion's *ask no questions get told no lies* policy meant its regulars were an asylum of misfits who all had something to hide, but mostly, they were ghosts living an after-life, because they could never return to the one they once had.

'The ah, the pub … it looks as though it's going to fall down,' grimaced Lizzy, finally opening the car door.

'Yeah love, and sometimes it bloody-well does.'

She took a tentative step onto the veranda, testing it to make sure that the weather-beaten timber would take her weight. Then, satisfied that it may be stronger than it looked, continued towards the door with Lucky and Shorty as attentive shadows.

'Who do I see about a room?' she asked, to no-one-in-particular while she inhaled the smell of stale sweat and failure.

Ten men, who looked like they might be regulars, looked at each other for a moment and then one-by-one, timidly raised their hands. An array of yellow-toothed grins smiled back at her and a few of them even tried to put some order in their greasy hair. Those who wore shirts attempted to button them. They needn't have bothered. Most were fighting a losing battle with their ample guts and fruitless attempts to attract the attention of two Swedish-looking girls trying to get phone reception by standing on rickety chairs.

After what seemed like an endless procession of drop-jawed stares, James, *call me Jimmy,* Orion introduced himself and ordered Shorty *to get the hell out the way and take the lady's bag to Room Two* then escorted Lizzy to the bar to register. It seemed an unnecessary formality, but nevertheless, she wrote her name and address in a thick, grease-covered book then pushed it back across the eucalyptus slab bar.

'That'll be fifty bucks, seventy-five if you want two nights,' said Orion, in a high- pitched whine usually reserved for jockeys and remote-control, model airplanes.

The noise came out of a fifty-something, skinny, leathered face with deep squint-furrows around both eyes. A bush of hair sprouted from each nostril of a pock-marked nose which shone. Probably from too many years drinking his own profits. Even though Orion wasn't much taller than Shorty Miles, somehow it seemed that he was. Perhaps it was his perpetually puffed out chest or his slicked-back hair which gave him an air of imperious self-possession. Then again, it may have been the orthopaedic lifts inside his battered crocodile skin cowboy boots.

Lizzy counted out fifty dollars. He looked disappointed.

'So, just the one night then?'

'I guess so.'

'Bloody pity that,' he whispered, under his breath.

'Excuse me?'

'Never mind love. I was just thinkin' out loud.'

The floral carpet in Room Two had clearly been part of another smaller room at some point during its long life. Where it fell short of the walls, shallow pools of dust and cobwebs had gathered, and the carpet's ends had frayed. Wafting up from it was the lingering odour of vomit and stale beer. Completing the olfactory stew was a healthy serve of mould. Lizzy gagged and as she looked around the room, she saw that pink paint had paid a visit to the walls in the distant past, but if appearances were correct, the paint and the walls had been feuding ever since. Now they barely spoke. In another corner, a knobby stem in a pot, with dead leaves attached, did it's best to impersonate a small tree. Covering the single window was a fly-blown Venetian blind which once may have been white. A sign on the back of the door pronounced, *No loaded guns, no feeding dogs, no oil drums, no repairing engines, no spitting,, no snotting out the window, no skinning dead animals. Toilet and bathroom down the hall to the left. To be used by paying guests only. No whores allowed in rooms by themselves.* It looked like it had been there for quite some time and was signed by *James Orion, Proprietor.*

In two small steps Lizzy reached a single bed and not seeing anything else which resembled anything to sit on, lowered herself down, but immediately fell into a deep trough. She leaned forward, trying to get to her feet, and when her backside finally rested on the bed's hard edge, she sat staring at a conga line of ants making their way along the skirting boards and disappearing into a hole in the floorboards.

'So, what now Andrew?' she mumbled to herself, 'What on God's earth should I do now you selfish bastard?'

In her mind, a thousand thoughts collided; if only she had never met Andrew Burns, if only she had been wise to his deception earlier, but mostly, Lizzy wondered why she had come to that alien world, which seemed to have no oxygen and no way back to earth. 'Houston, we have a problem.' quivered on the edge of her lips, but nothing came out. The glue of fear had done its job well.

The old-fashioned wind-up clock on the bedside table ticked loudly, keeping time with her heartbeat, while outside, the wind scratched at her window. In her sadness, she curled up in the hollow of the bed and clutched the small diamond pendant she always wore around her neck. She held it tightly, like it would escape if she didn't, and tried to hide from what she had to do.

CHAPTER 4

At seven o'clock Jimmy Orion knocked on the door of Room Two.

'Are you gonna be eating tonight. Last orders at eight and it's seven thirty already.' he yelled.

'Be there in five.' Lizzy replied, lifting herself off the bed.

Ten minutes later the swearing, spitting, arm wrestling and pool games stopped dead.

'Fuck me dead.' said one of the men, missing his mouth and pouring beer down his chest. Lizzy's hair was tied back, she was wearing a hint of make-up and the sleeves of her white shirt were rolled up to her elbows. It fell over a pair of faded jeans and her five feet-six inches was extended to five feet-nine with a pair of boots. Only the sound of the wind outside the pub interrupted the click of her heels on the floorboards as she walked towards the bar.

Lizzy had never thought of herself as an attractive woman, although many well-meaning mothers of girlfriends said she had 'potential' (whatever that is). The fact was, she was too busy worrying about how to make ends meet to care too much about how she looked; and after her husband died two years before, well, it didn't seem to matter all that much anyway. In that moment though, none of that was important to the motley collection of men. She had a pulse. That was all that mattered. Millions of years of primordial attraction were in play, regardless of their chance of success.

Approaching the bar, Lizzy tried not to make eye contact, because she had the terrible feeling that she was the last girl at the dance and was surrounded by life's leftovers who all had bad intentions. Even the two twenty-something backpackers wearing cowboy hats and University of Colorado t-shirts took a break from their pool game and licked their lips. She dusted off a bar stool and ordered a glass of wine, but the ferret-faced barman just stared at her as he cleaned the same glass over-and-over again.

'Got none of that wine stuff … not stuff you can drink anyhow. How about a beer?' interrupted Orion, pushing the mute out of the way.

'Okay, a beer it is. Thanks.'

'What brings a sheila like you to a shithole like this anyway?' asked Orion, pulling the beer.

'Well to be perfectly honest, I'm not really sure.'

'Nobody comes all this bloody way for no reason love. Even them tourist dickheads in them pretend cowboy hats are just tickin' something off their bucket list.'

'Have you heard of a man called Andrew Burns?' Lizzy replied.

'Yeah, he's that geologist fella, crazy in the head if ya ask me. He was in here the other night.'

'Really? Here? So, you know him?'

'Nah, I told ya that because I need ta tell a good lie every day. Of course, he bloody was.'

'Do you know where he went?'

'Dunno. He wanted a room, but we were full … first Thursday of the month … the hookers were … ah never mind about that … he just kept on drivin' east. That was the last I saw of him.'

'He has a mine. Do you know where it is?'

'Nah love. It's out there somewhere. Couldn't tell ya where though. That fella is like bloody Christmas. He comes in here once a year, shouts the bar and then disappears.'

'His mine is called Adamas. It's supposed to be at a place called Mistake Creek.'

'Posh mine ... it's got a name and all ... very la de da ... like I said ... it could be anywhere out there ... Mistake Creek isn't really a place though love, it's more like a convenient dot on a map on ya way to somewhere else.'

'I see.'

'Sorry that I couldn't be more helpful but let me tell ya this for nothin', if ya do decide to sort out ya curiosity, just remember that there's lots of room ta get lost out there and never be seen again. Happens all the time.'

'So you don't know where his mine is, but you do know Andrew Burns.'

'Yep that's about it, but one of them idiots over there might know where it is. Ask 'em.'

'Ya wanna play pool?' interrupted Shorty. 'I reckon I can get ya in ahead of all them other ratbags waitin'.'

Lizzy shrugged and walked over to a well-used pool table that had sides etched with an assortment of initials, blasphemy and crude stick-figure drawings that gave it the appearance of some-kind-of outback Karma Sutra. The once green baize top had faded to a vomitus yellow and sported a variety of stains.

'Do ya play?' asked Shorty, looking up at a chalkboard where the next player's name was written.

'A little.'

'Then you'll be playin' that bloke over there.' replied Shorty, nodding towards a man. 'His name is Henry, Henry Morgan; after the rum.'

Morgan was as black as the night, stood at least six feet-five inches tall and his greying whiskers needed a shave. Lizzy guessed he was about sixty, maybe sixty-five. He wore a faded khaki shirt, and matching trousers, held up by a wide belt sporting a saucer-sized buckle, which judging by the bucking horse engraved on it, was a rodeo award. Morgan was bare footed, held an almost empty beer glass and swayed like a sapling in a strong wind.

'Pleased to meet you, Henry,' said Lizzy, shaking his hand after he had wiped it on his trousers. He grinned but didn't reply.

The men who frequented Orion's reckoned that Henry got his pool practice using spears, emu eggs and the rolling hills as his never-ending table. Some said he was the only person who played on table a thousand miles on every side and never got tired of walking a hundred miles to play another shot. In truth, Morgan was a chameleon who lived a double life, whiter than white when he was around Orion's, and blacker than black the moment The Kimberley swallowed him up again. He was a will-o'-the-wisp, known to disappear for months on end, then reappear for a game of white fella's pool and too many beers.

Shorty Miles racked up the balls making a great show of his gentlemanly assistance.

'You break 'em. It might be the only bloody shot ya get.' laughed Henry.

She smiled, lined up the white ball and steered it into the triangle of balls that splintered and the 3 dropped into the right-hand corner pocket. Thwack! The two side pockets were filled with the 7 and 9 simultaneously. She moved around the table quickly, lined up her next shot and fired. Plop! In went the 11.

'Beginner's luck.' she smiled, then fired off her next missile which flew straight to the far corner and paused for a moment, before doing her bidding. Within minutes she had cleared all her balls except for the black. It was an easy shot, even a beginner could have sunk, but as she lined up the ball, she seemed to change her mind and turned to the men who had to quickly pretend they weren't staring at her rear end.

'Do any of you gentlemen know how I can get to Andrew Burns' mine? It's called Adamas. It's at Mistake Creek.'

All the faces remained universally blank until Henry spoke up.

'Yeah, this stupid black fella knows the way. But it's gonna cost ya plenty.'

Lizzy smiled, lined up the black ball and sunk the white off it. Henry had won.

'I'll take ya there in the morning.' laughed Henry. 'Nice of ya to lose on purpose, now all ya gotta do is play some other fella for a truck to get us there, unless ya wanna walk of course.' added Henry, slapping his knees and falling about until he was laughing so hard that the beer, he was drinking gushed out his nose like an exploding geyser. When it looked like he might choke, Lizzy slapped him on the back.

'Hey watch it. This black fella, he don't get bashed by no bloody white lady.'

He watched Lizzy's face turn to embarrassment and then erupted with laughter all over again and fell backwards onto a broken juke box.

'Okay, who wants to play for a loan of their truck?' she asked, but they had seen her skill, so no-one was game enough until Orion dangled a set of keys under her nose.

'You win, you got 'em for two days. That's it.'

'Sounds fair.'

They played shot for shot for the next ten minutes until finally only the black ball and white ball were left on the table.

'Looks like you're not goin' anywhere.' smirked Orion.

'Looks to me like you're stuck in this fine establishment for two days without a car.' she replied, lining up her shot.

'What do you think Henry?'

He shrugged. 'Dunno missus. Jimmy, he's won that trophy over there above the bar for the last five bloody years.'

The toilet-seat award had crossed billiard cues glued to it and sure enough, the name Jimmy Orion was emblazoned on it five times.

'Well, he might have to make room for another name.' she smiled, then without hesitation, pocketed the black ball.

'Mr. Orion, I suppose that means I get your truck.'

It was more of a question than a statement because the truth-be-told, Lizzy still didn't know how to be a winner. She never had.

'Two bloody days, that's all.' huffed Orion, throwing the keys on the table then stomping off towards the bar like a petulant child.

Ten minutes later Lizzy was getting ready for bed when there was a knock at the door. She opened it. Orion was wearing a clean shirt; his hair was slicked back, and he smelt like an after-shave factory. He was holding a bottle of cheap champagne.

'Is there something I can do for you Mr. Orion?'

'No, no, it ain't what ya thinkin.' he replied, preferring to take the coward's way out and give in easily, rather than admit his true intentions. 'I was just gonna tell ya that ya gotta be careful of that Henry Morgan fella. He's a brick short of a load ya know. He's just as likely to go walkabout while you're out there in the middle of nowhere. You gotta be careful that he doesn't just leave ya to the crows. I thought you should know what you're getting yaself into. That's all.'

'Mr. Orion, something tells me that it might be you that I need to be careful of.'

Orion tried to speak, but all that came out was a stammering barrage of *ands* and *buts* and *I thoughts*. Lizzy frowned, reached for the doorknob and Orion stepped out of her way. She was just about to close the door when she looked back to see Orion still standing there, despondently offering his bottle of champagne like it was a suitable replacement for his lack of coherence.

'Good night Mr. Orion. Sleep well.'

She closed the door before he had time to say anything else, locked it and pushed the pot with the dead tree in it up against it for some imagined extra security.

Only a small courtyard separated Room Two from the bar's toilets and the louvered windows allowed conversations to travel easily, so for a goodly part of the night, she had to listen to burps, farts and obscene comments about her *bits*. One man thought her *tits* were *bloody magnificent*. That made her blush, but one brutal commentator said her butt *hung lower than a snake's belly*. The resulting fisticuffs concerned her, and she wondered who her Sir Galahad might have been. Finally, sleep overtook her and as she drifted off, the voices inside her head tried to navigate the pathways of her memory to discover why her life had suddenly made such an odd turn and taken her to this place; this place where the wind was so hot that hell must not be far off.

CHAPTER 5

Lizzy woke before the sun was a crease in God's yawn and lay on the bed wondering what to do next. As she played possible plans over and over in her head, a small sliver of red and bright orange sun poked over the horizon, so she heaved herself out of the pit of her bed. Outside the window, two morose looking, black-eyed wild donkeys had come to raid the garbage bins, but when she opened the blinds, they just looked up for a moment and went back to their foraging.

The previous night Lizzy had resolved not to visit the conveniences down the hallway at any cost, but by morning she was fighting a losing battle with her bladder. She dressed quickly and opened the door, but when she did, a seated, cross-legged corpse fell into her room with a thud.

'What the ... !' screamed Lizzy, not knowing who it was.

The dozing body jumped to its feet, sporting the biggest black eye she had ever seen. Even on Morgan's ebony-coloured skin, the shiner was world-class, and she knew instantly who had defended her honour the night before.

'Ah shit. Sorry. I musta dozed off. Are ya ready to go? Let's go before it gets too bloody hot hey?'

'Henry, I'll be right with you, but right now nature calls.'

'Ah, don't ya bloody go down there.' he replied, looking down the corridor. 'The roaches, they're the size of bloody cows.'

She shivered.

'Mr. Orion, he's got what he calls the Royal Suite. It's this way. You come with me ... real quiet now. No-one is supposta know about it, especially me.'

Henry led Lizzy down the corridor through the empty bar, across the front veranda and up to a locked door where he reached up onto a ledge and after a few seconds of flying dust and fluff, located an over-sized key.

The door opened into a spacious room where three red, velvet couches formed a U-shape around a carved mahogany coffee table with magazines neatly fanned out on top. Expensive rugs covered the floor and large oil paintings of outback scenes battled to find spaces on three of the four walls. The remaining wall was lined from top to bottom with shelves which held leather-bound books, an ancient CD player, speakers, and a dozen small porcelain statues of women in crinoline dresses carrying delicate parasols.

'My god,' she said, taking in the room. 'I thought you were joking. This is well, quite a surprise.'

'It'll be a bloody surprise if Jimmy finds us here. Better be quick missus. In here.' said Henry, pointing to another door.

Lizzy opened it and thought she was on yet another planet. Black marble tiles covered every wall and flowed down to an impressive basin and vanity. Gold taps sat above it and long gold spouts, fashioned to look like flamingos, jutted out. To her left, a large black marble bath mirrored the vanity and a collection of white towels hung from a rail. The floor was alternate black and white marble checks and led straight to a black marble toilet and bidet with gold taps and levers.

She stepped in, slammed the door in Henry's face, but not realizing he was following, opened it again, apologized and rushed back in but then the door opened again.

'My God Henry, what's all this doing all the way out here?'

'Mrs Orion. Jimmy had to build it, way back, to get her to come and

27

live out here. She died ten years ago. Now he just uses it for his prostitutes.'

Lizzy turned up her nose but didn't object.

'I'm going to have a shower and I'll be right with you, okay?'

'No problem. I'll just sit here and read this,' laughed the hungover, sometimes stockman, holding a magazine upside down.

She emerged ten minutes later smiling, offering profuse thanks.

'Better go. Jimmy gets kinda funny about this place. No-one is supposed to know about it but them whores on Kitty Flanagan's bus, they just can't keep their bloody mouths shut,' explained Henry, rushing her out the door.

They were soon struggling along in Orion's Toyota making poor time towards Mistake Creek. There was other traffic on the road, motor bikes loaded down with camping equipment, dusty motor homes, dustier 4WDs and even a double-decker bus painted bright yellow, but they were all heading in the other direction like virgin burglars running from a savage Doberman.

'Where are they all going Henry?'

'Anywhere but here. See them black clouds, bloody rain is comin.' Wet time comin' here in The Kimberley. Pretty soon these roads won't be no good for drivin' no more.'

'You mean worse than this?'

'Sure missus, plenty worse.'

'How long will it take to get to Mistake Creek?'

'Coupla hours I suppose.'

Mistake Creek was only about one hundred kilometres to the east, but Henry had failed to inform her they would be driving through loose soil littered with razor-sharp shale, so just half-an-hour into their journey, Orion's Toyota flp flp flped to a slow stop.

While Henry changed the tyre, Lizzy lent against the bull-bar at the front staring out towards where the sun was spreading over the beehive shaped mountains she had seen from the plane. For a long time, she was silent, lost in a reverie of imagining, staring at the mountains, and wondering if she had made the right decision to come all the way from Sydney on what could almost certainly, be a wild goose chase, but then a question occurred to her. Perhaps she wasn't the first person to make the mistake of going there.

'Why is it called Mistake Creek, Henry?'

'Because a long time ago some white fella made a bloody big mistake missus, that's why,' replied Henry, starting to change the tyre.

'Yeah, I figured that, but what kind of mistake?'

'White fella tells one story ... us black fellas, we tell another one.'

'Will you tell me?'

'Sure missus, it's got a bit confused over the years. Shit!'

'Are you okay?

'Yeah, the wheel-brace just slipped off the bloody nut ...'

'Are you sure you're, okay?'

'Right as rain ... got another hand, so no problem ... anyway, white fellas say lots of my people got 'emselves killed at Mistake Creek. Some say they were eatin' a stolen cow and that white fella went and shot 'em. Fact is that cow was just out there runnin' around. But it doesn't matter now, it was a long time ago. Black fella's story is different though ... dis is da true way.'

'What is it?'

'A woman called Nellie and two black fellas were workin' on a cattle station. The woman lived with a station-hand called Joe Winn a long time ago, but she left and moved in with another black fella. His name was Hopples. Joe Winn and another black fella named Nipper, they rode into Hopples' camp and shot Nellie dead along with Hopples, four of Hopples' relatives and two other men ... bang, bang, bang ... they all gone. Three of them were just piccaninnies ... kids ya know. Three other men, they escaped and then the shit hit the bloody fan. Ah shit missus, didn't mean to say shit or nothin'.'

'It's okay Henry. Keep going.'

29

'The coppers, you know, the police, they tracked 'em down. Joe Winn was shot dead and Nipper, they made him walk back to Turkey Creek all tied up. They say Nipper was the murderer, but none of the people pointed their finger and said, *yeah, he was the fella what done the shootin'*, so they had to let him go.'

As Henry spoke, Lizzy felt the first drops of rain, the advance scouts ahead of the main deluge, but ignored the wetness on her face.

'That bloody big rain is comin' soon missus, not long now. We better get a bloody move on.'

Henry threw the punctured tyre into the back of the Toyota and started the engine, but Lizzy didn't move.

'Are ya comin'?' he yelled.

Even then, she just stood staring out to where the beehive peaks rose up, beckoning her from under a blanket of grey clouds. Ever since she had seen the strange formations from the plane, she hadn't been able to get them out of her mind. They had some kind of strange magnetic pull; a magic she didn't understand.

'Come on ... the tyre ... she's all done now. Let's go.'

'They're so beautiful.' she said softly, to no-one, and in the distance a single lightning bolt fractured the sky. Henry appeared at her side.

'Them rocks, that's what us *Kija* people call, Purnululu ...white fellas, they call it The Bungle Bungle, but it won't be so beautiful if we get bogged out here missus. Come on. Let's go.'

She finally gave in to Henry's cajoling, climbed into the Toyota and as they drove off, she turned to Henry. 'You didn't finish your story.'

'Not much more ta tell ... that Joe Winn, he was ridin' Mick Rhatigan's horse, he was the overseer at the cattle station, so them coppers arrested Mick Rhatigan for murder too ... one bloody mistake after the other ... that's what it was ... no bloody dead cow at all ... dunno, maybe that's why it's called Mistake Creek,' laughed Henry.

'You seem to know a lot about this ...'

'My mother she was there ... she was just a piccaninny, a baby ... her father was Hopples ... he's my grandfather, Nellie was ma kangkayi, you

30

know, ma grandmother ... she got no mother and no Hopples, so the white fella take her away and stick her at Texas Downs cattle station to cook and clean ... she was just a girl ... they paid her nothin' ... no wonder she was sad ... no family ... no nothin'.'

'Does your mother live around here too?'

'Yeah, she's still alive ... she's alcamen now ... old woman ... she's a good woman ... knows all the dreamin' stories.'

'The dreaming?'

'Yeah Ngarrangkarni ... it's our *Kija* law ... you white fella, you'll never understand it ... the dreamin', it's a long time ago, but today too. It's all about the making of the world, the sky, the rivers, the mountains ... them rocks over there ... the animals ... all of us ... it's how we came to be ... sometimes it's about bad things ... sometime it's about good things ... heroes that go with special places, things that make the colours on the animals ... this is our land ... we rest in it ... it's where we come from ... this all part of the dreamin' ... it's belonging to the past and my ancestors, but they belong to me too ... my mother ... she's called Rosie ... she tells me and my people all the dreamin' stories so we don't forget it all and so the dreamin' will be part of the future too. Our old people tell us, and we tell it the same ... pass it on ... it's where we come from, where we are and where we goin to ... the dreamin' it's all around us ... in every breath we take. Dreamtime is the beginning of it all ... now it's all part of our law, what we say and what we sing. We dance for da Dreamtime. Have ya ever seen a corroboree?'

'No Henry, I haven't. I hope I can someday. Your mother must be very wise.'

'She a bloody survivor ... I'll tell ya that. Them people at Texas Downs they say, *you walk over there to that mission school ... hundred and fifty miles* ... then they say, *now you walk back* ... then she got the leprosy and they sent her to the leper's place near Derby ... long time over there ... near the ocean ... she come back, and they say, *you fixed now ... you work two bloody jobs.* Then the bloody owner knocked her up and one day the coppers come around and took away all the half-caste kids like me and my sister. My grandfather was Hopples, he was a full blood, but they said I wasn't black enough … look at me. I'm as black as Jimmy Orion's soul, and that's bloody black as, but they took me away and stuck me in a mission school … Rosie, she cried when we went away … I've never seen her cry since. It's like she's all cried out … like she's got no more tears left.'

'She was crying for you and your sister Henry.'

'Na missus. She was cryin' for all of us black fellas. It was a bad time. Bloody sad that.'

As they travelled further and further, sweat glued Lizzy's spine to her seat.

'Mistake Creek is just over that hill.' said Henry, pointing into the distance. 'Don't know what that friend of yours is doin' all the way out there.'

'If I said that he was looking for diamonds, would that surprise you?'

'Sure would missus. Everybody knows there's no diamonds or nothin' there. The barramundi fish didn't go there … over there … Bow River and Cattle Creek … and up there where that bloody big lake is … where Lake Argyle is now … that's the dreamin' place … don't get me old mother started on that … she reckons you white fellas stole that land and stole part of her dreamin'.'

'Henry what do you mean that the barramundi didn't go there?'

'In the Dreamtime three women were chasing …'

'Daiwul,' she interrupted.

'Yeah. How do *you* bloody know Daiwul is the barramundi?'

'Never mind about that Henry. It's a long story. Too long. Please, keep going.'

Henry looked at her quizzically, but obeyed.

'The women, they tried to trap Daiwul in their nets, but that fish was too clever for them women. She jumped through the net and over the hill behind Bow River … up there where my mother Rosie worked a long time ago. Daiwul landed in the water goin' in ta Cattle Creek, but when she jumped over that hill, she scraped her belly and her scales

32

scattered into the country ... they're the diamonds ... where she jumped a big crack appeared in the hill ... that place is the proper Barramundi Dreaming ... not here, not this place. Those women, they gave up trying to catch Daiwul and went to Kowinji ... that's Cattle Creek, but they were turned into stone ... ya can see see 'em there today ... they're rocks now ... them rocks, they're my bloody ancestors.'

'What about the proper barramundi place?'

'It's all gone now missus ... that Argyle Diamond mine, that's on the women's sacred site ... they dug up the Barramundi Dreaming place ... it's not there no more ... like I said, don't get old Rosie goin' on about that one and what they done.'

'So why is Andrew Burns looking for diamonds at Mistake Creek? Why does he have a mine?'

'Dunno, but some people are mighty slow at learnin'. That fella has been comin' and goin' from up there for a bloody long time. Dunno why.'

Eventually, Henry's easy chatter gave way to peaceful concentration, as if he was preparing himself to be transported into another dimension, another space, an alternate reality. He sat low in his seat staring intently at the ochre mountains in the distance, watching the sun rise higher in the sky. He began to chant softly. Lizzy tried to make out what he was saying but couldn't. Her first instincts were to prod him and wake him from his haze, but somehow, she knew there was something going on inside Henry's head that she didn't understand. Perhaps it was his Dreaming. Perhaps his stories of creation were coming alive. Whatever it was, it was something spiritual; something which connected him to the earth, the mountains, and the sky. Henry was becoming the wind that blew across the gibber plains, the shadows of the rocks, the light of the sun, and the air they breathed. He was washing off the white fella and his bar-room pool games and dressing himself in a fine suit of respect for Ngarrangkarni. Henry was returning home.

CHAPTER 6

As they drove, Lizzy closed her eyes, and within minutes, her eyelids twitched, her breathing slowed, and she slipped beyond consciousness to dream and journey back amongst the patchwork quilt of her life.

Lizzy Lawson had been christened Anastasia Dimitriades, at a time when Australians called Greek immigrants *greasy wogs* and souvlaki and dolmades were strange, inedible wog food. These *New Australians* took all the dirty jobs, laid the best concrete, gathered in groups at seaside parks on weekends, played strange music on lute-like instruments, and always seemed to be having a good time. The more affluent among them worked day and night at their fish and chip shops or fruit stalls, while their less fortunate compatriots, like *Anastasia's* father, went door-to-door, selling the fruit and vegetables they grew in the over-worked plots set aside at crowded immigration hostels.

Her parents, Constantine and Eleni, had known each other since 1941, when, as small children, they huddled together in the streets of their village, Kondomari, on Crete, while their mothers were shot dead by German soldiers for refusing to prostitute themselves. Years later, the tortured image of their mothers begging for their lives still haunted them, but they carried the emotional scars alongside their resolve to succeed in their adopted country, and worked from dawn until long after dark, when they fell into bed exhausted. In their hearts they knew that if they worked hard enough, one day they would become more than just another wog nuisance hawking tomatoes.

Life was tough, but by the time Anastasia was six, her father owned his first fruit shop, and little by little, he scraped together the deposit to buy a rundown terrace house in Surry Hills. In the first year they lived there, her brother Alex was born, and Constantine and Eleni cheered when the Gough Whitlam's Labor government finally did away with The White Australia policy, allowing their relatives to join them. Anastasia excelled at school and even though the other children started off calling her a greasy wog or sometimes even a dago, her easy manner and ready smile eventually won them over. By the time she was ten, her father had four fruit shops, with plans for more, but the day she turned eighteen, Anastasia Dimitriades' life of semi-comfortable suburbia turned horribly sour.

Unbeknownst to her, her parents had arranged for her to be married to a second-cousin Milo, who had arrived two-months before, moved into their house, and taken a job managing one of their shops. When her father unveiled his grand plan just after she had blown out the candles on her birthday cake, she thought he was joking, but could tell by the stern look engraved on his face, and the expectant look on Milo's, that he wasn't. Of course she protested, but the more she protested, the more her father insisted. When that didn't work, he tried to convince her that it would all be okay.

'Don't worry, you can have your own opinion, you still can be your own person with your own pride, but never disagree with your husband. Let your husband always be right. He can do no wrong. The important thing is your marriage. Dear daughter...' he explained, '...you will be surprised that even though this seems to be a one-sided arrangement, in time your Milo will realize what a treasure he has, and he will come to you for advice. You will not only have your way, but his too ... ask your mother, she knows this only too well.'

Anastasia remained unconvinced and uncooperative, but nevertheless, plans for the marriage continued at pace all around her. When she refused to select a koumbara (maid of honour), one was selected for her, and even though she showed her intended not a whisker of encouragement, he took to presenting her with a new love letter every evening after dinner. They were all written in English, but Milo hadn't learned to speak or write any English beyond what was necessary to run the fruit shop. It didn't take long for her to work out that the quirks and foibles of the bastardized language in the letters belonged to her father, which made the letters well beyond weird.

Anastasia was a good Greek girl and a dutiful daughter, so for a while, she settled into a comfortable placation, but as her wedding day drew nearer, she began to fret and withdraw. When the thought of marrying the gruff and implacable Milo grew all too much she would collapse at her mother's feet and cry into her lap. 'Mamaka, you cannot make me do this terrible thing. I do not love this man.' But her mother was too well schooled in the traditional philosophy of *never disagree with your husband* to be any more than a good listener and a poor ally.

The night before the wedding, Anastasia snuck out of the house, not knowing where she would go, or how she would survive, vowing never to return. Of course, her father insisted that she had brought shame upon the family and promised never to speak to her again. In return she took an axe to her branch of the Dimitriades family tree and gave herself a new name. To hide among the twangs of home-grown Aussies, she wanted her new name to be so un-Greek that she would automatically be taken for a white Anglo-Saxon protestant who just happened to have a healthy tan and long, dark hair. She found inspiration for her new name on the few banknotes she earned waiting on tables at a coffee shop and chose Elizabeth after Queen Elizabeth II who appeared on the one-dollar note and Henry Lawson, the famous writer, who lent his image to the ten-dollar note. Elizabeth (sometimes Lizzy) Lawson was born, but she saw little of her namesake's images and struggled to make ends meet.

For the next eighteen years, life continued that way until one night, when she was working as a barmaid at a local pub, a man wearing overalls and muddy work boots, casually remarked, *you look just like my first wife*.

Of course, she asked, *how many times have you been married?* He replied, *never.* The man's name was Anthony King. Tony. An electrician.

Six months later Lizzy walked down the aisle without her father by her side. By then Constantine was the owner of twenty-two Fruit World mega-markets dotted all over the country. On the day of her marriage, he parked across the road from the church, but only saw his once-upon-a-time princess as she emerged, but then she was lost in a sea of kisses that he couldn't swim in. He cried quietly behind his sunglasses and drove off wondering how he could have been so horribly wrong to try and force his daughter into a loveless marriage and how he could have wasted all those years not seeing her or even remedying the problem.

Tony King was a warm and loving husband, who, despite his poor financial skills, managed to bring home enough to keep the wolf from the door, but that didn't matter. As far as Lizzy was concerned, life was perfect; well almost. They tried for three years to have children, but after too much *got to do it right now because I'm ovulating* sex, and too many failed IVF attempts, they resigned themselves to being childless. In the end they spent their time luxuriating in each other's company spurning pubs and friend's barbecues, preferring to be lost in their bubble. They existed at the epicentre of each other's universe and by anyone's measure, were deeply in love, but it all came to a shuddering halt when they least expected it.

On the evening of their fifth wedding anniversary Tony was running late for a special dinner Lizzy had prepared. He was speeding and didn't see the semi-trailer sweeping wide around the corner of the infamous Bigola Bends. He died tangled in three dozen red roses and a card which simply said, *Lizzy my darling, I will always love you.* The police also found a gift-wrapped diamond pendant in the wreckage of Tony's ute which they returned to Lizzy. She put it on and had never, ever, taken it off.

As it turned out, Tony's financial ineptitude would be her undoing, because the more she looked, the more Lizzy realized that his business, humble though it was, was a financial house of cards made up of second mortgages, truck leases, loans to mates and debts to a bookie. Without

Tony to hold it precariously in place, this edifice was about to come tumbling down. For what seemed like only a heartbeat in her life, it looked like Anastasia Dimitriades had found a certain kind of loving peace, but then all-of-a-sudden, she had nothing again; just like she always had. The bank took her house three months after the funeral.

Lizzy mourned Tony's death for longer than most people expected, and some tried to help her, but she was happier moping around her rented Pittwater cottage than pretending to enjoy their well-meaning attempts at comfort. Some days she would put on one of Tony's old track suits, just to feel him and smell him, then for hours on end, she would walk round and round an old pool table he had brought home from a demolition job. She would sink all the balls and then start all over again. The fact was, she always kept score for two and always talked to her dead husband like he was still in the room. Some days she would catch a reflection of her bedraggled self in a mirror or a window and wonder if she was going crazy.

When it rained, she liked to watch the seagulls dive in and out the boats moored in the small inlet near where she lived, and at night, she listened to the lonesome clang of the steel cable stays on their masts as she cried into her pillow. In her most lonely moments, she even wondered if in some small corner of the house, her father might be sitting, waving a disapproving finger at her. Deep down she knew that she never really left him and would always be his princess one way or another. While he might have erased himself from her life, she was secretly proud that he had done so well and thought of him often. One night, just over a year after Tony died, the phone rang.

'Lizzy.' she answered, but it was muffled by her pillow and barely audible.

'What are you doing?' asked a man's voice.

'Pole dancing.'

'Very funny.'

'Do you want some company?'

'Thanks, but I already have some.' she said, gazing at the photo of

Tony staring back at her from the bedside table.

'You've got to get out of that house more often. Have coffee with me.'

'What for?'

'Because you have to.'

'I don't have to do anything.'

'Then do it because I want you to.'

'Maybe next week.'

'You said that last week.'

'I know.'

'Have you got enough money?'

'I'll get by.'

'You only have to ask … you know that … don't you?'

'Thanks, but I'm okay. I've got the money megáli theía, great-aunt Delia, left me.'

'I'm having some people over for dinner next Saturday night. At least let me feed you.'

'I'm not coming.'

'Do you know my friend Fat Sam, the guy who has been teaching me karate?'

'The bouncer?'

'Yes. Either you come, or he comes and gets you. Which will it be?'

'Jesus Alex you're being pushy.'

'And you're being pathetic.'

'No, I'm not.'

'It's casual. Eight o'clock.'

'I already told you, I'm not coming.'

'I've got a key. Fat Sam is going to let himself in.'

'I'm *not* coming.'

The following Saturday evening rather than be dragged to a dinner, which she didn't want to go to, by a one-hundred and twenty-kilogram Samoan bouncer, Lizzy reluctantly dressed, did her best to put her hair in order and caught an Uber to her brother's house.

'Would you really have sent Fat Sam to get me?' she asked, as he opened the front door.

'He takes people for coffee too. Be careful.'

'It must be terrible having to force people to come to dinner.'

'Most of them come just because they're invited. You're the only one I need to threaten. You'd better be careful. I just got my black belt.'

'Yeah, and I know origami, so you better be careful too, or I'll turn you into a swan or something.'

'Oooo, I'm shaking.'

'You should be.'

Lizzy kissed her brother on the cheek. 'Thanks. I needed a bit of a push.'

'Consider yourself shoved!'

Alex Dimitradies ran the flourishing fruit and vegetable business with his father and was Lizzy's secret source of family news. On more than one occasion his father had told him things meant for *Anastasia's* ears. Births, deaths, marriages, and the progress of Fruit World were all reported with dutiful care, and whenever she was told one of these tasty morsels from her long-abandoned family life, *Anastasia* felt the golden thread of her past pulling her back. Unfortunately, she was just as stubborn as her father.

While Alex had a procession of women keen to take advantage of his Mediterranean good looks and assumed wealth, he had assiduously avoided marriage and happily played the field, gathering an eclectic swarm of friends and hangers-on. Some were like him; people from the wrong side of the tracks, made good. Others were builders, painters, plasterers, and labourers from his karate dojo, rough nuts, and fruit barons from the markets, fawning would-be models who only called themselves models because boys liked going out with models, jockeys and horse trainers and a smattering of second-rate rugby players. Sometimes there were even bearded, tattooed men who wore bikie club colours. But Lizzy knew that anyone invited to one of Alex's 'Beer in the Burbs' dinners was bound to be *interesting* for one reason or another. That night, she wasn't disappointed.

The tall, suntanned man sitting next to her was economic with his words, but a full life was etched into his face. His fingernails were cracked and broken and had a smattering of dirt under them.

'Andrew has been living in the Kimberley in Western Australia.' offered Alex, attempting to kick-start a conversation.

'And why have you been doing that?' said Lizzy.

'I'm a geologist.'

'A rock-doctor?'

'You could say that.'

'What have you been looking for?'

'Anything really, but mostly diamonds.'

'Oh.' she replied, subconsciously fingering the pendant hanging around her neck.

'How do you know where to look?'

'There are many ways, but as strange as it may seem, I followed a painting.'

'A painting?'

'An aboriginal dot painting.'

'For a geologist that's not very scientific.'

Lizzy's sceptical look roused the handsome stranger, and his trickle of words gave way to a flood of enthusiasm for a legend about the *Kija* aboriginal people who lived in the Kimberley. He said that they knew exactly where to find diamonds and had known where for hundreds of generations because old aunties and grannies had passed down stories about playing with *rain-stones*, but they had never told anyone exactly where to find them. Some people said the exact location was only known by a few elders and passed from generation to generation in the same way as their Dreamtime stories. The only trouble was, they had never told anybody. In fact, they flat out denied the existence of any diamonds, period.

'You mean to tell me there is supposed to be some kind of King Solomon's mine out there?' asked Lizzy.

'Maybe, but there are so many legends about diamonds it's hard to know what's true and what isn't.'

'Such as?'

'Well for example, Alexander the Great was supposed to have found a Valley of Diamonds during his campaign through India. The legend says they were guarded by snakes whose gaze could kill a man, so Alexander's soldiers killed the snakes with mirrors because they had to look at themselves. They threw sheep's carcasses into the pit of snakes, the diamonds attached to the fat and then vultures, attracted by the meat, picked up it up with the diamonds still attached. His men followed the vultures to their roosts and then picked the diamonds out of their droppings.'

'And people wore them?'

'Happily.'

'What about *your* legend? What's your valley of diamonds protected by?'

'Innuendo and rumour.'

'So, no one really knows what's what?'

'Yep, that's true, but the Dreamtime legends are also open to interpretation, so even if you think you've got it worked out in one area, the same interpretation probably doesn't apply twenty kilometres down the road.'

'Have you asked anyone?'

'There's no point. A lot of people have tried to bribe the elders to reveal the location, but they deny its existence. As far as they're concerned, the only diamonds they know about are the ones that are already part of their Dreamtime legend and have been mined at Argyle since 1983. Of course, that doesn't stop people from looking anyway.'

'People like you?'

'I'm afraid so.'

'Rocks in your head?'

'I wish I had a dollar for everyone who has said that to me.'

'No offence intended.'

'None taken.'

'But you still think that they're out there?'

'Well, maybe.'

'That doesn't sound too scientific coming from a *rock doctor*.'

'After the Argyle Mine opened some people said that the *Kija* people scoured their land looking for diamonds so geologists, like me, wouldn't find any surface traces. They said it was to discourage big mining companies from wanting to mine sacred sites.'

'Did they?'

'It was mostly dismissed as late-night pub talk. Besides, that's not how we find diamonds.'

'A jewellery store?'

'Pardon?'

'Isn't that how you find diamonds.'

'It takes all the fun out of it don't you think?'

'Sorry. I'm interrupting.'

'The *Kija* people call all this talk about diamonds *yilkurrum jarak*, bad talk. Along with everyone else, they never really took it all that seriously and for a while, nor did I.'

'But then?'

'I saw a painting done by an old aboriginal man in a place called Warmun, some people call it Turkey Creek … it's not too far from the Argyle diamond mine that I was talking about.'

'What was the painting of?'

'A barramundi fish the *Kija* people call Daiwul, a milk-bottle-shaped boab tree with a small plaque on it and painted men holding boards with religious crosses on them. When I asked the old man what the painting meant, he told me it was secret business. For a while I forgot about it, but then one day I worked out what he wouldn't tell me.'

'So, you *have* found diamonds?'

Burns smiled a wry grin and pressed on.

'Every *Kija* child knows who Daiwul is. The aboriginal storytellers always tell the story of Daiwul the barramundi being chased by three women—'

'You wish,' interrupted Alex.

Burns smiled, as if he was embarrassed by the comment, and continued his story about women trying to trap Daiwul in their spinifex nets, but she was too clever for the women and jumped through the net and over the hill behind a place called Bow River and as the fish cleared the hill, she scraped her belly and her scales lifted and scattered around the country. That was the Ngarrangkarni or Dreamtime legend about how all the diamonds at the Argyle mine were created.

'But something tells me that the fish is only half the puzzle. Am I right?'

'You catch on quickly. I worked out the other half when I went with a group of *Kija* people and some nuns to an All Souls Day celebration at a place called Mistake Creek. It's on the Northern Territory and Western Australia border. The *Kija* go there every year to pray for the departed souls of their relatives killed in a massacre years ago. Well, what do you think I found?'

'Let me guess. Diamonds?'

'Not quite, but there was an old boab tree with a plaque commemorating the massacre and there was *Kija* men painted in white holding elaborately painted boards covered in crosses.'

' ... just like the painting ... and you got to wondering if this Daiwul, this fish who was the creator of diamonds, had also paid a visit to this Mistake Creek place?'

'You're way ahead of me.'

Lizzy blushed. 'So, what about the diamonds?'

'I'm working on it.'

'Andrew is changing careers.' said Alex.

'Piano player?' asked Lizzy, playfully.

'Very funny. I've had a mine at Mistake Creek for a few years now.'

'So, you do believe the story.'

'A geologist doesn't start digging a big hole without digging a bunch of smaller ones first.'

'And what do your small holes tell you?'

'Now that, as they say in the military, is *classified*.'

Burns hadn't realized it, but for the last few minutes he had had the undivided attention of the entire table.

'Oh, I'm sorry,' he said, looking around embarrassed. 'I didn't mean to get carried away.'

'No, don't apologize. Passion is a wonderful thing.' said Lizzy, forcing a smile, but there was sadness in her voice, as if a great melancholy had suddenly settled over her.

CHAPTER 7

The next morning, Lizzy was drinking coffee and staring out a small crack in her kitchen curtains, watching the seagulls darting in and out of the yachts, when the doorbell rang.

'Andrew? What a ... a...' stammered Lizzy, pulling a well-lived-in cardigan across an equally lived-in pyjama top.

'I think maybe the word you're looking for is *surprise.*'

'Yes.' she replied, confused, and trying to put her recalcitrant hair in some order. 'Come in. You'll have to excuse my appearance. I've been out walking the dog ... there aren't any fashion police all the way up here. How did you get here anyway?'

'By cab and some good directions from an old man fishing on the jetty. Cute place. Very ahh ... rustic.' he added, trying to change the subject, but it was more of a polite remark than an accurate observation.

There was something chill and dank about her cottage that made him cautious about entering. All the curtains were drawn, and the only light was from a small electric radiator burning at the end of a long hallway. When the front door closed behind him, the cottage wrapped itself in the smell of rising damp, burnt toast, fresh coffee and another odd aroma which reminded Burns of the old people's home where his grandmother once lived.

As Lizzy ushered him down the hallway, past the other rooms, he couldn't help but think this had once been a comfortable home, but the joy seemed to have gone out of it. In between the sparse furniture, lakes of dust had flooded the polished floorboards and a parade of footprints had created an abstract backwards and forwards pattern in them. On the walls, what few paintings there were, hung askew as if someone had turned the whole house at an angle and failed to put it right. In the sitting-room fireplace, cold logs had burnt down to half-baked cheroots, but that must have been a long time ago, because now they were covered in cobwebs and dust. There were no photos or personal things in any of the rooms; no bric-a-brac of once-upon-a-times, just the emptiness where they once might have been. In the room at the end of the corridor, a white Labrador was curled up in front of the radiator. It looked old, slobbered, and smelt of wet socks and the seaweed dangling from the corner of its mouth. A mangled tennis ball had been read its last rites and lay buried between the dog's front legs.

'I brought croissants,' offered Burns, holding up a paper bag.

'Thank you. That's very handy. As you've probably realized, there aren't any shops up here.'

'You didn't eat very much last night. I thought you may need something to keep you going.'

'You're very kind.'

'Do you live here by yourself?'

'Just me and him.' she said, nodding at the dog. 'His name is Brutus.'

'Guard dog?'

'I think he'd lick a burglar to death.'

'Have you got some plates?'

'Yes, yes of course.'

With her head buried in a cupboard she asked, 'How did you know my address?'

'Your brother Alex gave it to me. He said it was either me or some guy called Fat Sam who had to make sure that you did something nice today.'

'Do you know Fat Sam?'

'No. Why? Who is he?'

'Never mind.'

Burns followed Lizzy out onto a small deck shaded by a flowering frangipani tree and while he swatted away mosquitoes, she fussed with butter and strawberry jam for the croissants, and worried about what to say next. She needn't have.

'Your brother thinks you stay at home way too much. He says you've become a hermit.'

'Does he now?'

'Yep. He says you're locking yourself up and letting the world go by.'

'Maybe I prefer it that way?'

'Do you?'

She stopped short. *Do you?* She didn't know. Ever since her husband died no-one had asked her that; no one, except Alex, seemed to care that she had become a hermit. Her old friends, that were mostly Tony's, vanished when he did. But that wasn't what concerned her most about Burns' question. The simple fact was, she hadn't even asked herself what she really wanted.

'I live a very quiet life these days.'

'These days?'

'I was married. He died just over a year ago. I haven't been out much since then.'

'I'm sorry. I didn't know; a small detail that your brother omitted to tell me.'

'That's alright. You're probably just part of his grand plan to get me back in circulation.'

'He's worried about you.'

'So, he sent you?'

'I wanted to come.'

Lizzy blushed.

'I'm not ready for anything like that.'

'For what?'

'Involvement.'

'Does lunch define involvement?'

'That depends.'

'On what?'

'What you're expecting for dessert?'

'Lemon tart.'

'Are you being rude?'

'No, there's restaurant I know that makes the best lemon curd tart you've ever tasted. At least that's what your brother says. I've never actually been there.' he smiled.

Lunch ran into dinner and dinner became a lingering, but cautious farewell at Lizzy's front door and over the next two weeks, she slowly fell for the ample charms of Andrew Burns. He was an unusual man, at least that's what her brother had thought when he met him at the fruit markets. Any man who could get a wily old operator like George Papandreou to cut his price for apples to almost nothing, without blood being spilled, had to have something going for him. Alex had struck up a conversation and it didn't take long to find out that Burns was more interested in rocks than Golden Delicious apples, but their mutual love of fast cars sealed their friendship, even if it was lopsided when it came to who could afford what.

Although Burns seemed to have gathered no more possessions than he could carry in a suitcase, he possessed a certain worldliness which most people couldn't quite put their finger on. There was just something about the way he carried himself and the way he spoke about the unusual as matter of fact which made people sit up and take notice. He was softly spoken but forceful, confident without being arrogant and knew when to listen and when to talk, which Lizzy thought made him a rarity among men. She could also tell he was probably more at home in a tent than a house. He told her that he could go for weeks, sometimes months, without talking to anyone. It was this unusualness mixed with his laconic easiness that attracted her. His free spirit somehow seemed to lighten the burden of her life and made her want to live again; to breathe out. She enjoyed his quiet persistence and easy-going manner, revelled in his quirky sense of humour, and at times even found herself having a good time; a feeling she thought she would never have again. He didn't push her too hard, and she respected him for that. When she wanted to be alone, he bowed out gracefully, but he also had a way of knowing when *alone* meant *hold me* and *see you tomorrow* meant *don't come* and when she changed her mind, he was never too far away.

They discovered that their childhoods were similar. Burns had a tear in his eye when he told her about his father, a Hungarian Jew called Ishmael Bernstein, who had come to Australia about the same time as Lizzy's parents, and changed his name to Reg Burns so he would fit in. He told her about his mother, an Australian girl who Ishmael met while she was working as a waitress in a cafeteria. Ishmael had gone back again and again on the pretence of loving the beef stroganoff, when all along it was Joyce, the waitress, he had fallen in love with. Lizzy found out that Burns inherited his love of rocks and minerals from his father who worked three jobs to buy a small caravan and a second-hand Buick Roadmaster to wander the outback of Australia. He had promised his wife he would strike it rich, but never did, and in the end, died a broken man. Burns' mother was still alive, but he had fallen out with her after she took a job managing a brothel in the Kalgoorlie gold fields. He told Lizzy that after graduating from university he spent ten years living a nomadic life alternating between working in bauxite mines in Queensland and driving giant iron ore trucks in Western Australia. In between, he honoured his father's memory by wandering the deserts in a battered pick-up truck looking for the motherlode.

Burns prodded and poked looking for Lizzy's life story too, but each time he thought she was about to say more, she changed the subject, and in the end, all he really knew about her was a disjointed mélange of titbits about being poor, fruit shops, not having to repeat the sins of our fathers and something about a snooker game in heaven, which he didn't understand. He thought it better not to push the point, so never did.

The next few weeks drifted by in easy comfort. They lived in an unreal world where time was of no importance and tomorrow was of no concern and by the end of the fifth week, the photo of Tony on the bedside table was turned face down. Lizzy had fallen in love with a man she hardly knew. It made her happy, but it also made her cautious. If life had taught her anything, it was that all good things must end, because in her experience, they usually did.

'When will you be going back to your mine.' she asked, as they watched the sun go down one night.

'Are you trying to get rid of me?'

'No, just wondering.'

'I've got to get some financing in place, then I can go back.'

'Financing? What for?'

'The mine.'

'But why do you need that if you don't even know if there are any diamonds?'

Burns stared at Lizzy wondering if he should answer. He bought some time by opening another beer, but then after a long sigh, began to speak.

'I'm going to tell you something, but then you need to forget I ever told you. Can you do that?'

'Sure. What is it?'

'Promise?'

'Absolutely.'

'Do you remember the story I told you about the old aboriginal artist when we first met?'

'Sure, the Mistake Creek painting.'

'Well, he wasn't right, but he wasn't wrong either. I think it was more of a hint than anything else ... or maybe just a coincidence ... I don't know ... but whatever it was, I think I've found a major diamond bearing lamproite pipe ... not kimberlite like most diamonds are usually found in, lamproite, just like that bloody big Argyle mine just up the road from it ... well actually a couple of hundred kilometres, but who's counting.'

'You *think* you have, or you *know* you have?'

'About five years ago I found a few small stones, diamonds, in what was probably a creek bed millions of years ago, then I backtracked along it and found more diamonds and before long I was up near Mistake Creek.'

'Really?'

'Yes, really. After some initial drilling, the signs are all good.'

'You're pulling my leg, right?'

'No, I'm not. I conservatively estimate there are over five hundred million carats. It just needs a little bit of rip and cut.'

'Rip and cut?'

'It's how they mine it.'

'You've kept this so quiet. I would've been jumping out of my skin.'

'I didn't want to spoil it.'

'Spoil what?'

'This.' he replied, waving his hand to her and back to himself.

'How would that spoil it?'

'Because I have to go away soon,' he replied, taking her in his arms.

'When?'

'As soon as I get some money.'

'When will that be?'

'I dunno. I've never been too fond of banks, don't really trust 'em ... but if you know someone with some spare cash ...'

'So, you're going to raise money to get your mine going and leave me here by myself.'

'See, I told you I didn't want to spoil it.'

'How much do you need?'

'Quite a lot.'

'How much is quite a lot?'

'Stage one is about twenty million, but I only need about one million to get started. It's for deposits on equipment mainly. After that, it really depends on what we find.'

'And if there's plenty of diamonds, raising the extra money will be easy I suppose.'

'Exactly.'

'And what does one million buy an investor?

'About ten percent.'

'And all this is based on *your* own geologist's reports I suppose?'

'Yes, but the core samples don't lie.'

'Core samples?'

'Samples from deep in the ground.'

'And where are they?'

'In a vault.'

'I see. Don't the local aborigines have land rights or something? They're not all that keen on mining from what I know ... something about scared sites ... you told me, and I've seen it on the news.'

'That's true but it depends on where those sites are. That's the only real issue. I'm trying to deal with them and sort out the Native Title Act so that everyone is happy. Negotiations are, as they say, ongoing.'

'Do you see any problems? Besides the money that is.'

'That Argyle mine got going pretty quickly with something they called the Good Neighbour Agreement. It was straightforward and lasted for twenty years. If I play my cards right, I can probably do the same. Now they've replaced it with what they call the *Argyle Participation Agreement*. Bloody tough negotiations required though. I've got Miriwung, *Kija*, Wularr and Malginin tribes ... they're the traditional owners and then there's the Kimberley Land Council to consider as well. I've got to get into compensation agreements, employment opportunities for the locals, management plans for sacred site protection, training and employment, land access, land management, decommissioning of the mine when we're done ... all that stuff costs a fortune.'

'So, you value the mine ...'

'Adamas.'

'Adamas?'

'That's what I'm calling it. It's Greek for diamond.'

'My Greek is a little rusty I'm afraid ... so you value *Adamas* at ten million dollars.'

'That's just a notional value so I can get some early investors. The real value is probably billions.'

'That's a big call for someone who hasn't mined a single stone yet.'

'I didn't say that.'

'You only said the core samples, whatever they are, were promising.'

'They are ... were ... so I started digging.'

'By yourself?'

'Pretty much.'

'In the middle of nowhere?'

'Yep.'

'And you found?'

'A few little baubles.'

'Are you teasing me?'

'Maybe,' he smiled.

'So, you're going to raise a million dollars then pack up and leave me. Is that about it?'

'You make it sound so final.'

'Well, isn't it?'

'It doesn't have to be.'

'It is. It always is.'

'I'm not planning on dying or anything.'

Lizzy's face quickly changed to a wan blankness. 'Nor was Tony.'

'I'm sorry. I didn't mean it like that.'

'I know. I'm sorry. It's still a bit raw.'

That was when she realized, for two months she had assiduously avoided mentioning Tony's name, but suddenly, it was as if just by saying it, he might know she was considering another man. She had been too much in love to hurt him, even if he was dead. Burns picked up the change in mood and took a step away because until then, he only had to deal with an anonymous dead husband; someone from her past, someone who seemed so far away, but now that his name had been spoken, it was as if part of the spell had been broken; the magic shattered. Burns knew the past was now in the present and the future would depend on what he said next.

'Tell me about him.'

'You don't want to hear about that ...'

'You're right ... I don't ... but I do ... for you.'

'Can we just leave it the way it is?'

'I think we've gone past that now.'

Lizzy tried to describe Tony and all that he was, but the first tentative steps produced only an unaffectionate description which Burns knew couldn't possibly be the truth. He knew how she really felt was hidden in the white lies she used to try and protect her past and nourish her future. He also knew that to press her any harder would only result in more half-truths and the reciprocity for a half truth is another and another, until finally they would both be drowning in banal, incomplete sentences and half-finished thoughts; thoughts they foolishly imagined would protect each other's feelings but did the opposite.

'We could just walk away now,' he whispered.

'Do *you* want to?'

She was stung.

'No, it's the last thing I want, but I think there's a part of *you* that wants to. You think it would be safer.'

'I'm a coward.'

'I'd say you've been pretty brave so far.'

'All bravado. Why don't you want to leave? I'm hard work.'

'Yes, you are.'

'No, I'm not ... wrong answer.' she smiled, and playfully slapped him on the chest.

'We'll work something out. We'll find a way to keep this going.'

'And just exactly what is *this*?'

For a man like Burns there was no right answer to a question like that. From experience, he knew there were only wrong answers and wronger answers, so there was no use even thinking about giving one. If he did, it would almost certainly be wrong, even if it sounded right. No matter what he said, it wouldn't be a perfect match for whatever was going through Lizzy's mind, and anything other than a perfect match was imperfect, so would eventually lead to tears and questions which he had no answers to and in providing one, he knew that he would dig his own grave. While he thought, Burns took solace in the fact that she hadn't asked the one question which wrought most fear into the hearts of men who made their living in his dubious manner. He paused and was about to give an answer, which he thought was what she wanted to hear, but in the silence, she quietly asked, *Do you love me Andrew?* but quickly followed it up with, *I'm sorry. That wasn't a very fair question.*

'Love often gets in the way of living.' replied Burns, taking her in his arms.

'Live for love or love to live. Is that it?'

'You can have both.'

'Can *we* have both?'

'How do you feel about living in the middle of nowhere?'

She shrugged.

'Let's make a deal.' smiled Burns.

'What kind of deal?'

'I'll go back to The Kimberley to get things going, then, if the mine works out, you can come up.'

'What then?'

'One step at a time.'

Lizzy looked into his eyes. There was only honesty staring back at her. At least that's what she imagined. She breathed out and her shoulders fell. It was the kind of relief you feel after a storm has finally passed, when the winds of change have stopped blowing and life looks like it might settle into a gentle rhythm that you can finally rely on.

'There's just one more thing.' grimaced Burns.

'Oh?'

'I need to go to South Africa pretty soon.'

'South Africa? Why there?'

'Mining equipment. I've tracked down a few second-hand crushers, scrubbers, and gravity separators. I've even managed to get a good contact for x-ray sorting machines.'

'Isn't that putting the cart a bit before the horse?'

'You don't exactly pick up this kind of equipment on supermarket shelves. When it comes up, you need to grab it.'

'Won't that take money? Money you don't have.'

'Unfortunately,' he sighed, breaking the embrace.

'Can you borrow against the mine?'

'It's too early for a valuation. The banks would laugh at me.'

'How much do you need? What's the least you could get away with.'

'Fifty-grand I suppose. Look don't worry about it. This whole thing is probably just a pipe dream.'

'Where are all those documents you've been talking about? Tell me all about your dream.'

'They're in my suitcase.'

'How did I know that?'

'Because my whole life is in there.'

She frowned, feeling hurt.

'Well quite a lot of it anyway.' he replied, suitably chastised. 'Besides, *you* wouldn't fit.'

Burns had made few concessions to the twenty-first century, but one of them was a laptop computer, which had seen better days. The keyboard was choked with dust, the outer case heavily scratched and it looked as if it had fallen out of his pick-up truck and been kicked around, but somehow, it still worked.

'Did that fall off the ark?' laughed Lizzy. 'Did you steal it off a man called Noah.'

'Don't be so ...'

'Cheeky?'

'Yes that. I'll have you know that it does the job very nicely thank you very much.'

'We can stay in touch by email. Do you have an internet connection at your mine?'

'Satellite phone.' he replied, rummaging in his suitcase, and producing a sophisticated yellow device. 'It hooks up to old faithful here ... instant internet.

'You continue to surprise me.'

Burns spent the next hour going into detail about his mine and carefully taking Lizzy through his geologist's reports. He clicked from screen to screen on his computer explaining each morsel of information like it was the most important thing in the world. He showed her satellite infra-red imaging of tenement number 12967/99 located at 16 degrees 42 minutes 40 seconds South, 12 degrees 23 minutes 17 seconds East, Western Australia-350 kilometres South-East of Kununurra, 250 kilometres North-East of Hall's Creek, covering an area of 1,000 hectares. When she seemed to understand everything, he was telling her, Burns decided to press on with a full scientific explanation but the jabber of *volcanic pipes of diatreme, composed of olivine lamproite presented as tuff and lava and peripheral volcanic facies suggesting lamproite eruption formed in a maar,* eventually lost her. Nevertheless, he pressed on explaining that *at the margins of the volcanic pipe the lamproite was mixed with volcanic breccia containing shattered wall rock fragments mixed and milled by the eruption. Minerals in the facies include zeolitic minerals, micas, kaolinite and clays typical of post eruption and hydrothermal circulation ...*

'Are you okay so far?'

'Not really.'

'I'm boring you, aren't I?'

'No, not at all ... go on ... please.'

He did, but Lizzy wasn't really listening. While he was carrying on about the potential for diamonds within the intact core of the volcanic pipe as well as within some of the marginal breccia and maar facies, she had already jumped way ahead.

'How far away is this Argyle place?'

'175 kilometres north-west and it has the same geology as Adamas. At Argyle, the diamonds have been dated to about 1.58 billion years, while the volcano which created my pipe is between 1.1 and 1.2 billion years old. It's a small period in which diamonds could have formed, around 400 million years ago, which may explain the small average size and unusual physical characteristics.'

'Is that a bad thing?'

'No, not at all. Argyle produces mainly industrial diamonds which are worth less than gem quality stones. They have about forty-five percent near gem quality, fifty percent industrial and the other five percent is gem quality diamonds, but that includes highly valued pink diamonds as well as sparkling champagne and rich cognac diamonds ... but they have lots of them. That's what makes Argyle what it is. In fact, they found so many diamonds, they had to invent their own sorting technology to cope with them all.'

'That's a nice problem to have.'

'Well, I think I, we, just might have the same problem.'

'You're kidding me, right?'

'No, I'm not. Initial indications show an average ore grade or diamond concentration of 6.5 carats per tonne, which extrapolated shows a yield of approximately five hundred million carats over the life of the existing lease. I think we can pull out about thirty-five million carats a year once we're in full production.'

'That's a lot of diamonds.'

'At about $190 a carat it's a lot of money too.'

'Do you realize how much?'

'Like I said, billions.'

'And this is what you've kept quiet all this time?'

'It's just a pile of rocks at the moment.'

'But Andrew, this could be huge.'

'Let's not get ahead of ourselves.'

'I'm just so excited for you. What about costs?'

'Adamas has large reserves and high ore grade offsets with an estimated production cost of eight dollars per carat compared to Canadian mining leases of one hundred and sixty-five dollars per carat and African leases at one hundred and fifty-five dollars per carat. With large concentrations, a controlled area and low extraction costs by world standards this really could be something to talk about.'

'So, you're telling me you just followed an old creek-bed, and this is what you came up with?'

'I had a bit of help.'

'Help?' she replied, sceptically.

'A lot of these diamonds fluoresce blue under ultra-violet light, so I just went out looking for them on the most stinking hot days when there were no clouds in the sky and UV levels were though the roof. I just looked for the little blue flashes.'

'Blue flashes?'

'Okay, it's not all that scientific, I know, but it works.'

'And I thought that all this scientific mumbo jumbo of yours, actually meant something. What about the ones that don't have *itty bitty blue flashes*?' she smiled.

'Well, that's a problem. In fact, there's a road up in the Northern Territory that leads to a place called the Merlin Mine which has been built almost entirely from diamond bearing material that didn't glow. When they built the road, they didn't realize that twenty percent of gems didn't, so they threw them out and built a highway out of the rubble. It's not a sealed road so people can pick up small diamonds just walking along.'

'On a sunny day?'

'Of course.'

'What about the core samples and your baubles, which, by the way you're talking, I'm guessing aren't actually just *baubles* at all.'

'You could say that.'

'Really? Where are they?'

'In the bank vault ...with the core samples.'

'That's probably a good idea.'

By the time Burns had finished, Lizzy's head was swimming with facts and figures and scientific sounding words she really didn't understand, but by then it didn't matter. Burns seemed to know what he was talking about and that's all she cared about.

'It all sounds great. Maybe too great.'

'It will be nothing if I don't get fifty thousand soon.'

'Have you asked Alex? He might have a few spare dollars.'

'I mentioned it, but he said that it's not his thing.'

'It's a pity, because someone is going to make their money back, a million times over. Did Tony leave you anything?'

'Yeah, debt, but my great-aunt left me fifty thousand. Now that's all that's between me and the poor house.'

'So you won't be investing, will you?' he smiled.

'Andrew, I would love to but—'

'No, no, I wasn't asking. Sorry. Don't worry, I'll raise the money someway or other. Maybe I'll go sell myself at Kings Cross,' he grinned.

'I thought you said that you wanted to make some money.'

'Very funny,' he replied, taking her in his arms.

'Do you really have to go away and leave me?'

'It's not leaving, Lizzy. It's making a better future for us. Both of us.'

Burns hugged her. She sighed and rested her cheek on his shoulder. Maybe she should give him her inheritance. Maybe he was right. Maybe she would make her money back a million times over, and then everything would be alright. She wouldn't have to struggle anymore.

They spent the rest of the day at the beach, swimming, horsing around and watching the sun dance on little blue flashes when the wind whipped up the waves.

'I might have to mine the ocean. I think I saw some of your little blue flashes,' joked Lizzy, emerging from the water.

'I should've stuck to the scientific mumbo jumbo,' replied Burns, looking Lizzy's dripping wet body up and down.

'It was very impressive.'

'You're impressive.'

Lizzy blushed and began towelling herself dry.

'You know, my father used to warn me about men like you.'

'Really?'

'He said they would steal my heart and then nothing else would matter.'

'Have I?'

'What?'

'Stolen your heart.'

'Maybe.'

'Only maybe?'

'Possibly.'

'Then I'll take that as a possible *yes*.'

'What did you say this morning?'

'When?'

'When I was getting excited about your diamonds.'

'I forget. What did I say?'

'Let's not get ahead of ourselves.'

'Then I'll take my own advice. It's probably safer.'

Lizzy kissed Burns on the forehead and lay down on the beach next to him but could only stare at the clouds drifting by overhead. A few minutes went by before she turned to him.

'I am in love with you, you know. I really am.'

CHAPTER 8

Two weeks later Burns came home and told Lizzy he had the money he needed; a cousin had invested. That's what he told her. He also asked her what her bank account details were. He said he felt bad about freeloading for so long and wanted to show his appreciation by depositing some of his new-found wealth. *Call it love-shack rent,* he said. She gladly accepted.

A week later he left for Africa but as he walked out the door with his beaten-up suitcase, she couldn't help but wonder if she would ever see him again. She didn't know why, but there was something about a man who lived his life like he was always ready for a quick escape, that made her worry. That night she tried to sleep but couldn't. She just tossed from side-to-side, willing sleep to come but her mind kept buzzing.

Eventually her eyes twitched, her breathing slowed, and her heartbeat dropped as she drifted off to a place where the dappled light of the sun's rays broke through thunderhead storm clouds. In the distance she saw a red glow, but then it sped towards her, swallowing her in a tunnel of crimson light. Beyond it was a blue ocean that sparkled like a million mirrors; each one reflecting an image of her but every image, though similar, was different, and blended into a confusion of colours and patterns like in a child's kaleidoscope. Her mind manipulated the images over-and-over again until she had no idea where it began, and the blue ocean became a clear pool and next to the pool grew grass the colour of emeralds. She saw herself lying there, enjoying the softness on her skin, but then the light in her dream flickered and she was standing in a place she didn't know that stretched for miles. Its open gibber plains shimmered with heat-haze, but the sun didn't hang in the sky like it should. It hovered just above the dry ground, frying all but the most distant of objects. A hot wind blew on her face, cutting her skin and, in her dream, she screamed, but in the nothingness, the noise was lost. She felt completely alone. For a moment she panicked, but then a hand tapped her on the shoulder. She turned. Her father looked younger than he ought to be. She took a step towards him, hesitated, but then moved forward again. His open arms were too inviting to ignore. She ran to him. She tried to embrace him, but when she did, he wasn't there. Lizzy looked left, then right, but there was nothing. She waited, unsure what to do, then off in the distance, she saw a black rectangle and walked towards it. A door. She opened it and stepped into a mysterious place where domes of giant red ochre bee-hive domes dotted the landscape and the air felt new; like the planet had been cleansed. She walked a little further and there was an old aboriginal woman sitting under an odd, bottle-shaped tree. The woman's dress was torn and faded, and her face looked like a crumpled paper bag, but her eyes pierced Lizzy's heart like two laser beams. She hesitated when the old woman's craggy finger beckoned her to sit down, but then took a step towards her and stopped. *I can't,* she said. *You must*, whispered the old woman, *you must*. Lizzy turned away looking for the door again, for a way out of her dream, but it was gone and when she turned back, the old woman had disappeared too. In her place Lizzy's husband, Tony, stood smiling at her. '*Be happy*, he said, *I understand.*' '*Do you?*' she asked, but before he could answer, the heat-haze swallowed him too. '*Come back*', she cried, as she tried to run towards him, but her feet were glued to the ground, and in a heartbeat, he was gone too. In his place Andrew Burns was laughing an almost maniacal laugh as he spilled a handful of diamonds onto a black granite block at his feet. Lizzy looked down and realized he was standing on a gravestone, but she gasped and took a step back. The inscription on the plaque read *Anastasia Dimitradies. Born 05.08.1975, Died 15.01.1993.* The year of her passing was the same year she turned eighteen; the year she became Elizabeth, Lizzy Lawson. She woke sobbing into her pillow, but it wasn't the dream that upset her, it was the return from it. She wanted to hold onto it and find Tony. She wanted to be with him just one more time, but in his place, there was only a ticking clock accompanied by the distant and lonely clang of the steel stays on the yacht masts in the inlet.

After a few minutes her heartbeat slowed, and she returned to the world she had left; disappointed, and full of questions that had no answers. She shivered as she remembered the old woman. Who was she? Where had she come from? Where had the hot wind come from and who was the woman who looked like her, lying on the impossibly green grass? She wanted to know why she had seen her own grave. After all, she was still alive, at least she thought she was. She touched her cheek to be sure, but as she lay in bed wondering, the dream replayed itself over-and-over again; all its images rushing at her in fast-forward. She tried to stop them, but they paid no attention. She wanted to yell *STOP, GO BACK*, but it was no use. Tony was gone. She licked her lips. Dry. She threw back the covers and walked to the bathroom and splashed her face with water and drank out of her hands. When she looked up, the old aboriginal woman was staring back at her from the mirror waving her bony finger from out of the darkness. *You must. You must.* Lizzy blinked, and the woman was gone.

She couldn't sleep after that so sat down at her computer to send Burns an email, but in her Inbox, there was a curious message from her landlord. The money for her rent hadn't been deposited and that was odd, because it was set up as an automatic payment on the fifteenth of every month. She opened her account. $234.00. How could that be? She had over fifty thousand in that account; her inheritance. She clicked on *transactions* and there it was. For the last eleven days someone had made a transfer of $4,500; just short of the $5,000 that meant she would automatically get an email from the bank to tell her. What the hell was going on? Who could have taken it? Had she been hacked? Cyber pirates? Burns? No, it couldn't have been. Could it? His cousin had invested. He had his money. He loved her. But then, in a moment of blinding clarity, she knew it was him. It had to be. The conversation three weeks before.

'Write down your date of birth.' he said. 'I'll get you a birthstone in Africa. It's the least I can do for all your kindness.'

She had dutifully complied, but now she knew she had made a mistake. Her PIN number was her birth date. She had told him that one night after too much wine. 5875. He already had her bank account details from when he deposited the love-shack rent. It had to be him. The fucker!

CHAPTER 9

With tears streaming down her face, she slammed her laptop shut and picked up her phone. She needed to find Burns. She had to know if it really was him; if he could have done such a thing when he said he loved her. People who love you don't do that. Do they? She wiped her eyes and punched in his number.

'Andrew Burns' phone,' answered a woman's sweet voice.

'Hi, I'm looking for Andrew Burns. I need to speak to him urgently,' she said, calmly.

'He's not here. Can I take a message?'

'Where is here?'

'Perth.'

'Perth, Western Australia?'

'Yeah. How many Perths are there?'

'Is he actually in Perth?'

'How should I know?'

'Do you know where he is?'

'I'm just an answering service love. He forwards his calls to here and we answer them. He could be anywhere.'

'Why does he do that?'

'What?'

'Forward his calls to you?'

'I don't know and it's probably none of my business, is it?'

'Can you tell him we have, tell him I, just ask him to call me please. Lizzy Lawson. He has the number.'

She hung up, hesitated, then punched in another number.

'Hello?'

'Alex, hi it's Lizzy. You haven't seen your friend Andrew, have you? I need to speak to him.'

'Who's doing the chasing now?'

'It's not what you think.'

'It never is.'

'I haven't seen him for a week. Can this keep? I'm in the middle of training.'

She ignored him. 'He's not answering his phone.'

'People do that. Maybe you're coming on too strong.'

'Do you know why he would be in Perth?'

'Perth? I thought he was going to Africa to—'

'Yeah, so did I.'

'We're supposed to be racing motor bikes tomorrow. Sounds like we're in the same boat.'

'Yeah, well right now, mine's called the Titanic,' whispered Lizzy, not intending Alex to hear her.

'Get him to call me if you hear from him, will you?'

'Of course. Can I help you with anything?' soothed Alex.

'I think it's already too late for that.'

'Fuck, you're not pregnant, are you?'

'You bloody men; one track minds. Listen, I've got a question.'

'Fire away.'

'Do you know anyone who knows anything about diamond mines?'

'Andrew.'

'Besides him.'

'Fuck Lizzy, what kind of question is that for six-thirty in the morning?'

'Think. It's important.'

'Why?'

'Because dear brother, your friend has cleaned out my bank account.'

'Yeah right. Tell me another one.'

'Alex, I'm fucking serious.'

'Why would he do that?'

'Because he loves me.'

'You're confusing me.'

'Now you know how I feel.'

'You're serious, aren't you?'

'Totally!'

'Jesus wept! Do you know where he is?'

'No Alex, I don't.' she replied growing frustrated.

'You're not going to do anything stupid are you?'

'I think I've done enough of that.'

'Promise me.'

'If I don't know where he is it's a bit hard to do any bloody thing.'

'Promise me you'll take a breath.'

She ignored her brother and repeated her question. 'So, do you know anyone who knows about diamond mines or not?'

'Why do you need to know?'

'I just want to find out how much crap your mate Andrew has been spinning.'

'Fuck Lizzy.'

'Alex, for God's sake, do you, or don't you?'

'There's this one guy. Peter O'Leary. He's some kind of chairman. Black Peak Mining I think it's called; something like that. Fucked if I know really, but Fat Sam thinks the sun shines out of his arse. O'Leary hires him to do security for his events. Black tie shit. At least that's what Sam says, but it could all be bullshit.'

'Ask him if he can set up a meeting for me.'

'He's right here. Ask him yourself.'

After minimal pleasantries Lizzy established that O'Leary was more a friend of Fat Sam's than an employer, and according to him, if anyone knew about mining, he did.

After he promised to call O'Leary, Fat Sam passed the phone back to Alex.

'Lizzy, promise me you're not going to do anything stupid.'

'Define stupid.'

'Lizzy?'

'Gotta go.'

She hung up, dropped the phone on the kitchen table and held her temples tight, trying to stop her head from exploding. Then, as she stared out the window, with her dog nuzzling up to her leg, rain started to fall. She could see her reflection in the glass. Her tears were just part of the storm that had set in.

CHAPTER 10

It was three days before O'Leary had an opening in his calendar. They met at Machiavelli, an Italian restaurant that money-market types, politicians, and high-rise miners used as their staff cafeteria. The place oozed power and privilege. Lizzy walked in, looked around, hesitated, and preened her dress. She felt like she didn't belong. Her unease must have shown because an old woman, who carried herself like she owned the place, sidled up beside her.

'Too many biga swinging dicks,' she whispered, with a strong Italian accent. 'You'll be fine. They're just people and they puta their pants on one leg at a time just like you and me.'

'I suppose,' replied Lizzy, politely.

'Look at you. Too skinny. Come, we feed you good. Who are you meeting?'

'Peter O'Leary. Do you know him?'

'Everybody knows him. Come, come, he is already here. I have an excellent table for you.'

Lizzy followed the old woman through the canals between the tables to where O'Leary was playing with his phone. He saw her and stood up.

'You must be Lizzy Lawson,' he smiled.

'Yes, yes, I am. Thank you for seeing me.'

'Your friend Fat Sam can be very persuasive, if you know what I mean.'

'So I believe,' she replied, sitting down.

The old woman interrupted, 'No menus today. I do something special for you, okay?'

They both nodded, intuitively knowing that to say otherwise was pointless.

'What can I do for you Lizzy?'

'Mr O'Leary, if you don't mind, I would like to pick your brain. Would that be okay?'

'Well for a start, call me Peter, but then help yourself, pick away to your heart's content.'

Lizzy spent the next few minutes telling him about Adamas and Andrew Burns but left out anything about the stolen money. When O'Leary asked to see the geologist's report she reached into her bag and pushed it across the table. While O'Leary ate, he read it, but she wasn't sure if the occasional *mmmm* was because he was questioning the contents of the report or he was enjoying his meal. Finally, he put down his fork.

'Look, this is all a bit unusual. Exploration results like these usually contain a complete set of sieve data using a standard progression of sieve sizes per facies as well as bulk sampling results and global sample grade scale per facies.'

'Excuse me?'

'It's a fancy way of saying that you drill some holes spread apart and if that looks promising you drill some holes closer together. The closer together, the sooner the mine can start talking about a *resource* rather than a *reserve*. You can raise money against a *resource* but only gamblers and fools put money into *reserves* ... I assume your friend is looking for investors?'

'Maybe.'

'Is this all JORC compliant? I don't see any mention of that in this document of yours.'

'JORC?'

'Joint Ore Reserves Committee. They set out minimum standards and guidelines for the public reporting of exploration results. If you don't have that, then no public company is going to go near you, and nor will any savvy private investors.'

'What is it?'

'It's a pain in the ass, that's what it is, but if you want big money, you don't have a choice. Everything must be done independently in labs. This report of yours just scratches the surface ... no pun intended. While we're on that subject, let me also say that I think it was prepared by a pretty average geologist; amateur even.'

'What do you mean?'

'Well, there's no mention of indicator minerals like ilmenite, chrome spinel, magnesium rich olivine or chrome diopside.' He turned the page, '...and nothing about diamond quantity by screen size per facies or depth. Are you sure this report is for real? I think someone might be pulling your leg.'

'What do you mean?'

'Faking the report. It just doesn't smell right. There's too much missing and the stuff that's covered is information you or I could get off the internet without too much trouble. Does your friend have core samples?'

'Yes, yes he does. At least he says he does.'

'They're going to be the key. He needs to get those into a lab before he goes hawking this report around ... maybe tell him to get himself a real geologist to prepare a proper report while he's at it.'

Gravity took hold of Lizzy's face and her hound-dog eyes probably said everything she was suddenly feeling.

'You've got to be careful Lizzy,' added O'Leary. 'This business is full of con men and charlatans, all out to make a quick buck from unsuspecting punters. I'm not saying that this is the case here, but it sure smells like it to me. You get a nose for these things after a while. No matter what business it is, when there's a lot of money at stake people don't always think too clearly ... they're often blinded by dollar signs I'm afraid. You know, my grandfather used to tell me about old gold prospectors who used to load up their shotguns with small amounts of gold and shoot it into the mine walls. It fooled a few people for a while ... usually just long enough to sell the mine ... but I'm sure your friend doesn't have to worry about that kind of tomfoolery, does he?'

'No, no not really. I suppose not,' she replied, dreamily.

'I can put you in touch with some good people if you want.'

'Yes. Thanks. That would be great.'

'You look disappointed.'

'It's not quite what I thought,' she replied. 'Tell me, how much money would a person need to get a proper diamond mine going?'

'That all depends.'

'On what?'

'Well, a whole bunch of things. The Canadians are draining lakes to get to diamond deposits and then building open cut mines ... that's bloody expensive ... and then it depends on whether it's wet or dry mining.'

'It all sounds expensive.'

'Well that all depends too. It's all risk and reward. You've got to put a lot in to get a lot out, but for this mine, if what the report says is true, which I must say, I doubt, you'll need two maybe three hundred million, and then some, just to get going, and even if you had the money, getting your hands on the right equipment can be bloody difficult.'

'What about fifty-thousand dollars? What would that get you?'

O'Leary laughed. 'That's going to buy the tea and biscuits for the workers for maybe a week.'

'So, if someone was talking about just a million dollars or so to get it going ...'

'They would bull-shitting you, big time I'm afraid. Mining isn't for the faint-hearted or the poor.'

'I know that feeling.'

On the bus ride home, Lizzy was sure she could hear the laughter of Burns' voice drunk with victory, but all she could do was quietly berate herself and wonder how she could've been so naively trusting. How could she have let her guard down so easily? She hated herself for not listening to the little voice inside her head when Burns arrived with his whole life in one suitcase.

'Fucking prick bastard!' she whispered, thumping her handbag but it was just a little too loud and earned her a stony-faced scowl from the old woman across the aisle.

She may have felt gutted, but the truth be told, Lizzy was angrier with herself than the man who robbed her. The money was important; it was all she had, and she had been too poor for too long for it not to be, but it was the ease of Burns' betrayal that hit her like a bullet, tore out her heart and left her gasping. She thought it was love that she felt. She thought it was real. She thought she could start her life all over again, but she had opened the door and he had slammed in her face. Now she felt unclean, like she could feel Burns' slimy hands on her. She wanted to scrub her body until the skin disappeared; until even the memory of his smell was erased.

Part of her wanted to believe Peter O'Leary was wrong about the report; she wanted to believe Burns really did love her, that he really had found diamonds and that he would come back to her, but the more she searched for a rainbow lining, the more she knew Burns was long gone, and so was her money. His love, his easy, unaffected ways were just an act; a contrivance, a scam, a plan, a pitiful lie, which only a woman in love could possibly have fallen for. At that moment she hated herself, but as the empty winds of loneliness raced through her mind, she tried to decide what to do next.

At first, she was rational and cool-headed, but as each possibility of quick retribution disappeared, the demons of her mind's hidden recesses poked their heads out for a better look. Eventually tears formed a soft film over her eyes, and even though she tried to hold back the flood, the dam-wall burst, and she began to sob. It was a private moment conducted in a very public place, but the other passengers were plugged into iPhones and their own lives of quiet desperation, so they didn't hear her; except for the old woman.

'Are you alright dear?' she asked, but Lizzy had fallen deaf; buried under a thousand layers of pain.

As her emotions ebbed and flowed, one minute she was an avenging warrior, prepared to rise up and lead her army against the evil love-rat and the next, she was a little girl, lost in the forest crying out for her father to find her. But then, she licked back the salty tears and found a tissue at the bottom of her handbag. Revenge may indeed be sweet, but she knew it was a dish best served cold. Besides, before she could even consider retribution, she needed to know why Burns had betrayed her. She knew the world was full of flawed, broken individuals, but this was different. This was a calculated plot to bring a person who was already on her knees, completely undone. What kind of person did that? Who mothered such people? How did they live if they had no scruples, no morals? She wanted to look Burns in the eye, so he could see the hurt she felt. She needed him to know he had stolen more than what little money she had. She needed to know if beneath the surface of the laconic, good-natured man, there lived an ounce of regret. But she also knew she had to see Burns to assuage her own guilt and to believe she hadn't been totally wrong about him. She had to find him. She didn't have a choice.

CHAPTER 11

Five hours after Lizzy and Henry had set out, she thought she saw a small building in the distance, then, as the wind ebbed and flowed, a dilapidated wooden and corrugated iron shack, marooned in the middle of a nowhere. A few kilometres from it, a small mountain range teased the tumble-down building with the possibility of shade and except for a few spindly trees, and a single desert-oak, there was nothing but spinifex grass and the occasional nub of a bush for miles.

The shack looked like it had been randomly added to over the years by amateur builders, with varying degrees of skill, taste, and availability of raw materials. One half was made of wood and additions either side had been concocted from tin, hessian, and a good dose of wishful thinking. A torn canvas awning was attached to the front and propped up by two weathered saplings. Surrounding the shack was a motley collection of fuel drums, agricultural pipes, rusted tools, engine parts and car tyres. To the right of the front door, was an old couch worn through to the inner springs. A dusty pick-up truck was parked outside.

'He's here, at least someone is,' said Henry, as they approached.

'He won't be expecting us, so we'd better be careful.'

'Ya tellin' me that he doesn't know ya comin'?'

'You could say that.'

'Ah, this is startin' ta smell pretty bad. Does he want to see you?'

'Probably not,' replied Lizzy. 'In fact, definitely not.'

'Who is this fella to ya anyway?'

'Dead to me.'

'Ah, maybe this isn't such a good idea. Maybe we should go home.'

'It's too late for that now, Henry.'

'I'm not so young no more. Can't handle myself the way I used to.'

'It's alright Henry. Everything will be okay.' replied Lizzy, as they pulled up next the truck. 'Is *this* it?'

'Yes.'

'*This* is a diamond mine?'

'Yeah, sure is, but I've seen worse.'

'We'll wait and see if he comes out,' said Lizzy. 'Toot the horn.'

'What if he's got a gun?'

'Then we'll get the hell out of here. Leave the engine running and toot.'

Henry did as he was told, but no one came. They waited a few more minutes. No one. They waited longer. Still nothing.

'Are you sure this is the place Henry?'

'Yeah, this is it alright.'

'Maybe he's asleep.'

'Nah, most of that shack is made from corrugated iron, so inside, it gonna be about one hundred and ten degrees. No one is sleepin' in that at this time of day.'

Lizzy looked perplexed. 'Then where the hell is he?'

'Maybe in his mine?'

'And where's that? I don't see any mine.'

'Could be any bloody where.'

'Toot again.'

'If he's here, he heard the first one. It's not like there's a freeway goin' by his door, just us.'

Henry switched off the engine and when he did, they heard the whir of a motor running.

'Generator. Probably out the back,' he said.

'So he must be here.'

'Someone is.'

Lizzy felt her heart pounding and wondered what would happen if she got out. She waited, but then Henry pulled open her door. She looked at him enquiringly, her eyes asking if it would be okay. He nodded.

'Maybe you're right Henry. Maybe this really is a bad idea.'

'Too right, but it's a bit late for that now.'

She got out slowly, as if acclimatizing herself to the heat and to the fear welling up in her belly. To the unknown. To the possibility that she might encounter a version of Andrew Burns she had never experienced before. An angry version. Finally, her feet hit the ground.

'You got to be bloody careful around here. Plenty of holes ta fall inta,' said Henry, removing his sweat-soaked shirt and throwing it onto the back seat.

'My God Henry, where the hell are we?'

Lizzy turned her face out of the wind, but when she turned back, Henry had disappeared, just as Jimmy Orion warned he might. She ran around their vehicle, hoping he was playing a joke, but he was nowhere to be seen and, in her loneliness, she thought perhaps he really had become the wind. After all, that was all that was left of him.

Her throat tightened.

'Henry! Henry! Where the hell are you?'

No reply. There was only one thing to do.

Approaching the shack, she was startled as two blue Alexandra parrots and a brightly coloured mulga parrot went squawking off into the sky and as her foot hit the doorstep, a zoo of desert insects and two thorny devil lizards, which had taken up residence behind an old car tyre, scuttled for cover. Inside the shack, the black hole of the unknown grabbed her like a giant spider wrapping its sticky web around her and gluing her to one spot. All she could manage was a timid, *Henry? Andrew?*

To her right, something scuttled across the floor, pushing her left, but in that direction another invisible, and probably imagined, creature forced her back.

As her eyes adjusted to the darkness, she could make out what she thought was a fridge but couldn't be sure. She felt her way towards it, opened the door and breathed a sigh of relief as the light of temporary salvation flooded the shack. She quickly memorized the layout, fearing the light would disappear, but out of the corner of her eye, she saw a cord by the doorway and pulled it. Light!

Next to the refrigerator was a dirty sink, with no taps and no pipes, propped up on old milk crates. Above the makeshift sink, two torn Playboy magazine centrefolds blew exaggerated kisses and stroked their pendulous breasts. The western side of the shack had a small window which looked like it could be pushed out, and propped up with a wooden pole, however, it had been installed on the prevailing windward side, so remained shut.

Four camp stretchers lined the walls. Burns' old suitcase was on one of them, and on another, a rectangular case with Remington 105CTI embossed on it. Lizzy opened it. Empty, but clearly designed for a shotgun.

'Fuck.' she complained to the emptiness.

A simple, unpainted wooden table, with four mismatched chairs, occupied the centre of the room. On it, there was a half-drunk long-neck beer, alongside two empties.

On the other side, was an open box of shotgun shells, and on a saucer near it, shot that had been removed from some. Burns' dusty laptop was open with his satellite phone connected. It looked like he had been working but had stopped mid-beer. A chair was lying on its back on the floor. Lizzy picked it up, sat down, tapped a key and the screen sprang to life throwing a soft glow on the empty bottles.

'So you must have left just recently.' she said to herself. 'It hasn't shutdown yet.'

Lizzy checked Burns' email to see if he had received the four messages she sent and quickly found them at the top of his *deleted* file. She shook her head as she read the message from someone called Ellen Hansen. *I'm looking forward to seeing you this Saturday. I thought we might go down to the Margaret River and stay at a wonderful bed and breakfast place I know. We can discuss the investment you were talking about then.* She opened his *sent* file and at the top was a return email to the same woman, *yes that sounds great. I'm just tying up a few loose ends in Africa. See you Friday night.*

There were messages from an assortment of other women too, but it was the one from a Hotmail address, dated two days before Lizzy noticed her money was missing, that made her want to cry. *Has that moron Lawson woman given you her PIN number yet?* Burns' reply made her feel even worse. *I got her drunk. It was like taking candy from a baby. Just a couple more days and I'll have the money and then she can go jump off a cliff for all I care*…and that's exactly what Lizzy felt like doing.

'My god, what have I got myself into?' she said, to the emptiness, slumping in the chair with the distant ark, ark, ark of a crow serenading her.

She sat there for a moment, calculating her options, but soon realized she hadn't thought her mission through. What was she going to do when she saw him? Demand her money back? Was he just going to give it to her? Unlikely. So, what the hell was she doing here?

'This is stupid,' she bellowed, thumping the table.

She got up, wiped the sweat from her forehead and opened the door.

'Henry! Henry, where the hell are you?'

No reply.

'So I guess that I have to wait for you to show yourself do I Andrew? Okay, well, I've got all bloody day, so you can play your fucking game of hide and bloody seek if you want, but I'll still be bloody here when you come out.'

A crow laughed at her.

'And *you* can bloody-well shut the hell up,' she replied, turning to go back inside.

At first, she sat down to wait but then turned her attention to Burns' suitcase. In it were crumpled clothes and dirty socks, a passport, which had never been used, and an airline confirmation; Perth-London-Zurich, with a departure date, five days away. Underneath it all, she spotted a dog-eared manila folder. She took it over to the table, opened it and stared open-mouthed at the photo in a newspaper clipping. The caption read, LOCAL TRADESMAN DIES IN HORROR CRASH and below that, a photo of Tony's wrecked utility. Yet another clipping read, BIG BANANA POWERS ON-OPENS FIFTIETH STORE. The magazine story about Lizzy's father had a small section highlighted in green, *His estranged daughter has not left her home since her husband, died six months ago.* There were another ten or so articles, but what was underneath the clippings made her gasp. Photos. Her walking her dog, Brutus, on the beach, filling her car with petrol, drinking coffee at her window and even one kneeling beside her husband's gravestone. Lizzy couldn't believe what she was looking at. It was as if the everydayness of her sadness had been recorded by a spy; a peeping tom who had ferreted his way into the sadness of her life.

As she flicked through the photos, she realized that Burns had been tracking her life for over a year. There were other files just like the one with her name on it and all of them had photos and newspaper cuttings of other women whose lives mirrored hers in so many ways. Even in her own misery, she couldn't help but feel especially sorry for Ellen Hansen. Her husband and two children had died when the roof at a shopping mall collapsed, and according to the newspaper article, the damages payout she received was in the tens of millions. The more she read the various files, the more the bile of hate rose in her throat, until finally, she swept them off the table with an angry swipe of her arm.

'Where the hell are you Andrew?' she screamed.

No answer.

The temperature was rising and so was her fury; she was a volcano ready to blow.

'Fuck this,' she said, to herself, then tied her hair back and headed for the door.

CHAPTER 12

Lizzy knew that Burns had to be around somewhere, but where was the mine he had talked about so optimistically? Beyond the shack, it looked like there was nothing, nothing at all. However, twenty meters from it, she found out she was wrong, and stepped off mother-earth into a giant hole, without even realizing it was there. It grabbed her by the feet and crashed her half-way down a makeshift ladder before showing some compassion and guiding her flailing arms to a rung. For a moment she hung there, gripping it awkwardly with one hand, but then death shrugged and sulked off into the darkness.

'Andrew?'

It was too soft to be heard at any distance, but the faint echo was enough to confirm that she was still in the world of the living. She took a deep breath and climbed down the rest of the way, descending deeper into despair as she went.

'Andrew? Are you here? Please be here.'

Suddenly a light went on behind her. She turned. It blinded her.

'Who's there? Andrew? Stop being a fool!'

The voice spoke softly. 'Ah, I don't think this fella is gonna say too much today.'

Lizzy could hear flies buzzing, and as the light moved, she glimpsed the shape of a body propped up against the mine wall. She screamed. Half the body's head was missing and if it wasn't for the Levi jeans, faded khaki work-shirt and battered riding boots that Burns always wore, she wouldn't have recognized him.

'You did this!' she yelled, running towards the light, tearing at the holder with her fingernails, striking out as best she could, but strong arms held her back.

'Hey, take it easy. I told ya before, no bloody white lady is gonna bash this black fella.'

'You did this! You killed him.'

'No not me ... it looks like this bloody fella blew his own bloody head off, look!' explained Henry, moving the flashlight over the dead body.

Nestled under the shattered bone that once formed a chin and a skull, there was a shotgun pointed toward the remains of a head. Lizzy felt bile rise in her throat. It irrigated her mouth, and she sank to her knees, just as two rats scuttled off into the darkness.

'What the hell happened here?' she wailed. 'This can't be happening.'

'I told ya this bloody fella was crazy. He shot himself ... it looks like he did it with them bloody barramundi scales ... don't it ... bloody strange that.'

Lizzy grabbed Henry's flashlight and as she steered it over the greying body, thousands of small specks of bright light jumped and danced and somehow made it seem as if Burns was still alive.

'Are *they* diamonds?' she asked, not believing what she was seeing. 'They can't be, can they ... why?'

'Dunno, but somethin' is bloody wrong here ... maybe he's a yilkurruny jiyliny—'

'Excuse me?

'Bad man. Why else would someone do this bloody stupid thing?'

'If you had asked me that a few days ago, I would've said he was an angel,' replied Lizzy sadly.

'Too bad about that missus. Now he's parta the earth, parta the sky, parta the rocks ... we all are ... we just don't know it yet.'

In the darkness, Lizzy's face collapsed but Henry didn't see it, so he had no idea what was going on inside her head. In the light, her face would have betrayed her distress and misery, but in the dark, her silence said little. She wanted to cry and a small part of her even felt sad for Burns, but she was too shocked to do either, so she just knelt there, rocking backwards and forwards.

'Come on missus. No use starin' at him. He ain't goin' nowhere.'

Eventually Henry thought he heard her sob.

'Are ya okay?'

There was a long silence, but Lizzy finally answered. 'I've had better days Henry. I've had better days.'

'Come on. Like I said, there's no use hangin' around here.'

She took one last look, then they ascended the ladder in silence and pushed their way through the wind back to Burns' shack. When they got there, another Toyota was parked next to theirs. Jimmy Orion sat tapping his fingers on the steering wheel. He saw her and waved casually, like it was no surprise that she would see him in the middle of nowhere. She wanted to ask him what he was doing there, when he said that he didn't know where the mine was. She corrected course in his direction. He poked his head out the window and pointed towards the shack door.

'There's someone inside who wants to see ya,' he yelled.

CHAPTER 13

Lizzy groped in the darkness, searching for the light cord, but when the shape of a woman pushed the fridge door open with her foot, Lizzy screamed.

'Who the hell are *you*?' she bellowed. 'You frightened me half to death!'

'I could ask you the same question sweet 'art.'

'Who are you?' she yelled, again.

'Are you telling me that you really don't know?'

'I have no idea.'

'I'm his wife. Helena.'

'Wife? Whose wife?'

'Andrew's, you numb-skull.'

Lizzy's face dropped. She turned on the single light bulb and retreated to a camp stretcher until she could gather her wits.

The middle-aged stranger was attractive in a well-used kind of way, but her blonde hair obviously came out of a bottle and her lips were creased from smoking too many cigarettes. Her jeans hugged her body just a little too tightly, and small singlet top exposed her flat belly and considerable cleavage.

'Wife?' Lizzy asked, in disbelief.

'What's the matter? Don't you know what a wife is?' the woman replied, blowing cigarette smoke.

'Andrew Burns' wife?'

'No, bloody Santa Claus' wife. Who do ya think?'

'I just ... I didn't know he was married.'

'Yes, Andrew seems to make a habit of leaving that bit out when he meets women.'

'I, I—'

'I've never actually been all the way out here before. It's not much of a love nest, is it?'

'It's not what it looks like.'

'Listen, Andrew has been screwing little sluts like you ever since I've known him.'

'Look, it's not that. It's not what you think.'

'Why else would a pretty girl like you be all the way out here?'

'He stole some money from me.'

'Why?'

'Well, he said he needed money for his mine but by the looks of things I think that was just a story.'

'Yeah, it's not much more than a toilet in the desert, is it?'

'Yes. I realize that now.'

'How much did he take?'

'All I had. Fifty thousand.'

'Jesus H. Christ! He's ripped you off, hasn't he? Tell me you're not serious.'

'I think he's done the same thing to a lot of other people as well.'

'Meaning?'

Lizzy walked over to the folder of press clippings spread out on the floor, gathered them up as best she could, then handed them to the woman.

'What the fuck is all this?'

'A lot of women who have been taken for a ride.'

'Like you?'

'Yes, like me.'

The stranger flicked through the file looking up sceptically from time to time. 'Is this you?' she asked finally, holding up a clipping.

'Yes.'

'I had no idea about all of this. I just thought he was going to his damn mine just like his idiot father always did, when all the time, he was all over the country chatting up all these women … and you're telling me he took money off all of them?'

'I think so.'

'Fuck. He's been a busy boy.'

'You mean to tell me that you had no idea about all this?'

'Honey, nothing Andrew Burns does ever manages to surprise me, but this is all brand fucking new. As far as I'm concerned, he's got the 'Wandering DNA' that his dickhead father gave him.'

'Ishmael?'

'Who?'

'His father.'

'His father's name is Reg, Reg Burns.'

'But he changed it from Ishmael Bernstein when he came to Australia.'

'Yeah right. Old Reg was born and bred in the bloody outback love. He spent half his useless life wandering round the desert looking for God knows what. Who the hell is Ishmael?'

'I should've known that it was a lie too.'

'Old Reg couldn't wander three feet these days.'

'He's alive?'

'Just. Senile dementia. He doesn't know what bloody day it is. He found this place almost forty years ago … before he lost his mind, he always said this mine was gonna make him rich one day.'

'I think Andrew just might have achieved that, but not how his father expected.'

'Why don't you just ask him for your money back?'

'Yeah right! I wish I could.'

'Why not? Andrew is a pile of jelly when he's backed into a corner. Just ask. He'll give in.'

'I can't do that because Andrew is—'

'Yeah, I know, he's an asshole. Everyone knows that.'

'Helena, I'm afraid that your husband is ... well he's ...'

'Go on spit it out!'

'I'm afraid he's dead,' she whispered.

'What do you mean, dead?'

'He's down the mine ... he ... he killed himself. Didn't he Henry?'

Lizzy turned for confirmation, but for the first time since she had returned to the shack, she realized that Henry wasn't there.

'And just who is this invisible Henry person?' spat the woman.

'He was with me when we found Andrew. He drove me out here. He must be outside. I swear ... he was here a minute ago. He's probably down the mine. Come on, let's go. I'll show you,' she said, before adding an apologetic, 'It's not very pretty.'

Lizzy grabbed her flashlight and stood at the door, her eyes begging the woman to come with her, but it took a full minute before she reluctantly butted out her cigarette and got up from the table.

'Lead the way. I may as well get the full tour of failure.'

As they passed Orion, he wound down his window.

'We better not stay too long. It's gonna piss down soon and we don't wanna get stuck out here ... the roads.'

'Yeah, yeah righto Jimmy, keep ya bloody shirt on. Apparently, I've got a dead body to inspect. Your friend here is having bloody fantasies.'

As Lizzy and the woman reached the yawning opening to the mine, they stopped.

'Down there? You want me to go down there? No fucking way!'

'Please, if he's your husband, you have to see for yourself.'

'I don't *have to* do nothin' sweet 'art.'

The woman shook her head but eventually did as Lizzy asked and climbed to the bottom of the mine shaft.

'Is this what Andrew has been carrying on about? It's just a bloody 'big hole,' she said, inhaling the damp.

'Not much is it?' replied Lizzy, trying to find common ground. 'He's just ahead here. Be ready. It's not very pretty.'

Lizzy turned into the side tunnel and shone the flashlight where Burns' body should've been, but there was nothing. No body. No flies. No rats.

'But he was right here a minute ago. I swear. I must have the wrong spot.'

She swung the flashlight frantically in wide arcs, but it was gone, vanished into thin air along with Henry.

'You've got to believe me. He was here, right here!'

'Yeah right.'

'But he was. He really was.'

'Maybe you've had too much sun love. Maybe you're hallucinating.'

Lizzy began to sob softly.

'Come on.' said the woman, grabbing her arm. 'Lover-boy is up there having a beer and a good old laugh at your expense.'

Lizzy pulled away. 'HE'S NOT! HE'S DEAD! I SAW HIM! I DID. I REALLY DID!'

At that moment, in the bowels of the earth, the disappointments and tragedies of Lizzy's life welled up in her eyes, breached the spillways and rushed down her cheeks in an avalanche of tears that only the truly wretched will ever know. Her body buckled, and she bent over, wracked by giant sobs and jerky spasms of the deepest grief imaginable and collapsed to her knees in the dust, crying such a pitiful wail that even Burns' wife felt sorry for her. She tried to comfort Lizzy, but it was a half-hearted effort done with little finesse or enthusiasm, and even less understanding of what she was really crying about. She had no way of knowing that life had been so cruel to her and no way of knowing that Elizabeth Lawson was just one loose thread away from coming completely undone.

'Come on let's go,' offered the woman, but Lizzy was too buried in her sorrow and didn't hear her.

She knelt, gasping for air, desperately trying to suck in oxygen, but she only managed deep guttural sobs that sounded like they might tear her lungs out. Eventually, she succumbed to her misery and curled up in a foetal position on the red soil and pounded the earth with her fist, sending puffs of dust into the air which stuck to her sweat. After a short while, she was just what Henry had told her she would eventually be; she looked like *parta de earth*. Burns' wife tried to look away, but couldn't, nor could she bring herself to reach out and help a woman she suspected was sleeping with her husband.

'I'm going back up now, no point in wasting any more time down here looking for that ratbag. C'mon let's go.'

When Lizzy didn't move, the woman shrugged and left without another word, then stumbled in the dark back towards the ladder, swearing under her breath as she went.

After a few minutes Lizzy called out, *Hello? Hello? Is anybody there?* but the stranger was gone, so she pushed herself up to a sitting position and turned the flashlight on the spot where Burns' body should've been. She needed to be sure she wasn't losing her mind, so took one last look. The body was gone, but just a little further along from where she thought it once was, were what she assumed were splinters of diamonds and bone fragments, implanted in the mine wall. As she moved the flashlight over the remains of the diamonds, they jumped and sparkled like the clear waters in the dream after Burns left. Lizzy wiped her eyes with her dirty hands and as her last tears seeped out, slowly rolled down her face, over her chin and plopped in the dust, she groaned and sank back into the dust, sobbing.

'Fuck you Andrew. Fuck you to hell.'

CHAPTER 14

Twenty minutes later, Lizzy pulled herself together and dragged herself back to the shack where Burns' wife was waiting in the Toyota, but there was no sign of Orion. As she stumbled up to the vehicle, Helena wound down her window, exhaled a large cloud of cigarette smoke, looked her up and down and shook her head.

'If you see Andrew, tell him I stopped by, will ya?'

Lizzy brushed hair out of her eyes. 'I know that you don't believe me, but he *really* is dead.'

'More likely he's wandering around out there somewhere looking for those little blue flashes of his … or maybe, just maybe, he's looking for another cute little brunette to replace you.'

'You'll see. I'm telling the truth. I really am.'

'Yes luv, of course ya are … tell lover-boy that I laughed when I saw his *mine*. I should've come sooner. I needed a good laugh. Tell him he's a dreamer just like his old man, oh, and tell him not to bother comin' home. I've had enough of his bullshit shenanigans.'

Just as the woman finished talking, Orion rushed around the corner of the shack doing up the buttons on his trouser fly. He was inside the truck before Lizzy could ask him why he said that he didn't know where Burns' mine was. Perhaps she had underestimated him and wondered if the woman who claimed to be Andrew Burns' wife had, at some point, paid his price of a night in the Royal Suite to get directions.

Lizzy watched until a long trail of dust finally blotted out their departure and jagged bolts of lightning dissected the midday sky. The rain was coming, just as Henry had said it would. She waited for a moment, taking in the beauty of nature, unfolding over the ugliness of her life, then shoulders hung, dragged herself back to the shack.

'We gotta go. Big rain is comin' real soon,' chirped Henry, as she stepped inside.

'Where the bloody hell have *you* been, and more importantly, where the fuck is Andrew's body?'

Before Henry could answer, she lunged at him attacking his head. All he could do was hold up his arms and try to fend her off.

'I tell ya before, ya can't bash a bloody black fella. How many times have I gotta tell ya that? Gubment says you can't. It's all official, written down and everything.' smiled Henry, with his tongue firmly implanted in his cheek.

But Lizzy was relentless. With Henry's reappearance her sadness turned to anger and unfortunately for him, he was in the wrong place at the wrong time. Her fists pounded at him until finally, she was spent and sank to the floor, sweating, sobbing, and swinging limp punches. Henry could only stare open-mouthed.

'Are ya okay?' he said.

But she didn't answer, so Henry lifted her onto one of the camp stretchers and did his best to comfort her until she fell asleep, but as she slowly drifted off, he could hear her mumble a soft but discernible, *you must, you must.*

While Lizzy slept, the blistering-hot day gave way to night and then a chilly morning. In the shadowland of half sleep, she lay very still, hoping someone had stolen all her troubles. She heard a noise but was too afraid to open her eyes and discover the truth, so drifted in and out of consciousness searching for the dream where she had seen her dead husband. Then in the pre-dawn darkness, she thought she could hear rain falling and the trickling of small streams. Behind her, the drip, drip of water on rock soothed her, and in another dimension, she could make out an eerie wind as it whistled through trees thrashing branches backwards and forwards. It was then she realized something was terribly wrong because the hut where she had fallen asleep was in the middle of an almost treeless plain. She opened one eye and saw Henry sitting not far from her. At first, she thought she must have imagined the wind and water, but as she reached out her hand to him, she could still hear it.

'Henry?'

'Ah there ya are,' he smiled.

'Is everything all right?'

'Oh yes. All okay 'cept for ma bloody sore head.'

'I'm so sorry Henry,' she apologized, softly.

'That's okay. I got a hard head ... just like the rocks ... I tell you before ... I'm part of the land.'

'How long have I been sleeping Henry?'

'Oh missus, sun went away, so long time. It'll be mornin' soon.'

As Lizzy's senses returned, she could feel hard earth and the comfort of what she thought might be a warm, animal skin beneath her. The claustrophobia of the shack had disappeared, and an unfamiliar peace surrounded her.

'Henry, where are we?'

'It's all okay. We're at Purnululu ... the Bungle Bungle ... that place what I told ya about ... you good here ... the rain come like I said it would. It was too wet at that mine, so we come 'ere ... no problem 'ere ... very dry.' insisted Henry.

'But Henry, what about Andrew? Where's Andrew?'

'Mr. Andrew ... he's dead ... you saw him.'

'Yes, I know, but where is his body?'

'Back to the earth missus ... dust to dust like ma catechism teacher used ta say.'

Lizzy was confused.

'Are we in a ... in a cave Henry?' she asked, incredulously, inspecting the jagged walls.

'Yes missus ... big one ... the world is just out there...it's rainin' bloody hard.'

The old man pointed to where the darkness of the cave finished and gave way to a subtler grey as a hint of moonlight peeked through a gap in the rain clouds. To the right of him a small fire flickered and as he stood up and moved to the mouth of the cave, the orange and red of the fire lit up the face of an old woman sitting rock-still while the light danced over her. When she saw the woman, Lizzy gasped, and hid her face behind her hands. She must be dreaming again. They weren't in a cave, there was no rain and no trees ... she *was* dreaming ... she *had to be* because the woman sitting next to the fire was the same one she had seen in her dream.

'Henry, that woman. Who is she?'

Lizzy tried to whisper, but the urgency in her voice turned her words into an anxious interrogation.

'Ah missus, that's my mother Rosie. She doesn't say much no more. You go on back ta sleep now.'

Rosie's round face with its narrow eyes and grey hair sat motionless on a well-lined neck which emerged from a yellow cotton dress which had seen better days. Her hands hung loosely in her lap, palms upwards, accentuating the wizened fingers of someone who had worked hard all their life. The old woman smiled a tight smile and motioned for Lizzy to lie down.

'You sleep now young girl ... get a proper good sleep.'

'But I ...'

'Sleep,' commanded Rosie, waving her hand a little more aggressively.

Lizzy was too startled and confused to say anything which resembled something intelligent, so she lay down until the first rays of the new day's sun crept over the horizon. By then the rain had stopped, but dark clouds still hung in the sky. Lizzy rolled back her animal skin blanket and looked over to where the red embers of the fire still smouldered. The old woman slept peacefully resting her head on a rock, but on the other side of the cave, Henry's bed was empty. Above it, were the shape of human hands painted on the cave wall and underneath them, the outline of a crocodile's mouth yawned towards the entrance where the cave opened out to a ledge ten metres above the ground. She walked over to it and looked down to where a shallow stream jumped and bubbled over large pebbles then flowed quickly past, dived over a small ledge into a pond and curved around a bend where it disappeared.

The wind had stopped, and tall palms dripped water like a thousand leaky taps. Then, as the sun rose a little higher, a rainbow caressed the gorge. Moments later, wild budgerigars and rainbow bee-eaters darted in and out of the high rock faces like miniature fighter jets at an air show while she stood silently marvelling at the beauty in front of her. To her left there was a rocky path leading down to the stream, so she edged her way down to where the water tripped over the rocks. As she knelt to scoop up some water, the silence of the morning was broken by a parrot's screech echoing in the distance. She looked up to where she thought the noise came from, but all she saw was an empty sky. Under it was a rocky chasm where rock faces butted up against each other like two giant loaves of burnt bread.

'It's Kaleruny ... him bring da rain,' said a voice behind her.

She jumped and turned, mouth open, holding her beating heart.

'Kaleruny dats da Rainbow serpent ... he makes the seasons ... sends down the rain ... he's da giver of life.' continued the voice.

Lizzy was too shocked to say anything.

'In the beginning that Rainbow Serpent, Kaleruny, took the water and filled up the creeks, the waterholes and of all the rivers. He had already made the mountains, the rocks, and the sky ... they were all part of his long time ago jobs. See that waterfall there? See that rock it runs over? That was a crocodile. He turned it into stone to stop the fish goin' back upstream ... a long time ago, that crocodile rock helped my sisters proper good.'

'I ... I ...'

The voice continued. 'In there, in that water, there's the spirit of the children waitin' ... waitin' to be born. They're all waitin' with that big old Rainbow Serpent.'

'I'm Eliz...Lizzy ...'

'Henry he's already tellin' me who ya are ... yeah, I know dat.'

'You're Henry's mother ... Rosie?' she asked, hopefully, finally recovering her voice.

'He's ma child alright. Henry is a good boy. He listens to me proper good. Are you good for listenin'?'

'I suppose so. Where am I?'

'You're where you need to be ... that's where, and that's all ya need to know for now,' laughed Rosie, as she hobbled off over the rocks, in and out of the submerged spinifex grass, past the miniature fan palms, and finally, out of sight.

'Are you coming back?' called Lizzy, but all she heard was an echo of her own voice. For a moment she thought she might cry again but then an unusual strength, a strength she didn't understand, made her brave. It was a new feeling that would probably take some getting used to, but for the moment she wore it like a pair of new shoes ... slightly uncomfortable, but with a bit of wearing in, she would probably get used to it.

She followed the stream until she came upon a still section where the water flowed off into a pond the size of a small swimming pool. Standing guard over the pool were dozens of eucalyptus trees. The leaves and bark still glistened from the rain and growing all around them, and up to the edge of the pool, was the greenest grass she had ever seen. Long, soft stems, the colour of emeralds, swayed in the hint of a breeze. Somehow, she imagined that the trees and the grass and the water were calling her.

She walked slowly towards the grass, watching its reflection swaying in the water expecting the mirage to disappear as she got nearer, but it didn't, so she knelt and ran her hands over the green carpet. Then she slowly lay down and as her cheek touched the grass, she shivered. A tingling sensation ran down her spine and in this faraway place, all alone, Elizabeth Lawson exhaled as the misery of her life ran out of her. The years of struggle, making ends meet, seemed to leach out of her and even the pain of Tony's death subsided long enough for her to smile. Lying on that grass she felt as though she was cocooned in a special kind of warmth; a love that at first, she didn't understand, but then, she realised that it was inside her. It was bubbling up from a place she had long forgotten and as the euphoria grew, she somehow knew Rosie was right. She was in the place she needed to be. This was her special place; her dreaming place, the place that held the answers to who she really was. It was too wonderful to be anything else but that. It had to be. But why here? Why this place?

In the solitary confinement of an all-embracing peace, she rolled onto her side, looked into the water, and staring back at her was the smile and sympathetic eyes of Anastasia Dimitriades, the person she had long forgotten. While she stared, she imagined she saw her father reading to her; simple story books that taught him English and her, the fantasies of faraway places. She saw her mother covered in flour, kneading dough to make pita bread and chopping zucchini, potatoes, myzithra cheese and mint to make her favourite dish, Chaniotiko Boureki. She saw herself laughing in a school playground and serving customers in her father's first fruit shop. She saw her newborn brother, Alex, when he was no more than a ball of wrinkled skin, and she saw the love and joy in her mother and father's eyes when they pulled her in close so that a photographer could record the moment for posterity. She saw herself playing hopscotch with laughing children on the pavement at the migrant hostel, a pimple-faced Colin Kenny arriving with a corsage to take her to a school dance, sharing watermelon with her family on the beach. She watched her teenage self swoon over John Bon Jovi and his gyrating hips. They were all recollections of sweet, wonderful moments, moments that dried up when Milo came into her life. She stared at the reflection for a long time but before she could reach out and touch her past, she saw Henry's reflection in the water. A tin billycan dangled from his left hand and under his right arm was a green–brown object the size of a small melon.

'Mornin'.'

She jumped for the second time that morning.

'Henry, where have you been? I thought you had run off again.'

'Nah missus. Gotta get da breakfast. Sugarbag and bush melon.'

'Sugarbag? Bush melon?'

'Bush tucker missus. Bloody good. The sugarbag is wild honey. You wanna try it? That melon tastes like, well, it tastes like bloody melon don't it.'

Suddenly Lizzy realized she hadn't eaten for two days and readily agreed even though the thought of Henry's bush tucker didn't sit well.

'Drop ya finger in, like this, and just scoop it out,' instructed Henry.

She twisted a small scoop around her index finger and hesitantly placed it in her mouth, half expecting to spit it out, but to her surprise, it really did remind her of honey, albeit sweeter and cleaner than its city cousins.

'What do you do with the melon?' she asked.

'Ah, almost bloody forgot ... my minds goin'.'

Henry broke the melon open on a rock and with a flat stick scooped out the black seeds in the middle, then broke off a portion for Lizzy who ate hungrily with none of the hesitation of the first scoop of sugarbag honey.

'Do ya like it missus?'

'It's delicious Henry, and I thought bush-tucker was just those little witchetty grub things.'

'Nah missus ... the land is like a bloody supermarket if ya look close enough ... besides we just like to trick you *kartiya*, white people, with them witchetty grubs ... we like to see ya squirm while ya eat'em.'

'Really Henry?'

He smiled a cheeky grin. 'Ya never know, do ya. Ya never know.'

Suddenly she lost her smile. 'What did you do with Andrew's body?'

'Ah missus he's over there.'

'I don't see anything.'

'That's because he's over there now,' said Henry, pointing in the opposite direction.

'Henry?'

'He's all around us now missus ... he's the sky, the rocks, the land ... even the bush melon there.'

She spat out the melon she had been enjoying and wiped her mouth ferociously. Henry laughed.

'Henry, tell me what you did with Andrew's body.'

'I left him in the fridge in that shack missus. Took out all the shelves and that beer and put him inside ... had ta break his legs, but then he fitted okay... filled up the generator out the back with diesel ... he's good for two, maybe three days.'

'You ... put ... him ... in ... the ... fridge?'

'Sure.'

'All of him?'

'Yes missus.'

'In one piece?'

'Sure. You thinkin' that us *Kija* blokes is cannibals or somethin'? Chop him up and have him a little bit at a time ... is that what you're thinkin'?'

'No Henry, no I'm not ... I was just—'

'Bloody big fridge that, but I had ta tie a rope around it to keep it shut.'

'I'm sorry Henry. I didn't mean to—'

'No worries. Old Henry has got a thick skin ...we gotta have that 'round you white fellas.'

'I'm sorry.'

'We gotta get him back to Jimmy's place. He's got an even bigger fridge ... then the police can come get him. If we don't take him back, they'll think I bloody shot him ... always the black fella ... that's where they'll be lookin' first.'

'Just like a long time ago at Mistake Creek hey Henry?'

'Yeah, just like that.'

'When can we go back?'

'We can't do anything until the roads dry out a bit, but if this rain keeps on goin' then we've got no bloody chance at all. It looks like you're not goin' nowhere either so you're gonna be me and Rosie's house guest for a bit. If there's no more rain, we go back ta see Jimmy in two days, maybe three … more rain … we're bloody stuffed.'

'This place is beautiful Henry. What's it called?'

'Purnululu. All of this place is Purnululu. It's the place ya told me you saw from the sky. I already told ya that.'

'No Henry, this place.' she replied, indicating the towering rocks and giant chasms all around them.

'Ah, this place right here, this place … on the map it's called Cathedral Gorge. We're on the edge of the gorge … more rain comin' … down further … over there, there's gonna be proper lot of water runnin' by soon.'

'Cathedral Gorge,' repeated Lizzy, with the soft respect normally reserve for holy places.

'It's just like a church, ain't it?' said another softer voice.

CHAPTER 15

'This place is just like them places I have seen in the pictures with the Pope,' smiled Rosie, dipping her finger in the leftover sugarbag. 'Did you try somma this melon? Ma mother used ta cut off bits and put a stick through ... dry it out ... keep it 'til the dry season ... bloody good,' said Rosie, biting off a juicy chunk.

'You've seen the Pope?' asked Lizzy, incredulously.

'Na, just in the pictures, while I was livin' in Derby ... had that leprosy ... de kartija, you white fellas, had a place there to fix it all better ... long time ago now.'

Lizzy took half a step away.

'It's okay. I don't got that leprosy no more ... just took my leg ... lucky I'm still here, but the good God up top, he saved me.'

Lizzy looked down and for the first time, noticed Rosie hobbled on an artificial leg which was nothing more than a stainless steel post stuck inside a dirty running shoe.

'This place is just like a big church, don't ya reckon?' repeated Rosie, shaking her limb to show Lizzy it was attached.

'It beautiful.'

'Are you the prayin' kind?'

'Lately, more than you know Rosie.'

'I'm not the prayin' one, but then I'm gettin' that leprosy. I got pain all day, so the station manager up at Texas Downs ... good fella old Jimmy ... dead now ... he sent me off to Derby to get better ... I was there for almost three bloody years. Them fellas there, they teach me to be a Catholic and all that stuff about the catechism. One of the nuns, Sister Mary, she used to come whisperin' and askin' if I wanna go to the church. She took me to see Father Tom, young fella with a round face like an orange and a squeaky voice like that Jimmy Orion's ... then I done the Holy Communion. I said to Father Tom, *what's that little white biscuit for?* He tells me, *you get it in your soul and it makes you very strong for everything ... it's God in heaven*, that's what he said.'

'Is this your church Rosie?'

'All this land is my church ... it's where I come from ...' replied the old woman, without thinking. 'All of this place, all of this land is my mother ... all of this is a part of Ngarrangkarni, the dreamin' ... all of it was made back then ... that Kaleruny he's doin' all this. We gave all of these places names ... not about what it is ... but about what happened there a long time ago ... in the beginnin' of time.'

Lizzy saw the faraway look in Rosie's eyes as she took herself back to a time when the rainbow serpent wound its way over the landscape creating all she knew. For a moment the old woman lost herself in the thoughts of forty-thousand-years, but just as quickly, snapped back.

'Let's all sit down. I wanna know ya good. Henry reckons you're a little bit wangala, you know, mad in the head. He reckons ya cry more water than the bloody rain.'

Lizzy turned to scowl at Henry but did a double take. While she was talking, he had disappeared, again. Rosie motioned for her to sit under one of the eucalyptus trees, which she did, and as the old woman squatted down, sat cross-legged opposite, and folded her arms under her considerable breasts, Lizzy couldn't help but notice that Rosie was so comfortably and so at ease, she looked as if she had grown out of the ground. The old woman stared at her, looking straight into her soul. At least that's what Lizzy thought.

'Why ya cryin' girl?' asked Rosie, getting straight to the point.

'Don't you ever cry Rosie?'

'Nope. No more cryin'. Done ma cryin' ... gotta get on with livin' now ... not dyin' ... ain't got no time for that cryin' thing no more.'

'Henry tells me that you've had quite a life.'

'Ah Henry, he dunno what he's talkin' about ... what ya doin' all the way up in this place anyway? Why ya comin' here ... is this ya holiday time?'

'Holiday time?'

'Up on that cattle station at Texas Downs, when the wet come we can't do nothing, so the boss sent us on holidays ... are ya on holidays?'

'No Rosie, I'm not on holidays. I came here looking for someone.'

'That dead *kartiya* fella eh? That fella what's got a head full of rain stones.'

'You mean he's got rocks in his head?'

'Nah, I was right the first time. My aunties, they told me about the long-ago time when they could play marbles with them rain stones ... long time ago ... you *kartiya*, callin' them diamonds ... that dead fella, he's got the rain stones all over himself.'

'You've seen him?'

'Yeah, I done seen him, at least what's left of him. Why do ya want ta come here to see half a bloody head with the rain stones? You *kartiya* ... bloody strange things that you been doin'.'

'Rosie, I came to see him because he stole money from me. He said he needed money for his diamond mine.'

'Never gonna get no diamonds all the way up there at Mistake Creek ... lookin' in the wrong place that fella was ... the diamonds, they are up over that hill there, over at the Argyle Mine ... that's the dreamin' place.'

'He said he followed a painting.'

'That fella has been diggin' in that hole for ten years...and his father before him ... he was diggin' there like a crazy man then he just left one day and never came back. A couple of years later that young fella showed up and kept on goin'.'

'He said the painting was done by an aboriginal man. It had daiwul and a big boab tree and—'

She hadn't finished her sentence before Rosie buckled with laughter. 'That paintin', that's old Possum Jack's joke on the young fella.'

'Possum Jack?'

'He got sick and tired of that fella askin' him where he could find diamonds, so he painted him a silly picture just to drive the young fella crazy. No diamonds at Mistake Creek ... they're all over there at Argyle. Bloody sad that.'

A forlorn look invaded Rosie's face along with a sliver of sunlight that pierced a gap in the giant boulders.

'Why is that so sad Rosie? What happened?'

'Ah no use talkin' about that no more.'

'But I'd like to understand,' replied Lizzy.

Rosie bit her lip and looked at her as if she was weighing up whether she could trust her or not. She scratched her forehead then fiddled with a blade of grass.

'When those mining people come, they don't ask us,' said Rosie, eventually. 'They never ask me or no proper boss. They don't say, *who owns this place?* They asked just a few people and then that lot went off to Perth and signed the bloody papers. We didn't know they went ... they just go and come back and said, *give it all ta them miners.* Now the ground is all dug up ... Mud Spring is all dug up. Then we walk up the road, that new car road, we walk up that. I tell you we all feel bloody sad. We can see the rocks where my relations followed that barramundi ... where the women used to roll that spinifex into nets way back in that Dreamtime. That place ... that's where the barramundi jumped away ... he jumped down into the little creek and then down along the big river ... making the diamonds ... now them minin' people, they blowin' up that Barramundi Hill. Very sad for me and those other *Kija* women, that's the women's place. Them miners, they didn't ask us. Right back from the Ngarrangkarni time, all those old women looked after that place and kept it safe. Then it was our turn and we failed. They should've asked us

... we'd tell'em not ta touch that side ... that's our side ... but nothin' is left now. Them fellas ... they can all have it now. When we see 'em we should say, *hey you were supposed to let us know that you were diggin' in the women's sacred site* ... we would have come and stopped 'em. Ahh, don't worry ... it's not worth talkin' about no more ... them *kartiya*'s put their heads down and that's it.'

'Rosie, when the Argyle Mine came did anyone actually understand how you and the rest of the women felt?'

'Two fellas never knew how much that place, that Barramundi Dreaming place, meant to us women ... first fella ... them *kartiya* what's runnin' the mine ... they try to do the right thing ... but understandin' was not part of what they is good at ... second fella, our own bloody men ... them silly blackfellas don't know the women's business, so they don't know about what goes on over there ... makin' our girls into women and such like ... they just took all that money what the *kartiya* give'em and used it all up on houses and water and pipes ... nothin' for the women. They don't bloody understand ... too bloody sad about that place.'

'It was Daiwul wasn't it Rosie?'

'Yeah, how you *kartiya* know about Daiwul? How you been hearin' about that barramundi fish?'

Rosie seemed surprised and fidgeted a little.

'When they dug up that barramundi place, we got nothin. Why don't them *kartiya* give some money to the women ... it was our special place ... that's what I been thinkin'. I been sayin' we get the money for all the people at Warmun, that's Turkey Creek ... you come through that place on the way to this place ... but why can't they say, *this money is for the women's scared place?* All of them men, they get the money ... I tell them ... this is what I say ... I say some goes to those men and some to us women. We got no motor car for the women's side ... no bus ... there's nothin' for the women ... anyway don't get me started ... what do I know about *kartiya* money ... I talk like that ya know ... anyway, you're taking me to another place. I was askin' why you're cryin' like that waterfall.'

'It's a long story.'

'Are you goin' some place in a hurry?'

'No, I suppose not.'

'Me neither.'

Under the black rain clouds Lizzy told Rosie the story of her fractured life. When she finished, Rosie asked just one question.

'You tellin' me that you gave away your name for someone else's?'

'Yes, I did.'

'Because ya couldn't get ya own way?'

'I suppose.'

'Them people over at the cattle station, they took my name away ... but I got no say in it. Rosie isn't my real name ... there was bloody Rosies and Dotties and Queenies and Mabels all over the place ... one of my people, the boss, he called her Buttercup, just like that cow she had ta milk everyday ... they call us these names because our real names are too hard to say ... get me this Rosie, do that Rosie ... easier than sayin' somethin' else ... but I don't give away nothin' as important as my name away, just like it's nothin'. I had no choice, but you, you had a choice.'

'But ...'

'No *buts* about it, ya gave away who ya are and now ya lookin' for it all over again. How are ya gonna be some other woman inside that skin you were born with? You are what ya are, that dead *kartiya* fella he saw, he knew, he knew that ya was lost ... dats why he took that money from ya.'

'I thought I loved him. I was just starting to heal when he came along.'

'Love has many enemies.' smiled Rosie.

Lizzy blushed. 'Rosie have you ever had the feeling that something new and wonderful was just around the corner and that you could almost reach out and touch it, but you didn't know where to start?'

'Ah sure missus ... all the time ... there's a season for everything. Just before the rains come, we got that Werrkalen time when da land is dry but there's new shoots. Them catfish is bein' caught and the bush turkey is makin' them funny mating noises and we is all waitin' for the rain to make everything all new again, that's the time of Kurlun … that's now … but that jalijkel, crayfish, comes on round … everthin' is wet and green, that's the Marlingin time and then there is Warnkan … gets a bit cold and we eat the emus eggs and tarntal. Those turtles, they're bloody good tucker.'

'No Rosie, I mean inside you. Do you ever get the feeling that you have to let go of yesterday to start tomorrow?'

'Sure, but yesterday is where we all come from missus, so no use tryin' ta run away from it … but you can think about it another way … there's a season for cryin' like you been doin' and there's a season for laughin' and a season for workin' and a time ta take your holidays … but you gotta move from season to season, lettin' nature have its way … 'cause soon the season for cryin' is over and then it's the season for laughin' all over again.'

Lizzy nodded and smiled the warm smile of appreciation of a daughter learning a lesson of life, and for the first time, truly understanding.

'Imagine if it only bloody rained here in Purnululu. I'd be talkin' to you from the bottom of that big Ord River up there in no time,' laughed Rosie. 'Rain follows dry, new beginnings follow the rain … see that grass there … two days ago it was the colour of straw … for the new season to start, another one has ta finish. You can't eat that sweet crayfish all the time … you'll get proper sick of that ya will.'

'What if I would rather forget some of my yesterdays?' asked Lizzy, turning away.

'Yesterday, that's the time of my dreamin'. Yesterday is special to me … it makes me what I am … it makes you what you are. Your ancestors come from there and pretty soon, you're gonna be someone's ancestors and what are they gonna think? What they gonna say? *Oh yeah back in the long time ago that* kartiya *woman she come down to Purnululu and she brings the rain … she's cryin' all the time and soon the land was covered in mud because of all her tears.* You're gonna be part of the Ngarrangkarni if you're not careful … you'll become a legend … maybe they'll do a corroboree about ya.' laughed Rosie.

The student and the teacher both laughed, and their laughter echoed around the gorge doubling their happiness, but Rosie suddenly stopped.

'The season is changin' while we're sittin' here missus ... you just gotta decide if ya want ta change with it.'

'I've seen this place before Rosie ... and I've seen you ... in my dreams ... I'm sure I have ... I've been here and looked at my reflection ... in this very pool.'

'That could be true. That thing in ya head has got a mind of its own sometimes ... takes ya to some bloody strange places ... ya see things ya don't normally see.'

'What do you see Rosie? What do you see when you look at me?'

Rosie scratched her head and thought for a minute. 'I can tell you straight or I can tell you crooked ... which one do ya want to do?'

'Tell me straight.'

'I tell ya straight in a roundabout way ... give me a minute.'

Rosie stroked her wrinkled chin and screwed up her nose, thinking carefully.

'You is like us black fellas more than ya know ... except we've had forty-thousand years to learn the way ... you're gonna have to learn it in about two, maybe three days ... 'cause if you don't, it's gonna crush you sure as if you'd fallen under that big rock there. I can see that in ya. I can see ya lookin', lookin' and not findin' nothin' ... your eyes, they're lookin' far away when it's here that you should be seein'. Your life has brung you to this place for bloody good reasons ... and it ain't for the cryin' ... as you can see, we got plenty of water for now.'

'Why do you think I'm like you Rosie?'

'Long time ago, all us mob, we been livin' here and then the men with the cattle came. The Duracks, Buchanans, Kilfoyles and over there in the west, them MacDonald brothers ... lots of their family too, they all comin'. We were a bit curious at first, but they didn't make no trouble, so we just watched ... but then the men came to mine the gold and they thought that we were some kind of animal that has to be hunted

... pretty soon all the killin' starts ... from 1890 to 1920 we call that *the Killin' Time* ... sad callin' somethin' the Killin' Time ... don't ya think? Lots of us black fellas done nothin' and got shot ... done nothin'. Some people they say half of us blackfellas in the east here, gettin' killed ... I dunno ... maybe that was true. Some people they're sayin' it's all a pack of lies ... like it never happened, but what do ya reckon ... if ya was in a shootin' party or poisoned a waterhole or rounded up a whole bunch of us and pushed us over a cliff, do ya reckon you'd talk about it or write it down in some history book ... we can't read and write so no good anyway, no good even thinkin' about it.'

'Only the winners write history Rosie ... and they write it to suit themselves.'

'Too right. One of them times over at Bedford Downs some *Kija* men got put in jail for killin' a bullock and then they let'em out, but the coppers they made'em walk two hundred miles back to Bedford Downs where they were put to work choppin' wood ... well they finished chopping that wood and then they fed 'em strychnine and they used that wood what they had chopped to burn their bodies ... bloody sad them Killin' Times. Bloody sad.'

'Was that when Hopples was killed?' asked Lizzy.

'How ya bloody know about Hopples? How ya know him? Has bloody big mouth Henry been talkin', talkin' too much hey?'

Lizzy nodded.

'Yep that was way back. I was just a piccaninny, a baby, then.'

Rosie's eyes glazed over and for a moment it looked like she might cry, but she didn't.

'That's a long time ago ... but that wasn't the *kartiya* ... that was the blackfellas fightin' over a woman ... nothin' has changed much hey?' she said, with a twinkle in her eye. 'Anyway, the *kartiya* no get 'em, then disease get 'em ... that cheeky copper no get 'em, then havin' no food made sure they were all gone.'

'Where do you come from Rosie?'

'You askin' me where I comin' from ... I comin' from this land ...

what you maybe meanin' is where I have been livin' ... is that what you're askin' me?'

'Yes, yes that's what I mean.'

'I've been workin' over at Texas Downs station like I told ya. It's that way a bit. I was doin' cookin' and cleanin' ... no bloody money ... just a blanket, bit of the flour, bit of tea and sweet sugar and a little bit of roof over our heads ... that's all ... not much ... in the wet, the boss he says, *go on holidays* like I already told ya ... but we can only take what we're ownin' and we don't own our clothes, so we're not goin' nowhere. All our friends, they walkin' long time to us for a sit down so it's not so bad. Well while we're waitin' for them to come, one of them *kartiya* boys, the big boss's son, he gets me knocked up ... ya don't fight 'em, if ya do ... they bash ya good and send ya on ya way with nothin' ... well I had the baby ... her *kartiya* name is Theresa, but her black fella name is Nyitparriya, that's her skin name ... well the coppers, that cheeky policeman comes one day and they say they're takin' all the half-caste kids away ... nobody asked us ... nobody tellin' us where they are goin' or when they comin' back ... they just throw 'em in the wagon and say to me *you not got a piccaninny no more* ... they took bloody big-mouth Henry as well. I never saw my Nyitparriya again ... but Henry, he was a bit older and could work at the station, so he comes back. He was much taller when he came back ... buggered if I can recognize me own boy ... they didn't tell me what happened to Theresa ... Henry, he dunno either. Too many of us women lost their children ... the newspapers today, they're call 'em the Stolen Generation ... have ya read about that?'

'Yes, yes, I have. It's so sad.'

'They should be callin' it the Cryin' Generation because that's all ya ever heard around the fires at night ... all the women weepin' and wailin' and cryin' for their babies. I reckon out there in the dark, the kids were cryin' just like us. Lots of us women just curled up and died of a broken heart when they stole our kids.'

Lizzy listened to Rosie's story wondering how one woman could endure so much yet show so much strength. 'It's so sad Rosie,' was all she could muster.

'That's not the sad part ... the sad part is we been losin' all them fellas to keep tellin' the dreamin' ... my relations. Some of the things we've been forgettin' because nobody has been tellin' ... that's my job now ... I'm doin' the tellin' ... lots of the women at Warmun do the tellin' ... keepin' it safe for the children and their children too.'

'What happened after they took Theresa away?'

'Ah that's too long ago now. Let's not talk on it no more ... I told ya that you're like me ya know.'

'How Rosie? How am I like you?'

'You're like me because you've been pushed out of ya life.'

'How do you know?'

'You got the look of the joey, that baby kangaroo. When the mother has been killed ... that joey he's lookin' around, lookin' to see what's gonna happen next ... he's got the empty eyes ... the baby eyes that are trustin' ya but not knowin' what you're goin' do to him ... he's been pushed out of his life in that mother's pouch ... you got that same look.'

'I need to find out who I really am Rosie.'

'Who you are is sittin' right here ... what you are is in here and here,' said Rosie, indicating her heart and head, ' ... but *why* you are ... well, that's another thing altogether ... why you are what you is, is for you to find out and for all them other fellas to discover a bit at a time ... do ya reckon you just find out why you are by lookin' at yesterday and sayin' *them fellas done somethin' that made me this way or that way?* Nah ... you is makin' why you are ... you're choosin' why, who and where and how ... it's all about what you choosin' ... not blamin' the other fella ... you've been choosin' ... you choosin' to come here ... to see the *kartiya* ... but he was dead ... so he's not gonna tell ya nothin' ya want to know ... I'm not tellin' ya ... that big-mouth Henry, he's not tellin' ya either ... so when it's all said and done, you need to be tellin' yourself.'

'Do you really think there's a season for everything Rosie? Do you think everything can start again?'

'You can sit and watch the river, but the time comes when it'll dry up ... there's nothin' there for ya ... or you can move on to another place where there's water and food ... if ya sit by that nice lazy river too long soon there's nothin' ... you can't see yourself in the water no more ... you can't see that other you that's lookin' back at ya ... remindin' you about who you really is ... when that river is dry, you can't see them no more.'

Lizzy started to cry again but the soft sobs weren't about her yesterdays, they were about her tomorrows.

'We're goin' walkin' now ... you comin' with me,' said Rosie, rising unevenly on her steel post leg.

Lizzy stood, desperately trying to hold back the sobs. 'Where are we going?'

'You're gonna meet my relations ... I gonna show 'em the nice *kartiya* girl what brings the rain,' smiled Rosie, helping her to her feet.

Lizzy attempted to straighten her hair and dry her eyes.

'You don't worry about that ... my relations are all blind ... but they see everythin'.'

CHAPTER 16

The old woman spent the next two days hobbling over puddles, avoiding storms and introducing Lizzy to the rocks and the land, the sky and the trees, the animals and the places of Ngarrangkarni. She introduced her to Jarrun, the kookaburra, Jikerrel, the kingfisher, Nyidbarraiya and Kularwun the two Purnululu hills. She told her the stories of morality and respect of the owl Dunbunji. She drew the dreaming paths that showed where men can go. Rosie showed her pupil the creeks where mowuntum, the white clay to make paint for the corrorboree dancing, comes from. In the distance she pointed out Rawoolilny and Wanambany, the two mountains to the north-east of Purnululu. She watched her jump as Goolarbool, the snake, slithered past with Loomoogoo, the blue tongue lizard, in hot pursuit. They saw Jirring, the kangaroo, feeding on new grass, while overhead, Ngamarring, the corella parrot squawked out an enthusiastic welcome.

In the caves and overhangs, Rosie traced her past with the help of ancient paintings done in red and white ochre and charcoal. She showed Lizzy burial sites and places of birth. She showed her the rounded rocks where her relations sharpened their tools and cooked their food ... and then in the shadows of the third afternoon, the old woman suddenly stopped and looked up.

'It's not gonna rain tomorrow ... you'll be goin' soon.'

Lizzy's face turned to stone. 'But I don't think I'm ready to leave. Not yet.'

The old women turned and looked deep into her student's eyes.

'You've been sittin' by that river of yours for too long. It's dryin' up fast and it's time for you to move on.'

'But there's so much to do. Besides, I like it here.'

'This is not where your river is ... you take your river, that place where you look back at yourself, it's with you whereever you go ... you goin' ... but one day you comin' back to see old Rosie ... one of these days. I know that for sure.'

When night fell, Rosie and Lizzy were back in the cave above the small stream and crocodile waterfall. Rosie stoked a fire, while her student sat staring out at the constellations of stars twinkling above them.

'Is this where you live all the time Rosie ... in this cave?'

'Nah, it's not like the old days no more. I came here just to look after you ... Henry, he's tellin' me that you need some peace and quiet ... this is the place for that. He knowin' you're not happy ... Henry, he's talkin' talkin' all the time, but he's a good listener too. He's got a big heart that man.'

'So where, where do you live?'

'I'm one of them women over there at Warmun. Some people call it Turkey Creek.'

'Why did you leave Texas Downs?'

'I learn in that catechism that the good Lord he gives, and he takes away ... well that's what happened. Government tellin' me back in '67 that we blackfellas, now we're proper good citizens ... we can call ourselves Australians ... don't want to get into that story, otherwise it'll have ta rain for a year before I finish tellin' you about how my people have always been livin' in this place ... we've always been here ... always been a bloody citizen ... citizen of what I say? Way back, they called all this beautiful land Terra Nullus ... nobody's land ... the bloody law back then said if there were no signs of growin' stuff and relyin' on the land then us blackfellas don't really live here. To them it was an unsettled land, so pretty soon, they began livin' on our sacred land and started usin' our huntin' grounds and takin' our fish ... ya hear that? If we don't rely on the land, they can do what they like ... them fellas didn't understand, we *are* the land ... we *come from* the land ... crazy *kartiya*. Anyway the government all of a sudden says we're bloody citizens and then says us blackfellas, we got to be paid same as them *kartiya* ... well them people what owns the cattle stations, they're sayin' *bugger that* ... they sayin' *Rosie you and all you others you get off my land now ... you go away ... I'm finished with ya, bugger off*...well, we go walkabout for a while livin' here and there, but back in 1970 my people stopped at places like Turkey Creek and sit there for a long time. Now lots of the people are there doin' paintin' ... keepin' the Dreamtime memories.'

'Do you paint too?'

'Nah no paintin' ... my job is ta do the tellin' ... keep tellin' the Ngarrangkarni ... Possum Jack and them others, their job is to do the paintin'. Some of them fellas are gettin' bloody famous. They got their paintings in all of them big old galleries all around the world.'

Rosie stoked the fire, and it crackled as the warmth of two new friends filled the cave and an easy silence fell around them, but it was soon disturbed. Henry reappeared at the entrance carrying something Lizzy couldn't quite make out in the semi-darkness.

'Brung you a barra ... bloody good fish this barramundi.'

'Where ya been?' asked Rosie.

'Checkin' the road back to Warmun ... still a bit slushy in bits, but if there's no rain tonight maybe we can go back tomorrow.'

Lizzy stared out into the evening sky watching a shooting star fall across her window into eternity.

'I'm not sure I want to do that.' she replied, absently as Rosie spread the coals of the fire out east to west as *Kija* custom dictated and lay Henry's fish down to cook.

'Smells good.' said Lizzy, after a few minutes, 'I could get used to this outback home delivery.'

While the fish cooked, she stood at the entrance of the cave listening to the croak of frogs in the stream below and the rustle of a growing wind in the palm trees. Suddenly Rosie was next to her. The old woman's eyes followed Lizzy's line of sight straight to where a full moon hung in the sky like a giant, white, dinner plate.

'Why would I want to leave here?' she whispered, '…with a beautiful moon like that.'

'Back in the dreamin' time the moon was a man.' said Rosie. 'He was called Karngin. One of them long time ago days, Karngin came back from huntin' and he saw a girl sittin' next to his mother. This girl, he saw, she was very beautiful with long black hair, just like you … well Karngin, he fell in love with her straight away. That woman was Darwool, the black-headed snake … she was also Karngin's mother-in-law, so it was forbidden for him to marry her. Well, them old people, they say, *who ya be wantin' for ya wife?* This Karngin he say, *doyen doyen, that one, that one there* pointin' at Darwool … but they say, *you can't do that, she's your mother-in-law, you gotta marry one of these nyawanas, one of Darwools daughters* … so they asked him again and he says, *doyen doyen, that one, that one* … well the people told him he must go away … he walked over there and sat down on top of that hill and he called out *Nungai Budenarr,* you mob die and then *ngyammon Mullin Ngynbingin,* only I will live forever. That's him up there now … that's Karngin, he's the moon and every month he comes back to life.'

'That's such a beautiful story Rosie … thank you for sharing it with me.'

'Belongin' to all of us … not mine to own.' replied Rosie quietly. 'Come on, we better eat the barra before Henry has it all.'

They ate in silence with only the soft sucking of fish bones and the smack of lips punctuating the evening silence.

'We'll get that Andrew fella in the mornin' and take him back to Jimmy's place.' said Henry, using a long, fish bone as a toothpick. 'We better get him before that fridge stops workin'. What do ya reckon?'

117

'I reckon I'd rather stay here for a while longer,' she sighed, already half asleep.

Rosie touched Lizzy gently on the wrist. 'Only Karngin livin' forever ... us other fellas we gotta get on with this life here.'

'Yes, I know. Unfortunately, we do.'

'Sleepin' now ... ya got a long way to go tomorrow.'

'But Henry, he said we're not far from Jimmy Orion's place.'

'That's not what I'm sayin' ... I'm sayin' that tomorrow you've got a long way to go.'

Lizzy nodded in the dark understanding what Rosie really meant and as she put her head down on her kangaroo skin bed, she heard the soft pitter-patter of new rain falling on the rock ledge outside the cave. Before long, the heavens opened and as she closed her eyes, a comfortable grin creased her lips. In her mind's eye she imagined that she was asleep on the grass in her Cathedral of New Beginnings.

CHAPTER 17

The deluge paused just before sunrise leaving a high gloss on the landscape and as the sun rose in the grey Purnululu sky, the wetness magnified the light and threw a strong glare directly into Lizzy's eyes. As she stood on the rock ledge overlooking her green grass and mirrored pool, she pulled the matted hair from her face and dusted off her clothes. She hadn't washed in days. The pool below her was too inviting to ignore.

A few minutes later she stood naked beside the water staring at her reflection.

'I see you,' she said.

Her reflection smiled back at her.

Lizzy washed her clothes, laid them out on the grass then stepped slowly into the pool, gradually sinking up to her waist, and as her confidence grew, her shoulders. The water felt so light, it was as if it had fallen off the wings of butterflies, so fresh, that it had the purity of a newborn baby, and so soft on her skin, that it reminded her of the clouds drifting above her. But it was more than all of that; the waters of Cathedral Gorge were her holy water, her sweet waters of renewal, and as she stroked her away through them, she felt an unlimited and previously unimaginable freedom. She was renewed. Baptized. Washed clean. Away from the world, in the middle of a land beyond most people's comprehension, Elizabeth Lawson gave herself up to the moment, revelling in the sweet waters of redemption.

'Sometimes them big old crocodiles find their way into these pools,' said Henry, standing behind her. Lizzy turned, startled, covering her breasts with crossed arms.

'Jesus Henry, stop bloody doing that!'

'Sorry, just tryin' to tell ya for ya own good but if you want 'em to eats ya bits, then you stay right where ya is.'

Rosie appeared behind her son, completing the domino of surprise.

'Henry, leave the poor woman alone. First you been tellin' her them stories about the witchety grubs and now you've been fibbin' about old Lalangkarrany, the crocodile. Get your skinny bag of bones out of this nice lady's bath time and make yaself useful ... get some of them good kunja, yams and jukurrah, them wild oranges, for our breakfast.'

'Dats woman's work.' yelled Henry, walking off laughing. He had finished having his fun.

Rosie turned to Lizzy in the pool.

'I keep tellin' people that he's not my son. He must have been switched at that mission school, no wonder I didn't recognize him when he come back ... you'd better be gettin' out of that pool now before that crazy old man comes back to play some more games with ya?'

'What will I wear?' asked Lizzy, looking at her wet clothes on the grass.

'That big smile of yours ... that's what you been wearin' this morning ... what you been thinkin' about? What are you up to? That sad joey look, it has done run away in the night.'

'Rosie, what will I wear?'

'You shoulda thought about that before you go makin' them all wet ... they'll be dry soon enough ... don't you worry about that.'

'But what will I wear until then?'

'You think I've never seen a *kartiya* woman with no clothes on ... I seen plenty ... and Henry, he's halfway to just about anywhere by now, so that he won't have to do that workin'.'

Lizzy sighed and stepped from the pool, water glistening on her body.

'There ain't nothin' of ya ... look at ya ... just skin and bones ... I seen fatter goannas in a drought.' laughed Rosie. 'What have you been eatin' to be so skinny? No wonder you were shiverin' in the night.'

Lizzy didn't know if she should hide behind a rock, cover herself with her hands or use her wet clothes as they were, but after several indecisive attempts at them all, her nakedness didn't seem to matter. A great peace fell over her and somehow, she felt as one with the earth and the rocks and the sky; like she belonged. She finally settled for sitting on the grass, cross-legged, like when she was a *wog* schoolgirl and her teacher wanted to read the class a story. Rosie sat down next to her and looked up at the sky.

'That rain last night, not so bloody good ... ya gotta stay here some more.' said Rosie, plaiting blades of grass into a bracelet.

'You know Rosie, I'm sitting here naked in front of someone I hardly know, in the middle of nowhere, after I've slept in cave on a kangaroo skin for three nights because there's a flood that's stopping me taking a dead body that has diamonds buried in what's left of its head back to a pub owned by the cousins of the hillbillies from Deliverance ... and ... I've lost all the money I had ... and ...'

'And what?'

'And I feel pretty damn good.' said Lizzy, almost a little too enthusiastically.

'I told you there was a season for everything.' whispered Rosie.

'Yes, but you didn't tell me that the seasons could change so quickly.'

'When ya open a door and walk through it, well then, you're on the other side. You close that door and there's no other side no more,' smiled Rosie.

'Thank you Rosie. Thank you for ... well, I'm not totally sure what I want to thank you for ... but I know that I feel this way because of you.'

'You feel the way you do because of you. This country has got a way of killin' a person and it got a way a savin' a person, but that person, *kartiya* or blackfella, don't matter, they gotta want to be saved in the first place.'

'How have you managed to live through all the things that you have Rosie? How do you keep smiling?'

'My heart, it done been saved by that Jesus ... religion for this alcamen, this old lady, it's simple ... Ngapuny, that's the God up top, he's the giver of life ... just like that spring at Turkey Creek, just like that water there that you been swimmin' in ... They are different, but they are the same thing. God and that Rainbow Serpent, Kaleruny, they're the same ... some of the people, they see 'em as different, but I see 'em as the same ... it's all about life ... all about livin'. Instead of lookin', lookin' for what's different about us blackfellas and you *kartiya*, we should be lookin' for what's the same ... seein' what your children and my children can do together.'

Rosie stopped talking and looked off into the distance, like she was thinking about something, but then began again.

'You're a different kind of *kartiya* than what old Rosie has met before. All them others, they just jarrak, jarrak, *talk, talk* and don't open them ears what God give 'em ... you got big ears ... you listen good to old Rosie.'

Lizzy touched her ears, suddenly self-conscious. 'My mother always told me that we have two ears and one mouth, and they should be used in the same proportion.'

'She's a smart lady that mother of yours.'

'I miss her. Maybe you'll meet her one day?' replied Lizzy.

'Like I'm tellin' ya, there's a season for everythin'.'

'Thank-you Rosie. I've learnt a lot.'

'Tell me somethin'.'

'What do you mean?'

'What is it that ya *don't* know yet?'

'Don't know?'

'Yes.'

'How can I tell you something if I don't know it yet?'

'We've all got somethin' inside us that stops the fish from swimmin' back to its water hole ... just like that crocodile rock over there ... somethin' that stops us from bein' who we want to be ... I already told ya about my tears.'

'You told me you don't cry anymore.'

'That's because I'm too scared that if I start again, I'll never stop ... too much water hidin' behind my eyes ... good old Noah, he'll be needin' his bloody ark again if I get goin' ... you've got somethin' stoppin' you too ... I know that.'

Lizzy bit her lip, suddenly feeling more exposed than she already was.

'Can you see inside me Rosie?'

'Maybe.'

'Then there's no use telling you a lie, is there?'

'Only tellin' fibs to yourself, not me.'

'Maybe I should get dressed.'

'You don't gotta tell old Rosie nothin' if ya don't want ta, but I tell ya, sometimes just sayin' somethin' out loud makes ya feel a whole lot better ... anyway ... off ya go, get dressed. Them clothes of yours will be dry by now.'

'It's not that I don't want to tell you, it's just that I don't know how to tell you.'

'First word, then the rest just comes out.'

Lizzy paused and stared off into the distance. Overhead the corellas squawked and up higher a strong wind blew the clouds away while Rosie waited patiently, plaiting more blades of grass.

'I, I think that maybe I'm afraid to love again,' said Lizzy, finally.

Rosie took her hand in hers. 'Love is yours ta give and not for others to take ... you'll be ready one day, take ya time ... what about that smart mother of yours?'

'What about her?'

'She loves ya.'

'I'm not so sure anymore. I haven't exactly been a great daughter.'

'Mothers have no choice ... you'll see, she loves ya ... question is, will you be lovin' her back?'

'Of course. Why wouldn't I?'

'It sounds ta me like ya already answerin' ya own question.'

'That's not the kind of love I mean Rosie.'

'I know that. I was just givin' ya a minute to come around to what ya really mean.'

The makings of a tear assembled themselves on Lizzy's eyelid.

'I loved Tony so much, and then he just wasn't there anymore ... and then when I opened my heart to Andrew ... well, you know what happened ... it's no wonder I'm afraid.'

'Sometimes love and fear is the same thing ... sometime there's no difference at all ... sometimes it's love that we fear ... that's the truth of it ... when that piccaninny of mine got taken away, I been fearin' to love anythin' ever again ... now I been lovin' God and he's been lovin' me back, so I ain't fearin' love no more.'

'There's a season for everything isn't there?'

'So ya say.' smiled Rosie.

'You're a remarkable woman.'

'Ahhh, not old Rosie. I've just been livin' while some others have been fearin' the shadows of their own life ... they've been lookin' over their shoulder ... not over there to where that sun sets over the horizon ... that's a long walk away ... I been thinkin' like that ya know ... lookin' to the future ... makin' sure my *Kija* people are going to be around for a while ... that they understand where they come from and where they're goin' to ... it's hard sometimes ... in the long ago time we had all we wanted right here ... food, and all we ever needed ... now we gotta play by your *kartiya* rules ... ya need money for that ... where are we gonna get money from?'

'Why don't the *Kija* people start their own diamond mine?'

'Ah, what do we know about the bloody big trucks and that stuff that blows up the side of that barramundi hill. What do we know about kartiya money and sellin' dem diamonds we've been findin'?'

'You've found diamonds ... here?' asked Lizzy, apprehensively. 'I thought that you said—'

'No missus, not here. This place is a bloody national park. You can't find diamonds 'ere. Even if they're here, they're not here ... no bloody mining allowed.'

'Then where?'

Rosie reached into an old hessian sack slung over her shoulder and as she opened the palm of her hand, the sun hit three grey rocks the size of the nail on her little finger. Even beneath the dirt, Lizzy could tell what they were.

Rosie pointed out to the east. 'Over there ... at Mount Parker.'

'You said the only diamonds were at the Barramundi Dreaming place ... at Argyle.'

'I did?'

'Why are you telling me this now?'

'I was just seein' if ya understand what I've been sayin' to ya for the last coupla days.'

'Do I?'

'I think you do. You understand what I've been tellin' you. You understand how important this land is ta us, so I know you won't say nothin' about these stones ta nobody. We've been lookin' a long time and found these just lyin' around ... but what are we gonna do with them? We're not tellin' them *kartiya*. They'll just send more of them trucks ... dig it all up ... no bloody way.'

'But what if you ... the *Kija* women owned the mine ... you could get all the things you need ... to continue your teaching ... to keep your stories alive.'

'Like I've been sayin', them white fellas know about gettin' them rain stones ... not us ... no point in diggin' into the backbones of all my relations and our special places.'

'I understand.'

'I knew ya would. That's why I told ya.'

'Cross my heart. I won't tell a soul.'

Rosie's face creased with a broad grin.

'We *Kija* people say that back in the Dreamtime fish and animals and birds and all of them reptiles were split up inta groups ... them people back then, they split up inta groups too ... that's what we call *skins* ... all of them groups got a skin name ... ya skin name tells ya where ya are and who ya related to and who is straight for ya ... tellin' ya who ya can marry and who's ya brother and sister ... my skin name is Nangari.'

'It very pretty.'

'I've been thinkin' that I'm gonna give you my skin name ... that'll make you my sister and if you're my sister, you'll have to come back to visit old Rosie.'

Lizzy stared straight at Rosie, but then, as single tear slid down her cheek like glycerin on glass, she reached out to hug the old woman and when she did, a similar tear ran down the old woman's cheek.

'Now look what you're doin' to me.' sniffed Rosie. 'It's been a long time. I thought I was all cried out.'

'There's a season for everything Rosie. Some just take a little longer to arrive.'

'Yeah, you're learnin' good. You understand.'

'Nangari,' whispered Lizzy softly. 'Rosie's sister.'

Rosie's bones creaked as she lifted herself up from the grass. 'You keep them three rain stones ... present from ya new sister.' said Rosie, wearily.

'Rosie ... Rosie I can't ... these are probably worth a fortune ... just one could probably buy the car the women need.'

'No good to us ... besides, waddya think would happen if old Rosie walks into one of them jewellers in Kununurra with a rock like that? Them *kartiya* will be on to us like flies on a carcass ... *Where did ya get 'em? Where did ya find 'em?* Nah, you keep 'em ... it's better that way.'

'Thank-you Rosie. I'll keep them safe for you.' replied Lizzy, gathering up her clothes and starting to dress.

As she closed the last button of her blouse, she could see Henry running towards them, waving his arms.

'I reckon that son of mine is a bit crazy.' smiled Rosie.

'I reckon he just might be the sanest person I've ever met. They don't make' em like that where I come from.'

Eventually Henry stopped in front of them, huffing and puffing.

'Where have you been Henry?' said Lizzy. 'Did you find any of those yams? I'm hungry.'

'No time for that. That rain last night, its only fallin' on this side of Purnululu ... bloody Kimberley rain ... you can have a wet front door and the back door can be as dry as anything ... over that side ... ' he said, pointing west, 'It's okay for drivin' ... we'll go that way ... get that fella with the diamonds in his head. By the time we do that ... if there's no more rain, I reckon we can get back to Jimmy Orion's and then Warmun where the road is good ... we're goin' now ... come on.'

'Do I have to Rosie?'

'I'm not tellin' you what you need to be doin'. Only you know that.'

'Is it time to find a new river?'

Rosie smiled. 'Yep, I reckon that's the thing to do.'

'Come on Henry. Let's get a move on. I've got a river to find.'

Henry looked at her quizzically, but his mother gave him a stern look which said, *don't ask.*

'Remember Rosie won't ya.' said the old woman, sadly.

'You're my sister now Rosie so I think I'll be coming back real soon. I've just got that feeling.'

'Some things ya just know, don't ya.' replied Rosie.

'And some things you just learn.' added Lizzy. 'Thank you Rosie, thank you for everything.'

'There's more of them rain stones where they came from.'

'Is that a bribe?'

'Dunno what a bribe is missus ... so how can it be one?' winked Rosie.

The two women hugged and when they finally let go of each other, Rosie turned and without another word, hobbled away.

'Come on. Time to go.' urged Henry.

After two hours of slipping and sliding through mud, they were back at Andrew Burns' shack. Henry extracted the body from the refrigerator, which by the smell of the body, had stopped running some time well before their arrival. They wrapped it in a dusty blanket and Lizzy sprinkled it with her perfume to keep the stench at bay. Henry put the beer and refrigerator's shelves back in and Lizzy gathered up all the press clippings from the floor, and then, almost as an afterthought, grabbed Andrew's battered computer and satellite phone, then, with what was left of Andrew Burns, they headed west. They drove in silence, not needing to speak and not wanting to inhale any more of Burns than was necessary.

With the moon rising and the red sun setting in opposite corners of the world they pulled into Orion's pub. Some thirty-four and forty-six wheel road trains, and a few muddy motor homes were scattered around like stranded whales waiting for the roads to dry out. Jimmy Orion and his cronies were drinking beers on the veranda. It was as if they were waiting for them.

CHAPTER 18

'Where ya been?' asked Orion, leaning on a post smoking a cigarette. 'Me and these other blokes, we were beginnin' to think old Henry there might've dumped ya in a hole or somethin'.'

The other three men lollygagging on the pub's veranda laughed. Orion stuck out his chest like he had told a great joke.

'We've got Andrew Burns in the back,' replied Lizzy, flatly. 'It looks like he killed himself.'

'Waddya mean, he bloody killed himself?' said Orion.

'I told that woman who you brought to the mine,' replied Lizzy. 'I'm sure she told you.'

'Yeah, but she thought ya were bullshitting!'

'Well, I wasn't.'

'He shot his self in the bloody head,' added Henry, a little too enthusiastically.

Orion threw his cigarette to the ground, walked over to his Toyota, looked in the open window and gingerly peeled back the blanket covering what was left of Burns' head.

'Jesus, he bloody stinks! What's all that shiny shit stuck in his bloody head?'

Henry started to answer, but Lizzy cut him off. 'It looks like he shot himself with broken glass. There were beer bottles in his shack ... it looks like he was celebrating something but then changed his mind...it's strange, isn't it?'

Orion turned to one of the other men who had come to see the body. 'I always said that bloke was a sandwich short of a picnic.'

'I reckon there's a shitload of stuff loose up there now,' cackled another man tapping his forehead. 'Jesus, what a fuckin' mess.'

'I thought that you said she was a real looker,' said one of the other men, just loud enough for Lizzy to hear him.

'That's what they bloody reckoned. It's all bloody bullshit if ya ask me!' replied another man, turning towards the bar.

Stung by the comment, Lizzy caught a reflection of herself in the side mirror of Orion's truck. Her clothes were wrinkled and stained, her make-up had long since disappeared and her hair stuck out in all directions. Nevertheless, she smiled back at her reflection and left everything just as it was.

'We should put him in that bloody big fridge of yours,' said Henry.

'Until the police can come and get him,' clarified Lizzy.

'They're already bloody here,' replied Orion, nodding towards the pub. 'Got here yesterday,' he smirked.

'Yesterday?' replied Lizzy. 'How would they even know?'

Orion shrugged. 'Dunno. Beats me.'

'Something tells me that you only remember what you want to remember Mr. Orion.'

'Sometimes it pays to forget,' he replied, with a grin. 'Looks like your new best friends want a word with you,' he added, as three men in police uniforms strode onto the verandah.

Behind them was a woman with bottle-blonde hair wearing tight jeans and a singlet top and smoking a cigarette. She smirked, but before she could say anything, everyone jerked their eyes skyward as a giant thunderclap echoed and bolts of silver lightning dissected the grey sky. Within seconds they were all drowned by an avalanche of rain and ran for cover.

'Are you Elizabeth Lawson?' asked a swarthy looking policeman with three stripes on his sleeve, as she took cover under the pub's verandah awning.

'I'm glad you guys are here.'

'Are you?'

'Yes.'

'I'm Sergeant Manfredi. We have reason to believe that you and Mr. Morgan are responsible for the murder of a man called Andrew Burns.'

She looked from left to right, first at Henry and then the other men and then at the woman. She grinned.

'You're joking? Right?'

'Do I look like I'm joking?' replied the sergeant.

'No. No you don't. What's going on?'

'Maybe you can tell me.'

'What?'

One of the other policemen pulled on a raincoat and headed for Orion's Toyota while another took Henry firmly by the arm and lead him towards a table near the bar. The sergeant escorted Lizzy towards the Royal Suite. Orion and the woman started to follow.

'Wait here,' demanded the sergeant, turning on them gruffly.

Inside, the interrogation began.

'We have reason to believe that Andrew Burns persuaded you to invest in his mine and when you realized it was worthless, you and Mr. Morgan killed him.'

'And who told you that fairy tale?' replied Lizzy, already knowing the answer. 'I didn't invest in anything. He stole almost fifty-thousand dollars from me.'

'That lady outside, that's Mrs. Burns, she became concerned for her husband's welfare and came looking for him. She says she found you at his mine and you told her that Andrew Burns was dead. Apparently, you also told her that you *gave* her husband fifty-thousand dollars.'

'I did no such thing. He stole it out of my bank account, and I most certainly didn't kill him.'

'He appears to be very dead though. What did you use? A shotgun?'

'He was already dead when Henry and I got there.'

'Why did you go to the mine in the first place?'

'To ... to ... I don't really know why.'

'His wife says you were in love with him and when you realized he was married you ...'

'I didn't know he was married until after she got there.'

'She says you found a file of women who he's been conning.'

'That part is true. By the looks of things, he's been ripping off women all over Australia.'

'And that's why you killed him?'

'Why would I?'

'Because you were in love with him and when you discovered there were other women you fought, and you killed him.'

'No. No I didn't. He was already dead when we got to the mine. I already told you that. Besides, why would I bring him back here if I had killed him?'

'To make it look like you hadn't.'

'Oh, for God's sake! What have you been smoking?'

It was the wrong thing to say and as soon as the words were out of her mouth, she knew it. The room went quiet. She was about to speak again when the door opened. A policeman in a raincoat stood dripping water on Orion's Persian rug, holding a manila folder and a man's wallet.

'Found this on the body,' he said, passing his sergeant a wallet.

He opened it and nodded.

'It's Andrew Burns alright.'

'You might want to look at this too sarge.'

The constable handed his boss the folder and whispered something in the sergeant's ear. The senior man nodded and casually flicked through the pile of newspaper clippings Lizzy had discovered.

'This boy sure has been busy.'

'I told you,' jabbed Lizzy.

'This looks like motive to me. That's not a good thing for you.'

'Listen, I could have just left him to rot out there, but I didn't.'

'That's not the point, is it?'

'Then what exactly is the point? You seem to think because that woman out there saw me at the mine, then I must've killed him. Christ, she didn't even see the body and she didn't believe me when I told her he was dead.'

'You told her that he was dead, and she didn't want to see his body? Unlikely.'

'I tried to, but it had disappeared.'

'The body?'

'Yes.'

'Disappeared?'

'This isn't looking good, is it?'

'And just where had it disappeared to?'

'Henry moved it.'

'So, Henry Morgan killed him.'

'No!'

'So why did he move the body?'

'I don't know.'

'And then it suddenly reappeared, and you brought it here?'

'No. Henry put it in the fridge.'

'The fridge?'

'The fridge in Andrew Burns' shack. We did that so that it wouldn't rot while we had to wait for the rain to stop.'

'And you helped him?'

'No.'

'But you were there?'

'I passed out.'

'Because?'

'Because I was ... I was unhappy. Alright? Because I just couldn't take any more crap.'

'It says here that your husband died,' said the sergeant, reading from Burns' file of newspaper clippings.

'Yes. He did.'

'Did you kill him too?'

'Oh, for goodness' sake. He died in a car accident. Check for yourself.'

'Don't worry, we will. My constable tells me the body has small pieces of something that looks like diamonds embedded in it. Do you have anything to say about that?'

'I don't know. They're probably diamonds.'

'And how would they have found their way into Mr. Burns' body?'

'How would I know? There was a shotgun. Maybe that did it. You're the damned detective.'

'We could save a whole lot of time here if just told me exactly what happened.'

'I have. I went to see if I could get my money back. We arrived, and he was dead.'

'How did you meet him?'

'In Sydney. He was a friend of my brother.'

'You came all the way from Sydney to do what? To ask him, *pretty please can I have my money back?*'

'No, well, yes. I just wanted to ask him why he stole my money when he said he loved me.'

'Did he say that he loved you?'

'Well no.'

'But you were in love with him?'

'I guess.'

The policeman held up the newspaper clipping about her father. 'It says here that your real name is Anastasia Dimitriades.'

'I changed it by deed poll years ago.'

'Why?'

'That's really none of your business.'

The sergeant glared at her.

'Listen, you're treating me like a criminal and I've done nothing wrong.'

'You're innocent?'

'Yes, and so is Henry.'

'Now, where have I heard that before?'

'Listen if you're not going to charge me, I'm going.'

'I don't think you'll be going anywhere for quite a while yet.'

'Do I get a phone call or is that just in the movies?'

'When we get to Kununurra.'

'Kununurra? You're arresting me?'

'I'm afraid so.'

'And Henry?'

'Looks like it.'

'Why don't you ask that woman out there what she was doing all the way out at Mistake Creek?'

'I already told you, she was worried about her husband.'

'A husband who's always running off with other women? For goodness' sake, he spends half his life wandering around the damn desert. Don't you think it's a strange coincidence she shows up on the day he was killed? You're telling me she suddenly starts to worry about him and just happens to show up the very same day ... yeah right! She told me she had never been to the mine before. Maybe she knew about all the money he was stealing off people like me. Maybe she wanted more? That's motive too isn't it? She sure seemed surprised when I said he had stolen fifty-grand from me. Maybe he was ripping her off, so *she* killed him ... funny how she turned up just after we found him.'

'She's the one who reported this.'

'To make it look like she hadn't done it?' replied Lizzy, sarcastically.

'We'll speak to her later.'

'Look, don't you think anyone who had been close-by when his head was turned into mush, would be covered in that shit?'

'Where are the clothes you were wearing that day?'

'I'm wearing them.'

'They look amazingly clean for five days out in all that.'

'I washed them.'

'Because?'

'Because they were dirty.'

'Or covered in blood.'

'Oh, for God's sake, why don't you just hang me now?'

'Innocent until proven guilty ... that's how it works up here.'

'Look, for the last time; he was dead when we got there.'

'We might have to let a jury decide that.'

'Jury?'

'Elizabeth Lawson, I am arresting you for the murder of Andrew Burns. Anything you say may be taken down in evidence and used in court against you. You have the right to legal representation. If you do not have any, it will be supplied for you ... turn around please ... do you understand what I have just said?'

'Are these really necessary?' stammered Lizzy, fighting the sergeant handcuffs. 'Where the hell am I going to run to?'

'It's procedure.'

Suddenly Rosie's last words filled Elizabeth's mind. *The lord giveth and the lord taketh away.* With one hand life had given her a new beginning, but with the other, had taken it away. This could not be happening.

'So much for a new river,' she whispered despondently.

'What?'

'Don't worry. Do you mind if I clean up a bit?' she asked, nodding toward the bathroom in Orion's Royal Suite.

'Know this place do ya? I thought so,' leered the sergeant, removing her handcuffs.

'Oh, for Christ's sake, get your mind out of the gutter,' she growled.

'Go on. You've got one minute.'

Lizzy splashed her face with water, willing what was happening to be a bad dream; a strange illusion that would disappear if she splashed long enough. Perhaps she was really sleeping. Perhaps it was only a dream, but no matter how much she wet her face, she knew her precious river was already flowing in a different direction. In a distant part of her mind, she heard Rosie again.

'I've just been livin' when some others have been fearin' the shadows of their own life ... they've been lookin' over their shoulder ... they should be lookin' over there where the sun sets ... that's a long walk away.'

CHAPTER 19

By the end of the four-hour drive north to Kununurra, Lizzy knew that Rosie's prediction was right. This wasn't in the plan. None of it. Not Orion. Not Burns' mine (or lack of it). Not Henry and his disappearing acts. Not the woman who claimed to be Burns' wife. Not Rosie. Not the connection she felt with that strange place called The Bungle Bungle, and most certainly not Sergeant Manfredi or being charged with murder. How could things have gone so horribly wrong? Was her life destined to be one disaster after another? What had she done to deserve this? There were too many questions she couldn't answer, and too many things that seemed totally out of her control. Why was life doing this to her again? It didn't make sense. None of it.

Peering through the cell bars, into a yard at the rear of the police station, Lizzy saw another 4WD pull in and two men remove a covered stretcher. Probably Burns' body. She hung on, feeling the sun-warmed steel bars, hoping they would disappear, but by then she knew that she wasn't dreaming.

Off to the right of her cell, down a short corridor, she could make out a small office where the constable who had dripped water on Orion's carpet was talking to the sergeant. He had Burns' computer and satellite phone and was reading newspaper clippings from the folder. The sergeant patted the constable on the back and mouthed something Lizzy couldn't hear, then the constable hurried off.

'It looks like you're here for a couple of days. The prison escorts won't be here until Wednesday,' said the sergeant, casually. 'They'll take you and Mr. Morgan over to Broome to see a judge.'

'You can't hold us.'

'If I have reasonable cause to believe you have committed a crime, I can do anything I bloody well want, including making you sit on your arse and wait two days, so get comfortable.'

'What about my call?'

As they walked towards the office Lizzy knew the only person, she could call was her brother. He was the only one she could trust.

'Alex?'

'Yes.'

'It's Elizabeth.'

'Lizzy? Where the hell are you? We've been looking for you.'

'Kununurra.'

'Where?'

'Kununurra. It's in the Kimberley. Western Australia.'

'What the hell are you doing all the way up there?'

'Alex I'm in jail.'

'JAIL! What on earth for?'

'They say that I murdered Andrew Burns.'

'YOU WHAT?'

'It's all a misunderstanding. I need a lawyer.'

'For fuck's sake Lizzy, are you telling me the truth? This is not the kind of thing you joke about.'

'Alex, I'm serious.'

'Jesus. Okay, I'm on it. Where are they supposed to go?'

'Kununurra police station.'

'Are you sure this isn't some kind of bad joke?'

'Alex, put down the phone and make a call. You need to do it *now*.'

'You *are* serious.'

'I've got to go.'

'Lizzy, just one more thing.'

'What?'

'Is Andrew really dead?'

'Very.'

'Fuck!'

On the way back to her cell she walked past Henry who was in a cell with three other men. They were scoffing down hamburgers while the contents oozed out the sides and down their arms.

'Don't worry Henry, the cavalry is coming. We'll be out of this place in no time at all.'

'No problem, It's good tucker in this place. Have ya had some yet?'

Lizzy and her impatience paced the cell, but the three aboriginal women who shared it, lounged wherever they could get comfortable.

'No use goin' up and down all day love. Ya feet will wear out before that bloody floor does,' said one.

'Are you *Kija*?' replied Lizzy.

'Mirriwong.' said the youngest of the three. '*Kija* is from down there at Turkey Creek. Are you from there?'

'Just visiting.'

'Whatcha doin' in 'ere?'

'They say I killed someone.'

'Hey Lois ... listen 'ere. This lady says she killed someone. Who did ya kill?'

'Yeah, who'd ya kill?' added Lois.

'It doesn't matter. I didn't do it.'

'Me neither.'

'What?'

'I didn't steal them groceries from that supermarket.'

'But that copper caught you with the trolley.' replied Lois.

'Yeah, but I didn't do it. I just found it outside. Some silly bugger must have left it there.'

The women laughed.

'Sit down with us.' said Lois, making room on her bench.

Lizzy joined them, and they talked long into the afternoon and early evening. Then as Karngin, the full moon, sat high in the sky, she finally fell asleep, leaning her head on the grocery thief's shoulder.

CHAPTER 20

Lizzy woke with a start early the next morning. Her body ached. The cell was in darkness and the only sounds were the women snoring and a wall clock ticking somewhere off in the distance. She began pacing up and down. The reality of what had happened had sunk in. She wanted to call out, but she had no voice. Every time she tried; the words seemed to get stuck in her throat. She guessed two hours must have passed before she saw a light go on down the hallway and a few minutes later, a constable appeared at her cell door. The old women were caught in the halfway land between sleep and wakefulness.

'There's some people here ta see ya.' said the constable.

'Some?'

'Yeah, they'll be along in a tick. You can talk to 'em here.'

Peering down the long corridor, Lizzy couldn't believe who was walking towards her. One had the unmistakable swagger of her brother, Alex, and next to him was a man she didn't know but guessed it must be the lawyer she had asked for. But the third man, she knew him well enough. Her chin began to quiver. The makings of tears welled up in her eyes and she was transported back to a time when her father had read her the story of the white-tailed deer, Bambi. Now she was the timid fawn who had been struck down by the evil of man, but approaching her, as fast as his old legs would carry him, was The Great Prince of the Forest, who had come to save her.

'Papa, papa,' she called, gripping the bars.

But Constantine was a blur, blocked out by tears.

'Anastasia ... my Anastasia ... ' called the distant voice, as he broke into a roly-poly jog.

And then suddenly her father was in front of her. The father she had lost so long ago, had come for her, to fight for her, to be her Papa once more. Their fingers met through the bars and for a moment they stared at each other, inspecting the lines and creases on the faces of the person they had each become. Their eyes mirrored the same sadness, but somehow, glued firmly in the middle, was happiness. Lizzy's father smiled, and said nothing, yet the look on his face told her everything was going to be okay.

'You shouldn't have to see me this way Papa.' she stammered. 'I'm so ashamed. How did you know that I was here?'

'Your brother ... he's not good at keeping secrets. Besides I tella him a long time ago that if you're ever in trouble then I must know ... your father must know.'

'I've missed you, Papa.'

'Time for all that later my little one. For now we must get you out of here.'

'Lizzy, this is John Murphy, the lawyer you wanted.' interrupted Alex. 'He takes care of some mates of mine. He's good. So, they say.'

Murphy nodded and did his best to look serious. 'What's all this about a murder?'

'I feel so stupid.'

'Have the police interviewed you?'

'Once.'

'Have they charged you?'

'I think so. Maybe. I'm not really sure.'

'It's a fucking kangaroo court. I'm going inside to sort out some bail.

Is there anything I should know?'

Lizzy spent the next few minutes bringing Murphy up to speed, filling in the details until finally the lawyer shook his head in disgust.

'Bloody country hick coppers. They wouldn't know their arse from their elbow...so do I have to ask you if you did it?'

'Not guilty.'

Murphy smiled. 'That's always a good start.'

Lizzy's father and brother stayed while Murphy stormed off in the direction of Sergeant Manfredi's office.

'Hey Miss Lizzy! Who's the good lookin' fella?' called Lois from the back of the cell.

'My brother.'

'Nah, not the young fella ... the other one.'

'My father.'

'Oh dear, you're in big trouble now girl,' laughed Lois. 'Big trouble.'

Murphy spoke with a growl, the result of too many cigarettes, too many *enthusiastic* cross-examinations, and, some said, a habit of gargling with gravel.

'What do ya fucking mean you interviewed my client without a lawyer present? Did you tell her that she could have legal representation before you talked to her?' bellowed Murphy across the sergeant's desk.

'Yes, we did.'

'Ah bullshit! This is going to be thrown out of court before it gets started. She wants bail.'

'That's not up to me ... the judge is in Broome ... he'll decide that.'

'So, you've got this ironclad case against my client, have you? Did you happen to notice that she didn't flee the scene of a gruesome murder? Did you happen to think about the fact she could've left the body out there in the middle of nowhere and it would probably never be found? And who brought the body back to you? Oh yes, that was my client. Listen sergeant, it doesn't sound like you've got much of a case.

My client is an intelligent woman not some numb-nut would-be miner, so if she killed this fellow Burns, why the fuck would she bring the bloody body back?'

'To make it look like she didn't do it.'

'You've been out in the sun too long son. That's never going to fly.'

'She tried to conceal evidence.'

'Where? Under your nose?'

'They hid the body.'

'In a fridge; to preserve the fucking thing. She's already told you that. In fact, she was doing you a favour in case you hadn't noticed. Preserving evidence.'

There was a knock on the door. The rain-coated constable looked anxious.

'Got a minute sarge?'

'Can it wait?'

'You're gonna want to hear this.'

'Out with it then.'

'I did what ya asked me to and got that body we brought in finger-printed.'

'Yeah, yeah and ...?'

'It's not Andrew Burns sarge.'

'What the fuck are you talking about? What about the wallet?'

'It musta been planted on him boss.'

Murphy rolled his eyes and tried not to look disgusted.

'Then who the fuck is it?' interrogated the sergeant.

'His name is Greg Wheeler. He's got some form ... assault, break and enter, malicious damage ... last known address is in Perth ... 12 Aldershot Crescent in Cottesloe ... that's a suburb I think.'

The sergeant shook his head in disgust and Murphy sneered.

'So if the body you have isn't Andrew Burns, have you charged my client with the murder of this Greg Wheeler fellow?'

'We might.'

'So, what about all this jilted lover crap not to mention all this con artist shit? Do you think she killed Greg Wheeler because she *wasn't* in love with him.'

'She might have … or that Henry Morgan fella might have done it … she might've helped him…or maybe he was the accomplice? There are lots of possibilities.'

'Come off it, sergeant. You already know Henry arrived with Miss Lawson and found the body … and then he came back with her. How many ways do you think an Aboriginal man has of disposing of a body in a place he knows very well?'

'He's got a point there sarge.' interrupted the junior constable.

The senior officer shot his underling a look which told him he better shut up.

'Listen …' said Murphy, ' … you haven't even worked out the rest of it, have you? Either this Andrew Burns bloke was never at his mine or he's still out there somewhere ripping off other gullible woman in mourning or … now here's the big surprise … *he* might've killed your Mr. Wheeler? How about that for a possibility?'

'I guess. Maybe.'

'Look, I suggest that you get my client and her friend Mr Morgan out of that cell before I start getting all nasty and start suing your arse for wrongful imprisonment. The politicians hate all that shit.'

'What about all the stuff Burns left behind, computer, satellite phone, files?'

'Now you're catching on. Burns was more than likely there, and he probably did kill this Greg Wheeler … it's not as though a million people are rushing to visit bloody Mistake Creek … so there aren't a lot of candidates, are there? And he left all that stuff because he had to leave in a hurry because he had just killed someone … probably someone who he wasn't expecting to be there. If I were you, I would be getting on the phone and letting a few people know that you're after Andrew Burns … or do we have to go to Broome and tell this bullshit story of yours to a bloody judge?'

The sergeant rolled his eyes. 'Let 'em go,' he instructed the constable, reluctantly.

The constable returned a few minutes later with Henry and Lizzy smiling like they had won the lottery. Lizzy's father smiled and held out his brawny arms and she ran to him and fell into them, happy to be his little girl all over again. She felt safe, safe like when she was a kid and their old house creaked, and she was sure that there was a ghost; safe like when she had come home from school crying because the other children had teased her about being a *greasy wog*; safe like when she had been confronted by the onset of womanhood, and his soft whispers and the cuddles of his work-honed arms that convinced her she wasn't dying.

'Thanks for coming Papa. It's not quite the reunion I had in mind.'

'You're my little girl and no matter how biga you get, you'll always be my little girl.'

'And you'll always be my Babaka.'

'Of course, I'm the only one you've got.' He smiled and hugged her again.

Locked in each other's arms it didn't take long before they both began to cry and their silent tears washed away the years of regret, forgave their mutual pig-headedness and wiped their slates clean. It took but a second; a heartbeat of love, for the golden thread of *family*, and all it means, to draw a father and his daughter back together again. In a strange way, Lizzy knew no matter how much she had come to hate Andrew Burns, she would always have something to thank him for. With her father hugging her and tears of happiness running down their cheeks, she knew her long walk towards the new horizon of her life could finally begin.

'Ya need to sign these papers,' interrupted the constable.

Murphy took care of the formalities while Lizzy, Henry, Constantine and Alex headed out the front door where the same hot wind which had assaulted Lizzy when she stepped off the plane in Kununurra, landed another blow. They were busy trying to flag down a taxi when Murphy joined them.

'Fuckwits,' he growled, handing Lizzy a small travel bag.

'They took this out of Jimmy Orion's four-wheel-drive. They said it must be yours.'

'Thank God. I don't think I could live in these clothes another day.'

'I was going to say something,' smiled Alex, but his sister ignored him.

'Sometimes I enjoy having sergeants for breakfast; especially that one,' scoffed Murphy. 'The man has terminal stupidity.'

'Speaking of stupidity,' smiled Alex. 'I know everyone has been telling you to get out of the house more often, but this is a bit ridiculous.'

'You're to blame for all this.'

'Me?'

'Yes you. You introduced me to him.'

'You needed a friend … speaking of which, who is your fellow criminal?'

'Where are my manners? This fine gentleman is Henry, Henry Morgan. I'd like you to meet my father, Constantine, this is my brother Alex, and this is John Murphy, the lawyer who got us out of here.'

Henry blushed, shook their hands, and tried to pretend he wasn't there.

'Whata do we do now?' asked Lizzy's father.

'Let's get back to Sydney.' smiled Alex, but his sister wasn't paying attention. She was too busy looking out to the distant horizon.

'I think I might hang around a bit and follow my river.' she replied, dreamily.

'What river? What on earth are you talking about?' replied Alex.

'I came here to find a man who stole something from me, but I found something quite different.'

'What are you talking about?' asked her brother.

'Me,' she smiled. 'I found me.'

All three men exchanged confused looks, but Henry grinned. He was the only one who knew what she meant.

'I know that look. What are you up to now?' asked Alex.

'I'm going to find Andrew and get my money back.'

'You're mad. Leave it to the police.'

'Those clowns?' scoffed Lizzy, nodding towards the police station.

'You're right. They couldn't find a beer in a bloody brewery,' grunted Murphy.

'And you can?' replied Alex.

'I think I know exactly where he is.'

'Where?'

'Margaret River, south of Perth. He's staying at a bed and breakfast with another person who he is about to separate from their cash.'

'How do you know that?'

'Her name is Ellen Hansen, and no, I don't know which B&B.'

'How are you going to find him?'

'I don't know yet. You guys go back to Sydney.'

'I'm not going anywhere,' sulked Constantine, folding his arms across his chest.

'Papa, you and John go back to Sydney. I'll be home soon. We can catch up then. Alex can come with me if he wants to. When we find Andrew, we'll get the police in Margaret River to handle it.'

'You no go near this man, you understand!' demanded her father.

'No Papa, we'll just see if we can find him and then leave it up to the police.'

'It's all crazy talk. Who do you think you are, Bruce Willis?'

'No Papa, but it would be nice to get my money back. It's all I have.'

'We got plenty of money now. Come home, forget about it.'

'It's not really about the money anymore Papa.'

Lizzy smiled tightly like she was hiding something and wasn't prepared to say what it was.

'How are you going to get there?' inquired Alex.

'Can you lend me the airfare?'

'That's what I thought. I've got a better idea.'

'Yeah, and what's that?'

'Papa chartered a jet to get us here quickly.'

149

'I wondered how you did that.'

'Papa and John can get a commercial flight back and you and I can take the plane down to Margaret River … we can't have you wandering off on your own again.'

'You know I can't afford that.'

'No worry. I pay,' replied Constantine. 'But on one condition. Alex goes with you.'

Lizzy smiled. 'Are you coming Henry?'

'Where to missus?'

'We'll drop you off in Turkey Creek. We can do that, can't we Alex? It's on the way.'

'Sure, why not?'

'I've never been in no bloody plane before missus.'

'As I'm discovering Henry, there's a first time for everything.'

A taxi pulled up, and as they drove to the airport. Murphy turned to Lizzy.

'Listen, I don't know if this is going to help, but apparently that dead guy's real name is Greg Wheeler. He lived in Perth. Last known address is 12 Aldershot Crescent. It's in Cottesloe.'

'But he's not going to tell us very much, is he?' smiled Alex.

Murphy shook his head. 'I must be crazy letting you run off and do this, but if you're anything like your brother, then there's probably no point in trying to change your mind.'

'Take care of my father,' replied Lizzy. 'He's the only one I've got.'

'For Chrissake, you don't do anything stupid,' frowned Constantine. 'If you finda this bastard, you get the police. He's already killed one man, so another one or two more isn't going to make a lot of difference.'

'We'll just find him Papa, then let the police handle it. That's all. I promise.'

CHAPTER 21

The jet lifted off from Turkey Creek, with Henry waving until the plane speared through thick rain clouds heading for clearer skies. When it levelled out, Lizzy opened a laptop she had found stored near a small desk in the aft section, plugged it in, connected to the internet, clicked on Google, typed in *5 star, bed and breakfast, Margaret River, Western Australia* and was rewarded with a page full of entries. Fortunately, only a handful were what she was looking for.

'Now let's see if we can find that bastard.'

'How do you know he'll go for something five-star?' asked her brother, peering over her shoulder.

'He won't, but she will. This Ellen woman he's meeting, her husband and kids were killed five years ago when a shopping mall roof collapsed on them. About six months ago she got two-hundred million dollars in compensation.'

'Shit. How do you know all that?'

'It was all in the file Andrew had. He's been tracking half-a-dozen women's lives, some of them for over three years. He targets either wealthy people who have had a recent death in the family or people who have just had a big payout ... or are about to.'

'But why you?'

'I don't know. I didn't have any money. He knew that.'

'How did he find out about your fifty-grand?'

'I told him, but I also told him that it was all I had.'

'He didn't pressure you?'

'No. I liked that, but he obviously had other plans.'

'It seems kind of sick doesn't it; preying on all those people I mean?'

'It's just plain cruel if you ask me.'

'And you think Andrew is going to take some of this Ellen person's money?'

'As much of it as he can get is my guess.'

'You just never know about people, do you?'

'Don't get me started.'

Lizzy scrolled down the search results looking for just the right bed and breakfast.

'This place looks like where I might go if I just got a couple of hundred million.'

'Next one down looks okay too.' offered Alex.

'…and this one.'

'Okay, let's go with these three, Noble House at Eagle Bay, Kauri Beach Guesthouse and Fernhill Homestead. I'll bet you a plate of mama's tomato keftedes they're staying at one of them … and if I'm right, they checked in yesterday.'

'I thought you said he had an airline ticket for Zurich.'

'He showed me a ticket for Johannesburg, but he didn't use that. My guess is that Ellen is going to be told he's off to Zurich and then she'll get a call with some cock and bull story…need the money in a hurry blah blah blah.'

'What are you going to say when you find him?'

'I don't really know. I really don't.'

'Maybe you should think about that. It would be good to have a plan even if it was crap.'

Three hours later they touched down at Margaret River. A soft, ocean breeze was blowing from the west, and around the terminal building, hundreds of eucalyptus trees swayed. High in them, they heard the warble of currawongs and the squawk of sulphur crested cockatoos. Between the trees and the ocean breeze, the air was filled with a sweet salt and eucalyptus oil perfume which after the humidity of the Kimberley, was a welcome relief.

'How long are you going to be?' inquired the pilot as they descended the stairs.

'Get comfortable,' smiled Alex, 'Something tells me that this trip is a long way from over.'

'Where do you want to go first?' asked Alex, as he slid into the driver's seat of their airport rental car.

'Let's try that Fernhill Homestead place in Yallingup,' she replied, opening Google Maps on her phone.

They drove in silence, taking in the lush coastal countryside, travelling through towering kauri forests and past fields ablaze with wildflowers, then vineyards, heavy with fruit. From time-to-time they could make out the Indian Ocean sparkling in the distance, and finally they pulled up at Fernhill Homestead.

'Are you ready?' she asked.

'What are you going to do?'

'Watch.'

In the neat entrance foyer, they were met by a man wearing shorts, a polo shirt, sandals, and a smile which seemed too big for his face.

'Welcome to Fernhill.'

'I have a reservation.' said Lizzy. 'Hansen, Ellen Hansen.'

The man skimmed his list but found nothing. 'Mmm,' he said. 'Just a minute, my wife must've taken it.'

He disappeared but was back a few seconds later with his wife drying her hands on a tea towel.

'Mrs. Hansen?' asked the wife.

'Yes?' she lied.

'I am afraid there must be some confusion.'

'Oh? Really?'

'Yes. When we spoke on the phone, I mentioned we were full this weekend. I thought that you were going to Noble House down at Eagle Bay? They had a cancellation; remember. I called you about it?'

'You did? Oh yes, excuse me … oh, oh, oh yes,' laughed Lizzy, turning to her brother, 'Oh dear, what a fool I am. Of course, that's where we should be going. I'm so sorry to have put you out.'

'No problem. You don't look anything like your picture in the paper. Much prettier.'

'Picture?'

'You've been all over the papers. I'm so sorry about your husband and children.'

Lizzy thought quickly and bowed her head.

'The money doesn't bring them back.'

'No dear, it doesn't,' frowned the wife.

As Lizzy and her brother got into their car, the woman turned to her husband.

'Poor dear. She must be in a terrible way. Imagine losing your whole family. No wonder she forgot where she was meant to be.'

Fifteen minutes later, Lizzy and her brother drove through the small town of Dunsborough and then along the rugged coastline towards Eagle Bay. Soon after, they saw a handsome house on a hill. With its sweeping gardens yawning with bottle brush, gardenias, hydrangeas and every variety of fruit tree, the magnificent stone and timber house stood like a silent sentinel watching over the bay. Noble House was certainly an appropriate name. In the distance, they could make out the white-washed tower of a lighthouse.

'Good afternoon.' smiled a man, as he opened their door.

'I'm Peter. Peter Fleming, your host.'

'Hi,' said Elizabeth. 'Elizabeth Hansen, Ellen Hansen's sister. I believe she's staying here for the weekend.'

'Why yes, yes she is.'

'We're having dinner with her tonight. Is she here?'

'No. I'm afraid not. They've gone to visit the wineries. Did you say you were having dinner with her tonight?'

'Yes, I did. Can you recommend somewhere?'

'The man she's with, he asked me to arrange a special dinner on the beach down at Eagle Bay tonight. Silver service, candles, the whole bit ... very romantic ... but he said it was only for two.'

'Mmmm, that's strange.'

'Look, it's no problem, no problem at all. I can do it for four if you want.'

'Really?'

'Of course.'

'Then let's make it a surprise. My new fiancé and I have some very special news for them. I'll call her and say we can't make it, then turn up after all. She needs some good news for a change.'

'Mum's the word,' said Peter, putting his forefinger to his lips.

'What time?'

'They've booked for eight.'

'Where's Eagle Bay?'

'Not far. I'll draw you a map.'

'Perfect. We'll be there at eight. I'll bring some champagne ... we're celebrating ... aren't we darling?'

Alex smiled politely, not knowing why she was calling him darling, what they were celebrating or who the hell her new fiancé was.

'We'll be at the southern end, near the rocks. Look for the white marquee and fairy lights.'

'Sounds fabulous ... how exciting ... Ellen will be so surprised.'

'It sounds like she has had a few hard years,' grimaced Peter.

'Yes, yes, she has, but we sisters must stick together at times like this.'

'She's lucky to have you.' smiled Peter's wife.

'What happened to calling the police?' asked Alex, as they drove away.

'What do you think they're going to do? Do you think Andrew is going to come clean just because we say he should? Do you think he'll just confess? Somehow, I don't think he's going to say, *oh yes that was me. I killed that man and blew his head off with a shotgun, and oh yes, I've been ripping off all those women and look, here are the bank accounts where I've hidden all your money … help yourself?* No, of course not.'

'Well, like John Murphy already told you, he's already killed one man. Doesn't that make him kind of dangerous?'

'We have to make him *want to* give my money back.'

'And just how do you propose to do that?'

'I don't know yet.'

'It's good to see you've finally got a plan.'

'There's no need to be sarcastic.'

On a hill overlooking Eagle Bay they waited in their car for an hour or more while the sun floated like a red ball on the horizon and then finally disappeared in a kaleidoscope of gold and purple somewhere out towards Africa. Once the light had gone, they looked down towards the southern end of the bay and sure enough, festooned in fairy lights, there was a small white marquee with the sides rolled up to let in the sea breezes. They could make out a man wearing a chef's toque busy at work and in front of the tent another man struck a match and threw it into a large bonfire which spluttered and sparked, but then took. In the distance the blink of the lighthouse shimmered on the ocean every few seconds then disappeared only to return momentarily but there was no sign of a woman or Andrew Burns.

'Are you sure you know what you're doing?' asked Alex.

'I'm just going to ask for my money back. He doesn't know I've been to his mine, and he doesn't know I know about the dead body, and he doesn't know that I know about all the other women.'

'He doesn't know very much, does he?'

'Exactly. As far as he's concerned, I'm still at home in Sydney waiting for him.'

'Do you think so?'

'How would he know otherwise?'

'He might have gone back to his mine and found all his stuff was missing.'

'Look, even if he did go back, how likely is it that he'll connect it to me?'

'How will you explain being here?'

'I don't know.'

'You don't know?'

'He's going to be so surprised he won't be able to speak.'

'That's your plan? You're going to surprise him into submission?'

'I guess so.'

'Shit Lizzy, you're out of your damn mind.'

'Maybe I am, but it's what I need to do.'

'No maybes about it, big sister. You're supposed to be madly in love with him and here he is having a romantic dinner with another woman, and you arrive ... on a beach ... in the middle of nowhere. What are you going to say? Oh hi ... just passing, saw your lights on, thought I'd drop in.'

'I didn't say that it was a great plan.'

'The man is going to be either completely pissed off or totally defensive.'

'Which would you be?'

'I guess I'd be ... I'd be surprised at first ... it would take some time to register what was going on and then ... and then, well, I could do just about anything.'

'So, we need to take control of the situation right from the get-go. The last thing he'll want to do is spoil his chance to get more money from this poor Ellen woman. If I don't go in too hard, he'll probably play along until he sees what the hell I'm up to.'

'I suppose, but what if he gets violent?'

'That's why you're here. Hasn't Fat Sam taught you anything with your karate yet? What use is that black belt you just got if you can't sort

157

out a dipstick like Andrew Burns?'

'Jesus Lizzy, you really are out of your mind.'

'Will you help me?'

'Do I have a choice?'

'No, just play along. You're my new fiancé.'

'I was worried you were going to say that.'

Just then a black Mercedes pulled up adjacent to the beach. The silhouettes of a man and a woman stepped out and the car drove away. The couple kissed passionately then walked onto the beach.

'Fucker,' whispered Lizzy, under her breath.

'I've got a bad feeling about this,' muttered Alex.

'You know Alex, I think that behind Andrews charming front he's just a bloody coward and you know what happens with cowards don't you; you push back and they fold.'

'Then you had better hope you're right.'

They waited until Peter had poured two glasses of champagne.

'Time to go.' said Lizzy, slipping off her shoes. 'Before they notice that there are four place settings.'

She ran the twenty steps across the sand to the marquee with Alex grumbling at her side and as the light of the bonfire flickered on her face Lizzy began the performance of a lifetime.

'Andrew. Oh Andrew, I'm so glad we found you. We have some wonderful news for you,' she said, running up and throwing her arms around his neck.

Burns' mouth hung open. Ellen turned to him looking for an explanation, but he was speechless. Lizzy could see him trying to form words, but nothing was coming out. So far, her *plan* (such as it was) was working.

'Oh, Andrew, you've hurt yourself,' frowned Lizzy, eyeing the sling draped over his shoulder.

'Small accident, my wrist ... nothing to worry about.'

'You poor dear ... oh I'm sorry ... you must be Ellen. I've heard so much about you. I'm Andrew's sister, Elizabeth, and this is my fiancé,

Alex. We just had to find Andrew and tell him our good news.'

'News?' asked Andrew.

'It's so exciting. We got engaged last night. You don't mind us crashing your dinner party, do you?' she said, pecking Burns on the cheek again.

'We're very close,' continued Lizzy, turning to Ellen. 'I just had to let him know. He would never have forgiven me otherwise. We drove all the way from Perth to find you. I could've called, but you can't drink champagne over the phone, can you?' added Lizzy, handing Peter the bottle she was waving about.

'Andrew loves that one, *don't* you Andrew?'

'Bit of a surprise heh?' asked Alex, playfully punching the stunned mullet in the shoulder.

'Ye ... ye ... yes ... big surprise. I had no idea, no idea at all.'

'Anyway, your friend Peter was kind enough to play along,' added Lizzy, not stopping to draw breath.

'How thoughtful, and congratulations,' said Ellen, finally speaking. 'Family is so important ... please ... sit down ... we have to help you to celebrate ... don't we Andrew?'

'Yes, yes of course,' he said, through gritted teeth.

'We're not interrupting anything are we? I know you two have probably snuck off for a dirty weekend, but I just couldn't resist. I'm, we're so excited,' said Lizzy, slugging back half a glass in one gulp. 'Where did you two meet?' she continued, putting her glass down next to her *brother's*.

Andrew closed his eyes and looked away. He knew what was coming.

'Oh, it was only quite recently, at a dinner party that my brother had. Andrew was so handsome, and he had such a wonderful life. I just couldn't resist.' smiled Ellen, stroking Burns' hand.

'Oh really?' smiled Lizzy. 'Is that right? Your brother had a dinner party heh?'

'Yes, that's right and then he started telling me all about diamonds and diamond mines and well, that was it ... he's a regular Indiana Jones, don't you think?'

'Yes, he's quite a catch ... aren't you Andrew?' teased his make-believe sister.

Burns blushed and tried to hide behind his champagne glass.

'And you two?' asked Ellen, nodding at Alex.

'Oh, we've known each other ever since we were kids.'

'How lovely,' smiled Ellen. 'Let's have a toast.'

'To Elizabeth and Alex,' she said, raising her glass.

'To Elizabeth and er ... Alex.' came the confused echo from beside her.

'How did you know we were here?' asked Burns, finally finding his voice.

'Oh, Helena told us. She knows everything,' replied Elizabeth, touching the side of her nose conspiratorially.

'Really? Helena? Are you sure?'

'Who's Helena?' enquired Ellen.

'Our sister,' replied Lizzy, jumping in before Burns had a chance to reply. 'She's the black sheep of the family.'

'I see. That's probably why you haven't mentioned her or Elizabeth yet, Andrew.'

Burns tried to hide his grimace. 'Yes, well, I think we all have our black sheep, don't we?'

'Yes, but some are a little blacker than others,' added Lizzy.

Ellen smiled, 'I can't wait to meet her.'

'Well, I'm sure you will,' replied Lizzy. 'You can't hide your relations forever, can you Andrew?'

'She sounds, interesting,' cooed Ellen, trying to be polite.

'Yes, yes, she is. Let's sit down,' added Lizzy. 'We've got so much to talk about.'

Lizzy could see Burns' cerebral cogs working overtime because with Helena's name now on the table, he had no way of knowing how much she knew. The fact that she knew the name of his sometimes wife was enough to push him back into his seat and wait for the next verbal missile. He also knew that if he didn't want to give his game away to Ellen, he would have to sit and wait for it to hit. It didn't take long.

Lizzy finished two glasses of champagne in quick succession, filling up the space with small talk and polite comments about lovely dresses, well-polished forks, and balmy weather.

'So, what made you choose Noble ... ' but as she spoke her hands fanned out and her champagne glass took flight, ending up in Burns' lap. He jumped up.

'Oh no. I'm so sorry,' smarmed Lizzy.

'Christ! Now look what you've bloody well done.'

'Andrew, it was an accident. It'll be fine,' chided Ellen, but Lizzy knew it was the perfect excuse for Burns to escape. He didn't disappoint.

'Look,' said Andrew. 'No problem. I'll just nip back to the room and get changed. It'll only take a minute.'

'Perfect, I'll come too,' said Lizzy. 'This champagne has gone straight through me. Alex, you stay and keep Ellen company for a few minutes.'

'Are you sure?' asked her brother, worried about her being alone with Burns.

'It's fine. Get to know Ellen. You might be related one day. Isn't that right Ellen?'

'But...' stammered Alex.

'I have a car. It's parked just over there,' added Lizzy, getting to her feet.

'I'm sorry, but I couldn't help overhearing. Are you going back to the house?' asked their host, Peter.

'Yes.' replied Lizzy. 'And we better make it soon,' she laughed. 'Or I'll burst.'

'Could I get a ride. I forgot the sauce for main course and the chef is having a hissy fit.'

'We can't have that, can we,' smiled Lizzy, but around the edge of her politeness, there was disappointment. She knew she had missed her opportunity to corner Burns and get the explanation she so badly wanted. She would have to bide her time and find a way to get him alone. All

161

three of them trudged off across the beach before anyone could say another word. Lizzy couldn't help but notice that Burns walked with a pronounced limp to complement his sling.

'They must take after different sides of the family,' said Ellen, as a car door slammed.

'Pardon?' replied Alex.

'They don't look anything like each other.'

'Oh yeah, you're right. No, they don't. Elizabeth is more like her mother.'

Lizzy drove. Peter was in the passenger seat. Burns sat behind him. They said nothing, but the owner of Noble House could tell that something was up. The tension in the air was so palpable that you could carve it, so he kept glancing at Lizzy then at Burns' reflection in the rear-view mirror, trying to work out what it was.

'Just pull in here,' said Peter, indicating a spot near a side door as they drove down the driveway. 'Andrew, your room is through the kitchen to the left and Lizzy, there's a bathroom to the right.'

'Thank you,' she replied, but Burns was already out of the car and striding off. 'What's his room number?'

'Six, but I don't think he'll be long. Let's just meet back here in say, ten minutes.'

'Sounds like a plan,' replied Lizzy, sweetly, getting out of the car.

She didn't turn left to the bathroom, but followed Burns, and just as his door was about to close, shoved her foot in.

'Surprised to see me?'

'What the fuck is going on?' spat Burns, hovering over his suitcase.

'It's quite a little scam that you've got going.'

'What scam?'

'Oh, come off it, Andrew. You stole my money, fifty grand, and you scammed a pile out of other unsuspecting suckers who fell for your so-called charms.'

162

'What money? What scam? I don't know what you're talking about.'

'Listen, cut the crap. You know exactly what I'm talking about.'

'Lizzy, I don't know what you're doing here, and I have no idea what the hell you're talking about so if you don't mind, I have a dinner to get back to.'

'I'm sure the police would be interested in talking to you about quite a few things.'

'Like what? Having dinner on the beach? You've got your wires crossed.'

'I doubt it.'

'Look, if this is your idea of some kind of payback because I'm having dinner with another woman, then I'm sorry, but as *you* said, you're, *bloody hard work*.'

'So, I had a chat with your wife Helena.'

'Ex-wife,' replied Burns, pulling a pair of trousers out of his suitcase. 'We were divorced three years ago. How did you know about her anyway?'

'Never mind. As my mother always used to say, *I always find out. The information always comes to me*.'

'Did she tell you that I would be here?'

'That's my secret. What about Africa?'

'What about it?'

'You were supposed to go there to buy equipment for your mine.'

'I've never been to Africa, and I can't afford equipment. You know that.'

'So, is Ellen your next victim?'

'What are you talking about? You've had too much champagne. Look, let's just move on. Why have you come all this way anyway; to be a jilted lover and make a scene?'

'I came for my money. Fifty thousand.'

'Fuck, here we go again.'

'I'm going to go back there and tell Ellen what you're really up to.'

'I'm up to nothing but having dinner, and I think it would be a good idea if you and your so-called *fiancé* make your excuses and leave.'

Lizzy didn't want to play her ace. She knew that if she told Burns she had been to his mine and seen the files and emails that he would also know she knew about the dead body. It irked her, but she had to keep that information to herself, or he might turn nasty.

'Look why don't you just transfer the money back to my account and we can forget the whole thing. Put it down to experience.'

'Lizzy, for the last time, I don't know anything about your money. You've got to stop behaving like some paranoid weirdo. We had a nice time. Now it's over. Can't you just accept that? Now if you don't mind, I need to get changed.'

'I'm not finished with you. Not by a long shot,' she replied, crossing her arms.

'Have it your way,' he gritted, dropping the trousers back in his suitcase, slamming it shut and heading for the bathroom door.

'Just go Lizzy,' he yelled, once it was locked. 'Go before you regret something.'

'It's easy to be brave from the other side of the door Andrew. What don't you man up and admit what you've done.'

'I've done bloody nothing.'

'Do you have your wallet?' she asked, hoping to catch him off guard.

'I've already told you. I'm not giving you any money because I haven't taken any. I know you're down on your luck, but this isn't the way to solve your problems. Listen, I'll just get changed and then we'll go back, and you can pick up Alex and be on your way.'

Now she didn't have a choice. The wallet hint had been too subtle for Burns. She had expected him to cave in and admit everything, or at the very least, become defensive, but his thin veneer of lies and bravado held. Now she was confused. Perhaps she would have to get the police involved after all. While Burns changed, she propped a chair under the bathroom doorknob so he couldn't open it, then dialled 000.

'Ambulance, police or fire brigade,' asked the voice at the other end of the phone.

'Police.'

Lizzy quickly told her story, being sure to mention Sergeant Manfredi in Kununurra, and after some explanation, hung up to wait for the police to arrive. Then there was a knock on the bedroom door. She opened it.

'Are you two ready yet?' asked Peter.

'He's still in the bathroom.'

'I see.'

Two minutes later he still hadn't come out, so Lizzy pounded on the door.

'Andrew, we have to go. Ellen will be getting worried about you,' she said, reverting to the role of dutiful sister.

He didn't answer. Another two minutes ticked by. Still no answer.

'Maybe he has fallen over and hit his head,' said Peter. 'Can I come in? Maybe I can help?' he added, looking at the chair blocking the door then back at Lizzy.

'It's a long story.'

'It always is,' frowned the host, inserting the screw-driver blade on a pocketknife into the small notch that allowed him to open the door from his side.

The bathroom was empty. The curtains were flapping in an open window.

'We were getting worried about you,' grimaced Alex, when his sister finally returned.

'Where's Andrew?' asked Ellen, as a worried look creased her face.

'Ellen, there's something you need to know.'

CHAPTER 22

The motel Lizzy and her brother found for the night was stuck in a 1950s time-warp, just like the sixty-something woman on the front desk, who was too busy watching a gameshow on a small television to be vaguely interested in what they wanted. She just pushed a key across the counter and pointed to the left.

'Room Five love. Stick ya breakfast menu on the door if ya wanna get fed. Settle the bill in the mornin'. No pets, no truck drivers, no smokin' in the rooms ... ya got all that?'

Room Five was a step up from Room Two at Orion's pub. The carpet fitted the room, there were two healthy looking single beds, and off to the right was a bathroom that smelled of bleach.

'This reminds me of the days back in the migrant hostel,' yawned Lizzy, stretching out on the bed next to Alex's.

'Pardon?'

'It was before you were born. The huts where we stayed, they were like small airplane hangars. The taps leaked, the windows let in the draft, the toilets never worked, the carpet ... well actually, there wasn't any carpet ... just red linoleum. It had a very strange pattern, so I used to lie on the floor and find strange animals in all the swirls and splodges.'

'Papa is always talking about those days. He still has friends that he met there.'

'The hostel was like the United Nations. It was full of people from all over the world ... Italians, Greeks, Turks ... all us *wogs* in together with the poms and the Irish, the Scots and a few people from Wales, who absolutely nobody could understand. *Populate or perish* that's what the Australian government said back then, so they let us all in. They were good days. I had forgotten just how good they were.'

'Those hostels don't sound like too five star to me.'

'You're too spoilt Alex, that's your problem. I remember lying in my squeaky bed listening to the rain on the tin roof, all wrapped up in a patchwork quilt mama made from scraps of material she found in bins. I can't begin to tell you how wonderful that felt. I don't think I've ever felt safer in my life ... except maybe in Tony's arms.'

'He had a way of calming you, didn't he?'

'Was it that obvious?'

'I'm afraid so.'

'I miss him Alex.'

'I know you do. We all do.'

Lizzy's mind wandered away, travelling deep into her own remembering. It was as if her body was still in Room Five, but the rest of her had gone to a place where she could be alone with her husband. She felt him stroke her hair and heard him say, *I will always love you. And I will always love you too*, she replied out loud, *always*.

'Always what?' replied Alex.

His sister smiled but didn't reply. She didn't want to speak, she wanted to hang onto her thoughts a little bit longer, but Alex was insistent.

'Well? Always what?'

She sighed and reluctantly let go of the memory.

'I will always remember how Babaka read me stories. I think that our father learnt half of his English by reading me Hansel and Gretel and Bambi. Sometimes he tried reading me the newspaper. That was so funny, especially the sports pages. He never did understand cricket...*why they bowl this maiden over,* he would say, *why is this a good thing?*'

167

'They did it tough for a while, didn't they?'

'After we left the hostel, we bought that little house in Surry Hills where you were born, and I think to pay for it there were days they went hungry so we could have something to eat. I remember having porridge for eight days in a row one time ... breakfast, lunch and dinner ... that's probably why I don't eat it now ... mind you, I'll probably have to learn to. Andrew has cleaned me out completely.'

'Everything?'

'I'm afraid so.'

'If you need money, you only have to ask you know ... what are brothers for?'

'I know. Thanks, but I need to do this on my own. You must be doing pretty well by now.'

'You mean Papa is?'

'You're running the business now Alex. Papa is getting old. You'll be taking over completely soon.'

'He doesn't think I'm up to it yet.'

'He's a worker Alex. He'll probably work until the day he dies. I'm sure he can't do what he used to do. He needs you.'

'He only comes in a couple of days a week now.'

'Because he knows you *can* do it.'

'I guess.'

'Look at you, six feet-three of karate chopping muscle and you're having a confidence attack.'

'Only with you, big sister, only with you.'

'I'm glad Papa came.'

'He loves you Lizzy. He loves us both. Look at what he did when you were in trouble. I didn't have to persuade him to come. He even hired that plane because there were no regular flights that could get there in a hurry.'

'I'm glad you told him. I needed to mend that bridge.'

'It's about time. He would like that. Mama would too. She misses you more than you know.'

'I miss her too Alex. So much.'

'Maybe we're all a bit too proud sometimes.'

'And look where it got us. If I could change it all I would.'

'Let's call it the wisdom of age.' smiled her brother.

'You know something Alex?'

'What?'

'When Tony died, I realized that nothing else mattered but love.'

'You loved him very much, didn't you?'

'More than I can say,' she replied, clutching the diamond pendant around her neck. 'I just feel empty without him. It's like I've got a permanent hollow in my stomach that just gnaws away at me.'

'What about Andrew?'

'What about him?'

'Didn't you feel something for him?'

'I guess I did, but once you've had the kind of love that Tony and I had, there's nothing that quite measures up. I think I let myself fall in love because I thought I had to move on, but I don't think you ever do, not completely anyway. There's always a part of you that belongs to a person you love but gets taken away. Have you ever been in love Alex?'

'Several times a week.'

He ducked as a pillow flew across the room in his direction.

'You'll learn.'

'What?'

'It's about being happy. It's about having meaning.'

'Lots of money will make me very happy and have lots of meaning.'

'That's not what I'm talking about. Before those idiot police took me off to jail, I met a woman, an aboriginal woman. Her name was Rosie, she's Henry's mother. You wouldn't believe the life she's had. Her father was murdered, one of her children was taken off her ... she never saw her baby again ... you've heard about the stolen generation, she lived it ... she lost a leg to leprosy. She has no possessions, yet she still remembers every day of her life like they were the most joyous moments ... and she looks forward to all her tomorrows, so she can help her family and friends remember the Dreamtime stories ... so they can know who they are and what they are ... where they came from and how they're connected to the places they live in.'

'Sounds like you're thinking of going bush?'

'No. No I'm not, but I've got to put a few things in perspective.'

'Like what?'

'Like who the hell I am.'

'What's all this stuff you've been sayin' about a river you need to follow?'

'Pardon?'

'You told Babaka and me back at Kununurra.'

'I did?'

'Maybe you got too much sun?'

'No, no ... my river is very real. Rosie told me about it.'

'Told you what?'

'It doesn't matter.'

'No, tell me.'

'You wouldn't understand.'

'Try me.'

'Well if you really must know, she said that life is like a river and you can sit and watch the river, but the time will come when it'll dry up ... and then there's nothing there for you ... or you can move on to another place where there's water and food. She said that if you sit by that lazy river for too long, soon there will be nothing ... you won't be able to see yourself in the water anymore ... that other you, the *you* that looks back at you and reminds you of who you really are ... when the river is dry, you can't see that person anymore.'

Alex's face was blank. 'I'm not so sure that I know what you mean.'

'It doesn't matter. I guess you had to be there.'

'Where?'

Until that moment Lizzy hadn't imagined how difficult it would be to explain what happened to her. She could hardly believe it herself. On the flight to Margaret River, she had mulled it over, but the more she tried to make sense of her recent life, the more it confused her. How could she tell people that she had lived in a cave with an old aboriginal woman and her disappearing son? How could she explain what those three days exploring every nook and cranny of the Dreamtime had meant to her? How could people possibly understand just how much it had changed her? The fact was, she didn't understand it herself, but she knew it had changed her.

In pondering the answer, she realized there was no need to tell anyone, anything, especially the people who inhabited the life she once knew. It was her personal journey, her personal awakening, and there was no reason to give anyone an excuse to smirk knowingly or to talk behind her back like she was some kind of crazy woman.

'I'll tell you all about it some other time.'

Her brother smiled.

'Does this river of yours have any water in it now?'

'I can see the mud at the bottom.'

'So why follow *that* river?'

'I think I've found a new one. I just need to find out how deep it is, before I dive in.'

'Now you're really confusing me.'

'This is not about a river Alex, it's about yourself. You take your river, that place where you look back at yourself, you take it with you wherever you go. It's what's inside you.'

'Self-respect?'

'Self-worth, self-understanding, self-development, self-actualization ... shit, it's all fancy psycho-babble rubbish. When you get right down to it, it's just about being able to look in the mirror and see the person staring back at you and be happy, truly happy with what you see. If the world goes to hell and someone pushes a little red nuke button, before that mushroom cloud eats me, I want to be able to say that I like who I am; just for a moment. That will be enough.'

'What about now? Do you like who you are?'

'I see possibilities. What about *you?*'

'What?'

'Are you happy with who you see.'

'No one has ever asked me that before.'

'I'm asking you now.'

'I don't know. I really don't.'

'You don't know if you like the person you see in your mirror?'

'I guess. I've never really thought about it.'

'That's my point. Nor did I. When I left home way back when I was eighteen, I knew I couldn't marry Milo. I knew it would ruin my life. I had to change rivers, but I went and sat by a lazy river of self-pity and worthlessness until Tony came along … I changed rivers because he picked me up … he saved me and took me to a new river … a wonderful new life of love, but after he died, I just didn't have the strength or the inclination to pick myself up and change direction again. I just kept following the same river, hoping that the rains would come and fill it up again, but Tony isn't coming back, he's gone. I need to move on. Rosie was right, there comes a time when no matter how much water has been in your river, it dries up and then there's nothing. You've either got to move on or die where you are.'

'Are *you* dying?'

'Part of me already has. I just don't want any more to.'

Alex smirked. 'Going after Andrew isn't about the money, is it?'

'Sometimes you really surprise me.'

'I'll take that as a compliment. Anyway, what's all this talk about dying? Is there something you're not telling me?'

'I'm not dying, but I don't want to die a little bit at a time. If I let Andrew get away with what he's done, then another part of me will almost certainly die.'

'Which part?'

'A very important part; my spirit, my will to do anything … my reason for getting out of bed in the morning. When Tony died, I think part of me died with him ... you saw what happened to me.'

'Yeah, you locked yourself away.'

'Yes, I did because I couldn't change what happened that night. I wanted to, but I couldn't.'

'You're way too smart for the likes of Andrew Burns. How the hell did he get away with it anyway?'

'Because he knew what I really wanted.'

'And what was that?'

'He gave me a way to live again, something to get my teeth into, a way be part of something; to be whole. He took his time, got to know me, then he put it out there. I bit, and then he took it away, and I wanted it twice as much. I could kick myself for being so stupid.'

Lizzy's eyes started to well up.

'Are you okay?'

'One day I'm going to be okay and maybe that crappy feeling in my stomach will go away too, but I know, I just know, that if I let him get away with what he's done then he'll have taken a lot more than just money.'

'So, if we get your money back, you get some interest.'

'I suppose it's something like that. We just need to get Andrew to tell us where it is.'

'What about all those other women?'

'I'm going to find their money too ... just you wait and see.'

'As you've discovered, the polite approach doesn't work.'

'I should've listened to you.'

'Where do you think he is?'

'He could be anywhere by now.'

'So, what do we do tomorrow?'

'There's an address in Perth, the one John Murphy gave me. Maybe if we can find out a bit more about this Greg Wheeler guy, that might lead us somewhere.'

'Maybe it will lead you to your river,' smiled her brother.

CHAPTER 23

The next morning, Alex and Lizzy's charter flight made the short hop to Perth where they rented another car, but as they approached 26 Aldershot Crescent, they saw a police car parked outside. They drove past just in time to see two policemen talking to a blonde woman wearing tight jeans and a singlet top smoking a cigarette while she watered a spartan garden. They didn't hear what the policemen said to her, but whatever it was, it was enough to make the woman throw her arms in the air and faint on the lawn. The garden hose fell out of her hand and started thrashing about like an out-of-control cobra and while one policeman tried to revive the woman, the other attempted to wrestle the hose to the ground. It would've been comical if it hadn't been so sad.

'That's the woman from the mine,' said Lizzy. 'She's the one who said that I killed her husband. It's Andrew's ex-wife, bloody Helena.'

'Ex-wife?'

'Back at Eagle Bay, Andrew told me that they were divorced three years ago.'

'You believed him?'

'I guess I shouldn't. He's not exactly known for telling the truth, is he?'

'Okay, so explain this, what's she doing living with our dead guy?'

'That's what I want to know too. Jesus, I wasn't expecting this little love triangle.'

They watched as the policemen helped the woman up from the lawn and took her inside. Ten minutes later they re-emerged and left her standing in the doorway dabbing her eyes with a tissue. Once the police car was out of sight, she shrugged, smiled like a Cheshire cat, threw the tissue in the garden, and closed the door.

'It looks like the mourning period is officially over,' said Lizzy, shaking her head.

'What's going on there?'

'What do you say we drop in for a visit?'

'And say what?'

'I think those coppers were just the local boys who had been sent around to do the dirty work.'

'Dirty work?'

'You know, *I have the sad duty to inform you that Greg Wheeler has passed away.*'

'You're confusing me.'

'Now that the police have discovered the body that I found isn't Andrew Burns, I think they were here to inform Mr. Wheeler's next-of-kin what happened to him. *Procedure.* That's what my good friend Sergeant Manfredi up at Kununurra would call it. Bloody procedure.'

'And so?'

'When Henry and I left Orion's place up north, everyone was sure that it was Andrew who had been killed.'

'Surely that moron Manfredi would've called her and told her it was all a big mistake.'

'Maybe he did, but Manfredi would have no idea that Andrew's *so-called* wife was living with the dead guy ... and you can be sure she wouldn't have told him that.'

'How do you know?'

'Because she had already told everyone, including the cops, that she

175

was Andrew Burns' wife.'

'Mmmm. You've got a point.'

'What could she say to the coppers ... *oh I'm sorry I made a mistake about which husband I thought I had?* If she got upset about Greg Wheeler carking it then the police would want to know why, and she would have to say, *oh he's my husband too.* No, I don't think so. She would've had to just wait for the local police to come around and tell her what happened, then act like she didn't know anything. And that's exactly what I think she has just done. The fainting was a nice touch, don't you think?'

'So, you're telling me that little miss tank top and this Greg Wheeler guy *were* actually at the mine at the same time?'

'Jesus Alex, no wonder Papa still comes into work. They had to be.'

Her brother tried to look hurt, but he was too intrigued to dwell on the insult.

'What do you say we go and see if she can fill in some of the blanks for us?'

Alex shook his head in amazement. Who was this version of his sister? He had never met her before.

They got out of the car, walked to the woman's door, and knocked. No answer.

'But she was there just a minute ago.' said Alex.

Lizzy knocked again.

'I know she's in there.' she added, pulling out her mobile phone and Googling Wheeler. G. 26 Aldershot Crescent, Cottesloe.'

She punched in the number and listened while a phone rang inside.

'Maybe she knows it's you?'

Finally, it answered.

'I know that you're there. Fuck off!'

'I just want to talk to you.'

'About what?'

'Andrew.'

'He's not dead. The police just told me.'

'Yes, I know, but your *other* husband is.'

The phone went dead. Soon after, the front door opened.

'Can we come in?'

'Suit yaself,' she sighed, walking back down the corridor leaving a pall of cigarette smoke in her wake.

The woman led them into a small living room that was sparsely inhabited by dilapidated furniture. In contrast to the rest of the room, an expensive looking plasma television sat on top of empty milk crates in one corner. The ashtray on the coffee table was full to overflowing and next to it were the bony remains of a KFC meal and four empty beer bottles. The house smelt like a pub after closing time.

'Waddya want?' growled the woman.

'I'm sorry to hear about your husband.'

'So ya know?'

'Yes, yes we do.'

'Anyway, he's not my husband. I left Andrew for him, but we never got married. I'm still officially married to Andrew,' mumbled Helena, lighting a cigarette from the stub of one she had almost finished.

'What was Wheeler doing up at the mine?' asked Lizzy.

'I dunno.'

'I think you do.'

'And you think I'm going to tell you, do you ... just like that?'

'Yes, I do.'

'Now why would I wanna do that?'

'Because your friend Sergeant Manfredi obviously hasn't put two and two together yet. Imagine if he knew that *you* were the dead guy's what ... de facto ... as well as being Andrew's wife. Do you think he might start asking some questions about why you were up at the mine?'

'That copper is a gold-plated idiot!'

'Yes, that may be true, but one call from me will sort that problem out.'

'How the hell did you find me anyway?'

'A bit by accident really. We came here to see if we could find out

177

more about your friend Mr. Wheeler.'

'You didn't know that I lived here?'

'No. It was quite a coincidence wouldn't you say Alex?'

'I guess so.'

'Then you can fuck off!'

Lizzy pulled out her mobile phone.

'One call ... that's all it takes. You tell me what I need to know, and I might not make it.'

'I already told ya, fuck off.'

'Have it your way. Let's go Alex.'

They were almost at the door when Helena changed her mind.

'Sit down.' she demanded. 'Here's the deal. I'll tell you some stuff and then you forget that you ever saw me here. Okay?'

'Okay.' replied Lizzy, after a long pause, '…but you'll need to make it worth my while.'

The woman stubbed out her cigarette and took a deep breath.

'Andrew has been running this scam of his for years. He was doing it when we were together ... when I left him, he stopped for a while. I reckon he didn't have the balls for it by himself, but then I heard he was doin' it again. I told him that if Greg and me, didn't get our cut, then we were goin' to dob him in.'

'Did he cut you in?'

'Some, but we knew he was getting way more than he was telling us. I almost choked when you said that he had knocked-off fifty-grand from you. Holy fuck, I thought, the prick had gone big time.'

'You hid your surprise well.'

'Yeah well, we didn't see any of it, did we?'

'Why was Mr. Wheeler up at the mine?'

'He went up there to frighten Andrew; to make him give us more money. As you can see, we're not exactly flush. I told him not to, but he wouldn't listen.'

'Frighten?'

'Yeah, frighten. That's all. He wasn't going to kill him or nothin' like

178

that.'

'So, what happened?'

'I don't know. My guess is that he wasn't expecting Andrew to have a gun. I know that.'

'Why?'

'Andrew hates 'em. His father was always shooting stuff when he was a kid. He begged him not to, but he always did, so he grew up hating bloody guns.'

'So why did he have one?' asked Lizzy.

'I really dunno.'

'Why were *you* there?'

'Andrew is always calling and saying we should get back together. He keeps sending me emails telling me how much he loves me. We talked about who he was setting up ... just like we always had.'

'Yes, I know, I've read your emails,' replied Lizzy, dismissively, 'You still haven't told me why you were there.'

'I wanted Andrew to think that I was going back to him.'

'So you would get more money.'

'Something like that. I dunno why I would even think about doing that. Greg and Andrew are two peas out of the same pod ... they look alike, dress alike...fuck, they even screw alike, but Andrew, he's a bloody dreamer. Greg wasn't much better, but he belonged to me, not every other bloody woman on the planet. I knew Greg would never amount to much ... look for yourself,' she said, sweeping her arm around the almost empty room. 'I was going to show up after Andrew had the shit scared out of him and be the—'

'Good guy?' asked Alex

'I guess, but I just wasn't expecting to find you there. None of his women have ever gone to the bloody mine.'

'It's all in his so-called geologist's reports ... exact location.' explained Lizzy.

'None of 'em as bright as you, I guess. The bastard got greedy. When we were together, he was only askin' for small amounts, five thousand here, ten there ... as you've probably discovered, he can be quite charming.'

'Too charming.'

'Yeah well, you're not the first to fall for it ... but it got too easy, so he started asking for bigger and bigger amounts but then he had to have stuff that people could see ... you know, real information. I said, *hey, keep it small*, but he wouldn't listen.'

'So why did you tell the police that I murdered him?'

'When Greg didn't call me to tell me how it went, I thought he might've got carried away or something. I didn't want him to go to jail.'

'So, you were going to set me up instead.'

'I didn't plan it that way. I just sort of made it up as I went along when I saw ya there. I guess I sort of maybe panicked a bit. If there wasn't a body even though ya said there was, then the police would thank me for at least reportin' what ya said and if there *was* a body, well then the coppers had no way of knowin' that Greg was there, and he'd be off the hook.'

'And I would go to jail.'

'Yeah well, it was better than the alternative. Doesn't matter now though, does it? Andrew's off doing his thing and poor old me is left with nothin' as usual.'

'You're a good actress. Are you acting now?'

'God's truth.'

'Why did Andrew plant his wallet on Wheeler's body?'

'I guess if people thought that he was dead then he could just disappear and have your money for himself.'

'But he had just killed his problem.'

'Yeah, but I could still dob him in, couldn't I?'

'So why did you tell the police he was your husband?

'He is. Like I said, we never actually got divorced.'

'Do you know where my money went?'

'He never told me what he did with all that money. I just got bits and pieces, a few dollars here and there from time to time. Shush money more like it.'

'Do you know where he is?'

'Even if I knew, I wouldn't tell ya.'

'He was never keen to hang around.'

'That's his life story. They'll write it on his bloody tombstone ... *Andrew Burns. He was never keen to hang around.*'

'Do you know who he's got lined up next?'

'Waddya mean?'

'I think he had the gun because he was shooting diamonds into the wall of that so-called mine.'

'Why?'

'A friend of mine told me that it's an old gold miner's trick to make it look like he's actually found something. My guess is that he's lining up someone for something big and that person wants to see a bit more than some fake geologist's reports.'

'I wouldn't know about that.'

'I don't believe you.'

'Yeah, well you don't have a choice, do you?'

'Yes, I do.' replied Lizzy, fiddling with her phone.

'Look, I don't know. If he was ready to fake his own death to keep all the money, do ya reckon he would tell me about some big score?'

'If you're telling the truth, then no, but I think you know exactly where he is.'

'I'm the last person who would know. He wants to disappear, doesn't he?'

'He was down at Margaret River yesterday ... we saw him.'

'With that Ellen woman?'

'Yes.'

'As far as I know she's the last little one. I think the big score you might be talkin' about is actually *you.*' she replied, turning to Alex.

'Me?'

'Andrew said you were good for quite a bit ... rich dad shit.'

'How much?'

'I'm not sure.'

'Bastard, no wonder he wanted to be dead.' growled Alex.

'Listen, I don't know where he is, and I've told you everything I know, so I think you had better just fuck off.'

They got to their feet. 'I have just one more question.' said Lizzy.

'What's that?'

'How do you know Jimmy Orion?'

'Who said that I know him?'

'Cut the bullshit Helena. I saw you with him at the mine.'

'Alright then, he's my brother. So what?'

'Brother?'

'Yeah. How do ya think I met Andrew in the first place? I was up at Jimmy's shithole pub visiting him one Christmas and in waltzes this tall good-looking bloke and shouts the bar. I was the only girl there. I think he had been out in the Never Never a long time and needed some company. You know how it goes.'

'Did Jimmy know Mr. Wheeler?'

'Hated his guts.'

'Enough to want to kill him?'

'Now listen ...'

'Okay, we got what we came for,' said Alex, ushering his sister towards the door.

'We have a deal. Right?' said Helena.

Lizzy looked at her, unsure what to say. 'Yeah, we have a deal, but if I find out you've been telling me lies then I'm making that call.'

They climbed back into their car but didn't drive away.

'Do you believe her?' said Alex.

'Not a damned word.'

'Are you going to call the police?'

'Not yet.'

'What does that mean?'

'It means *not yet* ... let's just see what happens next.'

As they spoke, the curtains of the house parted a fraction. Helena peered through the crack. A man, holding a battered suitcase, was standing behind her.

CHAPTER 24

The midday traffic was thick with cars going to and from the beaches at Cottesloe and Swanbourne, so Alex and Lizzy moved towards the airport at a crawl.

'Where do you think Andrew is?' said Alex.

'A rat never strays too far from its nest.'

'Do you think he'll go back to his mine?'

'There's no reason to go back there. He's got his money, but now that you mention it, I just can't help but think that he will. I don't know why. It's just a feeling.'

'Come on Lizzy. We're done. Call the police. Let's go home.'

'I guess we don't have much choice, do we?'

They drove in silence, neither willing to admit defeat, but unable to see what they could do. Part of Lizzy had resigned herself to Burns having won, but another part wasn't done. Not yet.

'I'm going to call Manfredi,' she said, finally breaking the silence.

'What about your deal with Helena?'

'She's lying. I know she is. Now that Wheeler is dead, she'll go for Plan B.'

'Andrew?'

'Yep, and now she knows that he's alive, she's going to try and find him.'

'If she hasn't already. Andrew could've called her from anywhere. He would've left up north at least two days ago and he has been down at Margaret River. If he wanted to get in touch with her, he could have, and so could she.'

'The thing that worries me is that she knew about *all* the women, and she knew about you. She said Ellen was the *last* one ... so she must have known about the *rest* ... she knew about me too. She knew everything Alex.'

'Maybe he's been telling her about all the other women to make her jealous, so she would come running back to him ... it's an old trick.'

Just then a light bulb went on in Lizzy's head. She turned to her brother.

'You're a genius, but he wasn't making her jealous, she *knew* about them all because she was in on the whole thing from the very beginning. If you believe her story, the less women Andrew told her about, the less money he had to give her, but she knew about them all ... and I think our Mr Wheeler found out and went to the mine to kill, or at least hurt Andrew; none of this bullshit *warning* stuff that she was carrying on about ... and it didn't turn out quite as he expected.'

'Not quite ...'

'As far as Andrew was concerned it was business as usual and he was up there shooting the mine walls full of diamonds so when people asked for core samples or whatever other stuff they wanted, he would have proof. I just don't think he was expecting Wheeler to ruin his little party ... maybe he interrupted him ... maybe the gun really did just go off.'

'So, if Helena and Andrew are in this together, that means—'

'He's back at that house we just left ... or he's about to be ... I'd bet on it ... fuck, that woman can act ... bloody Academy Award. If little Miss Tank Top is there, then that asshole is there too.'

Alex spun the steering wheel viscously. The tyres squealed as he threw the car into a sharp U-turn. Horns blared. Drivers shook their fists.

'These rental cars always seem to do that so much better than normal

185

cars.' smiled Lizzy, as they sped back down the highway.

'I'm just not sure what we're going to do when we get there.'

'That's probably when we should call the police.'

'Maybe.'

'Ah shit, don't you ever give up? Enough is enough Lizzy.'

'Didn't you say you just got your black belt?'

'They teach you to avoid a fight, not to go looking for one.'

As they slowed to a crawl a block from the house, they saw Burns put a sports bag into the back of a taxi and get in. Helena lent in kissed him and waved good-bye.

'It looks like she's staying.'

'Yeah, and he's travelling light so he can't be going too far or for too long.'

'What do we do now?'

'Follow him. Let's see what he's up to.'

For the next forty minutes they hid in traffic, playing a cat and mouse game trying not to be seen.

'I think he's headed for the airport,' said Alex, pointing at a traffic sign.

'If he gets on an international flight, it's all over.'

'This is it. The moment of truth,' said Lizzy, spotting the diverging arrows that showed the way to the Domestic and International terminals.

'Christ, he's taken the domestic. Where the hell is he going?'

They followed the taxi all the way to the terminal, where Burns paid the driver and limped inside.

'Get in there, see where he's going.' commanded Alex, as a parking inspector told him to move on.

'What if he sees me?'

'Go, we're going to lose him.'

Lizzy jumped out and ran towards the terminal with no attempt to hide herself, but just as she reached the automatic doors, she gathered her thoughts and slowed to a sensible, and less conspicuous walk. For a while she huddled behind tearful families farewelling relatives and hid behind every available pillar, but couldn't see him. Finally, after five minutes of searching, there he was. The woman at the check-in counter was attaching a luggage tag to his bag with the letters, BME.

'What does the code BME on luggage tags mean?' said Lizzy, to a passing flight attendant.

'Broome. It's up north, on the coast.'

'So, the rat doesn't roam too far from the nest after all.'

'Excuse me.'

'It doesn't matter. Never mind. Sorry.' replied Lizzy, striding off.

'What's he going up there for?' asked Alex, scanning Google maps on his phone.

'He's heading back to that bloody mine of his, that's what he's doing.'

'Why would he want to do that? He must know that people are onto him by now. Look here ... Broome is a million miles from this Mistake Creek place. If he drove there from Broome, it would take him ... ten, maybe eleven hours.' said Alex.

'Maybe he's flying from Broome.'

'I just don't think so. My guess is that he wants to be as low key as possible anywhere near that mine ... *if* that's where he's going.'

'What would you do if you had just killed someone?' replied his sister.

'Get out of the country, quick.'

'Yeah, me too, so he must be hanging around for a reason.'

'Listen, call your mate Manfredi. Tell him that Andrew is on a flight to Broome. They can pick him up when he lands.'

'Or maybe *we* could meet him at his mine.'

'Listen, you just can't go around playing cops and robbers like this. Someone is going to get hurt and that someone is probably going to be us. This new river of yours is going to get you, both of us, into a shitload of trouble.'

'I have to do it Alex. I just have to.'

'Why? I'll give you the fifty-grand if that's what's bothering you.'

'Like you said, it's not about the money. I want to be able to look in the mirror and like what I see.'

'You're out of your mind. You know that don't you?'

'I've got something loose in my top paddock according to some people.'

'What?'

'Never mind. Look, there must be some reason he's still here.'

'Yeah, he's an idiot.'

'I don't think that's it. I think something important is keeping him here.'

'Like what?'

'I don't know, but whatever it is, we're not going to find out sitting here playing Twenty Questions.'

'Okay, so what's the plan?'

'This is my guess. He'll fly to Broome … here,' explained Lizzy, stabbing the map. 'Then he'll drive from Broome to Halls Creek, here,' she continued, spearing the map again. 'Then head to his mine.'

'No Lizzy, we're not—'

'I'll make you a deal. We'll get ourselves to Andrew's mine and if he doesn't show up after two days, we'll go home, all finished … done. Okay?'

'Why are you so damned sure he's headed for his mine?'

'I'm not, but why else would he go all the way back up there? Maybe it's for some of these,' said Lizzy, reaching into her handbag and pulling out the rain stones Rosie had given her.

'What the hell are they?'

'Diamonds, very big diamonds.'

'You're kidding me. Where did you get them?'

'Rosie.'

'That aboriginal woman? Henry's mother?'

'Yep.'

'What have they got to do with Burns?'

'Maybe nothing.'

'Then why are we going traipsing half-way across the country to find him?'

'Look, Andrew told me he had core samples, and he probably didn't. He also told me he had a few baubles.'

'Like those?'

'Yes, he probably hasn't, but where did he get the diamonds that we found all over Wheeler's body?'

Alex shrugged. 'How should I know.'

'Rosie told me she found these just lying around and Andrew has been wandering those deserts for years, *looking for little blue flashes*, that's what he said.'

'Blue flashes?'

'Diamonds, they fluoresce under UV light ... sunlight.'

'You mean he just picked them up off the ground?'

'Rosie did. Maybe he did too.'

'So why didn't he take them when he left the mine?'

'He had just killed a man. He probably panicked, but it's more than that. When we got there, it was like he had only just left. His laptop was still turned on. So was his satellite phone. There was a half-drunk beer on the table. Damn, it was like he was interrupted and the more the pieces fall into place, the more I think he left something behind; something important to him ... all because he had to leave in a hurry.'

'So, you're saying he's going back to that mine because he left diamonds there ... you're crazy!'

'I know it's a long shot.' she said, shyly, as she fiddled with her phone.

Alex shook his head. 'Jesus Lizzy, remind me never to invite you over for dinner again.'

'So, you'll come?'

'Sure, but just how the hell do you plan on getting there?'

She held up her phone. 'There's a regular flight for Kununurra in three hours.'

'Why not just keep the charter flight and fly direct to Turkey Creek?'

'It's too conspicuous. People will talk. We need to be very low key.'

'Who do you think you are, bloody James Bond?'

Lizzy grinned. 'It takes about three hours to get to Kununurra, we'll rent a car, and then it's about two and a half hours drive to Turkey Creek.'

'Why go via Turkey Creek?'

'That's where we'll find Henry. We need him to show us the way.'

'He could be long gone by now…'

'I don't think so. He's got a job there. The Turkey Creek Roadhouse. His *Kija* people own it.'

'And how are you going to pay for all this?'

'Your credit-card of course. You said that's what brothers are for. Remember?'

'Fuck. Two days, that's it, then I'm out of here. This shit is getting way too crazy for a banana seller like me.'

Lizzy leant over and kissed her brother on the cheek. 'And remind me never to trust your friends again.'

'What?'

'Nothing. We need to buy a satellite phone.'

'A what?'

'A satellite phone … and a laptop … a demo model that's all set up and ready to go.'

'Jesus Lizzy, I'm not going to ask why.'

'Good. You go inside and get some tickets and we can be back in the city in twenty minutes for a little electrical shopping.'

Mission accomplished, they settled into the departure lounge where Lizzy opened her new computer, connected to the airport Wi-Fi and started pounding away.

'What the hell are you doing?' asked her brother, from behind a magazine.

'When people tell lies, there are usually more lies behind those,' she replied. 'I'm just finding out if that's true.' she added, turning another page in the document, *Adamas Mine, Tenement #12967/99 Summary of Geological Findings*

'What are you on about now?'

'I'm not sure yet. Read your magazine.'

As their plane accelerated down the runway, Lizzy stared out the window into another gathering storm, wishing she could hear the crackle of a fire and the splash of rain on the rocks outside her cave. Then as the ceiling of grey clouds gave way to blue sky, Rosie's soft voice came drifting back to her, ' ... *yesterday is where we all come from Miss Lizzy ... you can't run away from it ... but you can think about it another way ... there's a season for cryin' like you been doin' and there's a season for laughin' and a season for workin' and a time to take ya holidays ... but you gotta move from season to season, lettin' nature have its way ... 'cause soon the season for cryin' is over and it's the season for laughin' again.'*

Lizzy knew her time with Rosie had been a turning point in her life; she knew Rosie had been there for a reason, although she wasn't entirely sure why. But, as she turned her rain stones over and over in her fingers, she imagined her new river and knew she needed to follow it no matter how crazy Alex, or anyone else, thought she might be.

CHAPTER 25

The gravel crunched under their wheels when they turned off the highway into the Turkey Creek Roadhouse; a petrol-station, restaurant, motel and caravan park, guarded by lazy Brahman cattle lying in the shade of acacia trees. Lizzy spotted Henry, serving petrol, drove up behind the car he was filling and got out. A smile spread from one end of the old man's face to the other.

'I had a feelin' you'd be back sooner rather than later,' he chortled, replacing the nozzle in the bowser.

'Why is that?' replied Lizzy.

'Rosie told me that you two are sisters now.'

'Sisters?' replied Alex.

'You can call me Nangari.'grinned Lizzy.

'The only trouble is, it means I can't marry you like I was plannin'. You're not straight for me no more.'

'That's too bad Henry,' smiled Lizzy.

The old man smiled a toothy grin. 'Bloody sad that is. When ya dropped me off at the airport I told old Four-Eyes-Harold that I was gonna marry ya one day ... I didn't know you were my aunty then ... can't marry you now.'

'We can be friends though Henry.'

'Sure, top friends. Waddya doin' here?'

'Well, we're headed for Mistake Creek,' Lizzy replied, cautiously.

'Again?'

'Call it unfinished business. How are the roads?'

'Why do ya want to go back there for?'

'Because that's where my new river is flowing, Henry.'

'I dunno, you women talk a strange bloody language sometimes. My mother, she's the same, them other women in Turkey Creek, they all talk in bloody riddles.'

'Can we get there?' asked Alex.

'Yeah, I suppose. For the time being it's okay, but you see them clouds out there … more water in that lot than you got in your eyes.'

'Will you take us?'

'Ah, coppers were crawlin' all over that place … even towed Burns' old truck away … good old truck that. We could've used that.'

'What were they looking for Henry?'

'Dunno. This is all a bit strange if you're askin' me.'

'Strange is one way of describing it,' interrupted Alex, nudging his sister.

'For a while there, I thought they were waitin' there for that Mr. Burns to show up again, but they gave up and went back to Kununurra. What kind of bloody idiot would go back to the place where he just killed someone?'

'That's a good question Henry, a *very* good question,' replied Alex, sarcastically.

'Ya want to go there now?'

'Can we? Do you have to work?'

'All finished for a coupla days. We can get some rooms at Jimmy Orion's place.'

'No Henry, I don't want him to know we're here.'

'We gotta go straight past his place to get to …'

'He can't know Henry.'

'He knows everything that happens out his way.'

'Henry, Andrew Burns was married to that woman who said we killed him, and Jimmy Orion is her brother.'

'Fair dinkum.'

'Yes, but what you don't understand is that we think that they're in this together, so if he knows we're here, she's bound to find out and tell Andrew.'

'We want it to be a surprise,' added Alex.

'Okay, no problem,' replied Henry. 'I know a way that Jimmy won't see us ... them proper roads is new, but my relations they had them Dreaming tracks ... long time ago ... in the time of creation *when my ancestors came to Earth to make the mountains and the hills and all of them plants and animals. They moved through the land makin' the rivers and mountains and their journeys left very long tracks, they're called the Dreaming Tracks ... them tracks told us where our water was and where all of them trees with fruit was hiddin' ... they tellin' us where we should be huntin' ...* I'll take ya that way ... it's rough, but we'll get there okay.'

'Thanks Henry. I knew that we could rely on you.'

'Do ya wanna see Rosie before ya go?'

'Where is she?'

'She's at the school in Turkey Creek. Every Wednesday, she's sittin' under that bloodwood tree and tellin' the kids all the dreamin'. I know she'd like to see ya ... she cried when ya left ya know ... first time in bloody years ... everyone thought she was sick.'

'She cried?'

'Bloody strange that missus. I've never seen her cry before ... not in all my years.'

'Let's go see her Henry. I'd like my brother to meet her.'

'What are ya gonna do when ya get to that mine?' replied Henry.

'Wait.'

'For what?'

'Andrew Burns.'

'Mr Burns? You're crazy, he's not comin' back there no more.'

'We'll see Henry.'

'I told ya you women have got a funny way about ya.'

'You're not wrong Henry,' said Alex. 'You're not wrong.'

'I got me old Toyota out the back,' replied Henry, walking off. 'We'll take that. This road car of yours won't be no good out where we're goin'.'

CHAPTER 26

When they pulled up at the school gate in the Turkey Creek township, they could hear children singing.

Wanyanyakenji

Kurlu-kurlu parruma nguyu

Wangkarnal

Pulpampi pinpij nungju

You little children you be happy

The little crow will bring you a present

You little children, you be happy

The little crow will bring you a present

'They're getting ready for Christmas,' smiled Henry. 'You wait here, enjoy their little concert, and I'll go get Rosie.'

Wangkarnali, wangkarnali

Pulampi pinpija yuwu

Little crow you bring a present for us

Little children we are happy.

After a few minutes Rosie hobbled over, and if it was possible, her smile was even wider than the one Henry greeted them with.

'Who's this fella?' said Rosie, eyeing Alex suspiciously over Lizzy's shoulder as she hugged her.

'My brother, Alex. Alex, Rosie. Rosie, Alex.'

Alex put out his hand to shake the old woman's hand. She took it in her leathery paw and held on.

'You got good ears for listenin' like ya sister or you just jarrak jarrak all the bloody time ... which one is it young fella?'

Alex looked confused.

'He's got good ears Rosie,' smiled Lizzy.

'Good. What ya doin' back here? Have ya come to see ya sister or is ya after some more of them rain stones?'

'I'm following my new river Rosie. Just like you said I should.'

Rosie nodded knowingly. 'I suppose I didn't tell ya that some of them rivers wind back on themselves over and over again,' she said, drawing a snake in the dirt with the dirty shoe on the end of her steel-pole leg. 'The trick is to look at the new part of that river, not the part you've already seen.'

'Keep walkin' towards that horizon hey Rosie?'

'Sittin' down is not so bad sometimes. It's just a question of how long. I've been sittin' here at Turkey Creek for a long time now ... long time for me anyway, but when ya look at time, all time, it's not so long, just a minute or two ... if ya know where ya goin'. Do ya know where ya goin' Nangari?' asked Rosie, holding Lizzy's hands in hers.

'I think so, yes.'

'Today I'm tellin' all them piccaninnies, them children, about the Dreamtime ... one of these days that'll be your job for your family. You'll have ta tell the story of where ya been and what ya been doin', what happened to all ya relatives, like ya brother Alex here. When that time comes ya got to be proud of what ya done ... is ya gonna be proud when this is all done Nangari?'

'When what is all done?'

'When you've done what ya came back here for.'

'There are seasons for all things Rosie, you told me that. This is the season for starting again, but before I can do that, I have to finish a few things.'

'Well, you go do whatever it is ya gonna do and when it's all done you come back here ... maybe I can help ya with ya a new beginnin'.'

'Don't you want to know what I'm doing?'

'I already know. You got that hunter's eye now. That poor sad joey's eyes are all gone away. Now ya listenin' for the signs, looking left and right and way ahead. You're lookin' for that jagarra, that kangaroo, to spear ... you're chasin' somethin' ... ah what do I know? That huntin' is men's work ... I'm just a crazy alcamen, an old lady, who talks too bloody much.'

'We better go,' suggested Henry. 'More rain is comin' soon.'

'With some luck we'll get stuck in Purnululu again,' smiled Lizzy.

Rosie grinned back much like a loving mother would, then stroked Lizzy's cheek.

'I knew you were out of your mind,' jibed Alex, but Rosie shot him a stern look.

'This sister of mine is a kural ... mother ... not a mother with babies, but a mother with ideas ... just like the babies, you got ta feed 'em, and then they grow up to be big ideas ... just like this school here ... we used to teach over there under that big old tree, and then one day we said, *let's build a school*. Some people said we were crazy ... it'll never happen ... but look for yaself, there it is ... a proper good school. She's got ideas alright this sister of yours. Listen to her. That old Lizzy, that frightened Lizzy, she done gone away.'

Alex blushed, suitably reprimanded, and shuffled his feet in the dust.

'Off ya go,' said Rosie with a smile. 'The first step is the hard one.'

CHAPTER 27

'We're going to need some fuel for that generator at the mine,' said Lizzy, as they headed for Henry's Toyota.

He smiled a toothy grin. 'It's already in the back missus.'

'How did you know? I thought you said that ...'

'If ya had come back in two months or two years you would have been here for pleasure, but comin' back after two days, that means you're here for business and the only business you got is out at that mine ... either that, or Jimmy Orion's Royal Suite,' laughed Henry.

'Henry!'

'See, there aren't too many choices, are there?'

Alex looked puzzled but knew it was no use asking questions. His sister was too far gone.

'Whose truck is this?' said Lizzy, as they drove.

'It belongs to the *Kija* men ... royalties from the Argyle mine.'

'Do the women get anything?'

'You've been speakin' to Rosie haven't ya?'

'Maybe.'

'My mother, she got it in her head that the women need some transport, but there are other things we got to get first ... more houses, water, pipes, fix the school up some more, tools for the workshop, medicine for the clinic … she'll get her turn soon enough.'

'Maybe I could help,' offered Lizzy.

'What are ya thinkin'?' asked Henry, as he swerved to avoid a pothole.

'Yeah, just what's going on inside that crazy mind of yours this time?' added Alex.

'I don't really know yet.'

'Bloody hell,' grimaced Alex, from the back seat. 'I can see trouble ahead.'

Lizzy wasn't ready to reveal what she had in mind, so changed the subject, and as they drove, Alex grew quiet.

'Is everything okay back there?' asked his sister.

'Amazing land isn't it?' he replied, in a soulful whisper.

'More than you know.'

She knew Alex was too engrossed to talk, so turned to Henry. 'What was that song the children at the school were singing?'

'Ahh, that's a song about a crow … he's called Wangkarnal … the black crow with the long black hair … long time ago, he saw the eagle who had many bird wives, but that eagle, he never shared his meat with his wives … well the crow and the curlew stopped the eagle from finding the sugar bag honey and they stuck sharp sticks in his throat to punish him for his greedy ways and that made his neck stick out so all future men had that lump too—'

'Adam's apple?'

'Yeah, but then the curlew stole the only son of the crow and that Wangkarnal, the crow, he found it inside the body of the curlew. This good Dreamtime crow loved his son and was worried about all of them others too, so he watched, real careful like, to see that everyone had enough and if they didn't, he would always share his bush food.'

'The crow helped all the other animals even though the curlew killed his son?'

'My people say that the crow, he's like God the father, him Ngapuny, we call him the god up top … he sent his son Jesus to teach the people and then he died, but God up top, he kept on lovin' all his people …

didn't he?'

'I suppose you're right Henry.'

'Now that crow, he's just like your Santa Claus only he don't bring meat and bush tucker no more, he brings them presents for the kids.'

'So how can you believe in the Dreamtime *and* the Christian God?'

'Both of them ways, they're the same. Ngarrangkarni is when creation happened ... this Ngapuny story is the same. God the Father, he was the creator ... only difference is that Dreamtime is about animals and that mission school teachin' is about angels and people. Back in the Dreamtime we buried our relations up in the trees ... same as goin' to heaven don't ya think?'

'You could be right Henry.'

'Too much the same to be fightin' over who's right and wrong ... us *Kija* lot, we got rules for cookin' our food ... no different to gettin' that white bit of bread for the holy communion ... we keepin' our sacred places safe ... where do ya reckon that Pope fella lives ... he's keepin' that place sacred ... and he's goin' off to church to tell all of them people about the birth of a spirit child ... he's tellin' the story over and over again just like we do so no-one forgets ... and what do ya reckon is around them windows in all of them churches where they're tellin' the story? I'll tell ya ... pictures of what happened a long time ago ... just like what we do with our paintings ... no difference I reckon.'

Lizzy was about to reply when off in the distance she saw the glint of corrugated iron in the sun.

'What are ya gonna do if that bugger is already there?' said Henry.

'He's not. I reckon he's driving across from Broome and we have about a twelve-hour head-start on him.'

'Have ya got a plan?'

'Yeah right!' said Alex.

'Well no, not really.'

'So, what are ya gonna do?'

'She's relying on divine intervention.' sniped Alex, from the back seat. '... and we're just as crazy as she is for coming.'

The words were no sooner out of his mouth than they pulled up in front of the Andrew Burns' shack. Rainwater had pooled in the canvas lean-to attached to the front and a dozen or more brightly coloured mulga parrots were squabbling like children in a backyard swimming pool. The two scraggly trees off to one side of the dilapidated shack still shone from the rain, and underfoot, it was muddy enough to make anyone watch where they stepped.

'You've got to be kidding me,' grimaced Alex, uncomfortably. 'This is way worse than you said.'

'Wait until you see where you're sleeping.'

'You mean that this is where we're going to *stay*.'

'Yep,' smiled Lizzy. 'There's a cave I know back down the road a bit if you would prefer that.'

'You're serious aren't ya?'

'Sure am.'

'Do you honestly think that Burns is going to come back here if he has a pile of money from God knows how many women? Surely, he can afford a nice hotel somewhere?'

'Yes, I do. He's coming here. I just know he is.'

'You're mad, isn't she Henry?'

Henry covered his ears. 'I got jobs to do. I can't be talkin' about that stuff.'

With that, he turned off the engine, opened his door, grabbed the jerrican of fuel out of the back and trudged off.

'Do you actually have a plan that you're not telling me about?' asked Alex.

'Like you said, divine intervention.'

'I thought so. What are the laptop and satellite phone for?'

'We may need them.'

'To get some bloody help ... is there a save me now.com?'

'Very funny.'

'Then what are they for?'

'Andrew had a laptop and a sat phone when he was here. The police

202

have them now. When I got here, they were still turned on. I checked his email, that's how I found out about Ellen down at Margaret River.'

'I gotta give ya that one. Very smart.'

'Well, I also checked to see what websites he had been on,' said Lizzy.

'And?'

'Just one. BankWest.'

'So that's probably where your money is,' replied her brother.

'I think that's a fair assumption, so now, all he needs to do, is give me the account name and number and a password.'

'Sure, that should be easy. You'll just ask, and he'll give them to you. No problem.' replied Alex, sarcastically.

'When I went back to the hotel with him at Eagle Bay, he denied all knowledge of stealing anything from me.'

'You would probably do the same if you were cornered.'

'You know, the trouble with lacing a lie with truth is that it gives a person somewhere to start.'

'Excuse me?'

'Andrew's documents, the so-called geologist's report, apparently it was full of rubbish, but it gave me the tenement number and the latitude and longitude of this pile of crap.'

'So?'

'So, while you were reading your magazine back at Perth airport, I was working.'

'I still don't get what you're saying.'

'The West Australian Department of Industry and Resources has all the titles to all the tenements online. I just punched in Andrew's tenement number and guess what?'

'What?'

'Pretty soon it will be mine.'

'How, but more importantly, why would you bloody bother?'

'Under the terms of his lease he must spend ten thousand dollars a year to upgrade the property and then lodge a report. He hasn't done that for quite some time ... and he's also supposed to pay $14.52 per hectare rent every year ... he hasn't done that either ... that's $145.20 he owes them every year for the last fifteen years.'

'I thought you said he had a thousand hectares?'

Lizzy frowned. 'He's not exactly known for telling the truth, is he?'

'And you found out all this online?'

'Exactly.'

'So, what does it all mean?'

'It means that I have applied to have his tenement forfeited and for me to pick it up.'

'Why would you want this pile of crap?' asked Alex, getting out of the Toyota.

'Because little brother ...' replied Lizzy, reaching into her handbag and pulling out Rosie's rain stones, '...underneath it there are lots of diamonds. Lots.'

'Now you're really confusing me. When Andrew had the mine, there were no diamonds and now that you look like you can get your grubby little claws on it, it does have diamonds ... big ones.'

'Exactly.'

'So, are there diamonds here or not?'

'No.'

'Fuck, it's no wonder that I'm in fruit and vegetables.'

'Look, all we've got to do is to make Andrew believe that there are diamonds.'

'He knows there isn't, and from what you've said, he's been digging around out here for years, so he'll just be twice as cranky if he finds out you're trying to take it off him.'

'He can't hang around ... he knows that ... there's a small matter of a murder charge.'

'There might be a few more of those if we're not careful.'

'Hear me out.'

From the back of the shack they heard the generator splutter to life then settle into an annoying drone.

'It's quite simple, Andrew's father spent years out here before him.

Neither of them found anything, but why would they spend all that time digging if they didn't *think* there really was something?'

'Maybe to get away from that wife of his. She's not much is she?'

'Seriously, we've just got to convince him that there really are diamonds here and his heart will take over.'

'So, you think he'll trade the money he stole from you for *could be, maybe, perhaps,* do you?'

'I really don't know, but there's only one way to find out.'

'Shit Lizzy, you're out of your mind…take me on the grand tour.' he added, shaking his head.

They ducked under the canvas awning and felt moisture on their faces.

'It's going to rain again.' complained Alex, wiping water off his forehead.

'You're a real city-boy, aren't you?' teased Lizzy, looking up to where the birds were playing in the awning puddle.'

Lizzy reached up as the door squeaked open, pulled a cord and the black shack was suddenly bathed in light.

'Fuck me,' whispered her brother. 'A mega shit-hole.'

'There you go.' she said, sweeping her hand around the one room shack. 'The Mistake Creek Hilton ... sorry, no chocolate on your pillow and I don't think there are any of those little bottles of shampoo in the bathroom ... oops, sorry, no bathroom.'

'Room service?' asked Alex, as a lizard with a spiky collar disappeared between his feet into a gaping crack in the floorboards.

Lizzy shook her head.

'But you promised ...'

'I lied.'

Alex watched while his sister dropped her bag on a camp stretcher and dusted off the table with a dirty cloth.

'It's not much is it?'

'I just want to see the look on that bastard's face when I drop these rocks on the table.'

'Well, if we don't hide Henry's truck, you might never get the chance to do that. He might see it and just drive off.'

'When he comes, he'll be coming for a reason ... but you're right, we probably should get that thing out of the way.'

'Where's Henry?'

'I don't know.'

'He does this.'

'What?'

'He just disappears and then out of the blue, there he is again ... he's like bloody Houdini.'

'The keys are in it. I'll park it just over that ridge I saw. It looks like there are some trees there. I can park in the shade.'

'Come straight back.'

'And then what? Are we just going sit here and wait for Burns to show up?'

'No, we're going to have a beer,' she replied, opening the refrigerator.

Alex shook his head and walked out. 'Fuck Lizzy, this shit gets weirder by the minute. I sure hope you know what you're doing.'

Twenty minutes later, Alex fell breathlessly in the door as Lizzy was connecting her computer to the satellite phone.

'There's a trail bike out there, near the trees. It looks like someone crashed it ... there's blood all over it.'

'Where?'

'Just over the ridge, where I was going to park the truck.'

'Any tracks?'

Alex sneered. 'You're asking *me*? I'm the city-boy, remember.'

Lizzy thought for a second. 'That's the same way that Helena and Jimmy Orion left when they were here.'

'So?'

'So, it explains a lot of things.'

'Like what?'

'Like how Andrew got out of here when his truck was still parked outside ... it was here when Henry and I arrived, remember.'

'My guess is that Wheeler came in on the motorbike and surprised Andrew,' said Lizzy.

'Or he was already waiting here for him ... those bikes make a lot of noise ... it's not like you can sneak up on someone.'

'And then Andrew shot him?' replied Lizzy. 'Just like that? I don't think so.'

'Didn't you say that Wheeler's body was down in the mine?'

'Yes.'

'And didn't you say that the remains of his face were covered in diamonds?'

'Yes.'

'So why would he do that? You don't shoot some dipstick, who surprises you, with diamonds.'

'No you don't. There were shotgun shells on the table when I got here. The cops must have them now, but there was also a saucer full of those little ball-bearing things that go inside. It's like Andrew had taken them out on purpose.'

'And replaced them with diamonds?' smiled Alex.

'But why?' replied Lizzy, before it suddenly dawned on her. 'Bloody hell, it really is what O'Leary told me about.'

'Who?'

'Peter O'Leary. Fat Sam's friend.'

'What did he say?'

'Old gold prospectors used to shoot gold into the walls on their useless mines, so they could sell them.'

'So? What's that got to do with this?'

'Andrew was doing the same.' replied Lizzy. 'Only this time it was with diamonds.'

'But why?'

'Well imagine if he showed someone chunks of rocks with diamonds poking out of them. They might just fall for it.'

'So he had no intention of wrapping up this little scam of his.'

'It looks that way … and I think that he was in the middle of shooting up the mine walls when Wheeler interrupted him. They fought. Wheeler got shot.'

'Maybe it really was an accident?'

'Yeah but try explaining that to the cops and try explaining why the gun was full of diamonds.'

'So then Burns planted his wallet on Wheeler and left his truck to make everyone think that it was him who was dead.'

'Exactly, and the crashed motorbike explains Andrew's limp and the sling.'

'Okay, so explain this, if he crashed the bike and injured himself, how the hell did he get out of here?'

'Well, that's the big question isn't it, but it's just a bit too much of a coincidence that Helena and Jimmy Orion just happened to be here when I was.'

'Maybe they just happened to find Andrew after he fell off?'

'Well, they were here to help someone, but the question is … was it Andrew or this Wheeler guy?'

'Helena said Jimmy hated Wheeler's guts so I don't think he would have helped him.'

'Her whole story back at the house was total crap. She was leaving Wheeler for Andrew all along.'

'And Wheeler found out.'

'That still doesn't explain why Andrew would want to come back here.'

'I guess we'll just have to wait and see, won't we.'

Lizzy opened the door and peered out into the gathering twilight. On the distant horizon a patchwork quilt of purple, red, orange and yellow clouds was backlit by the setting sun. The day was growing dark but there was still no sign of Henry. She saw the silhouette of wild camels running in the distance and heard the croak of a frog, which seemed strangely out of place in the desert, but it was the sudden flicker of flames out to the left of the shack that grabbed her attention. Next to the fire, the shape of a man was staring into the flames. When she looked back into the hut her brother had collapsed on a camp stretcher and was already asleep, so she stepped outside and walked towards the fire.

'Evenin',' said Henry, looking up.

'Where have you been? You've got to stop running off like that.'

'Had to get us some dinner.' replied Henry, indicating a large goanna which lay dead next to him.

'We can't eat *that*.'

'Sure you can. I just gotta pull out the guts, clean out the stomach and then it's all good for cookin'.'

'But Henry ...'

'You liked the bush melon and that sugar bag ... even that bloody barra ... and them other things that you didn't think you'd be likin' so much. I tell ya, this goanna is bloody good ... it tastes like chicken.'

'Alex won't eat it.' she squirmed, trying to make it appear that *she* would.

'Tell him it's chicken ... he's a city-boy ... he'll never know.'

Lizzy smiled. 'I owe him one. I'll teach him to introduce me to ...'

'What's that?'

'Never mind. How long will it be?'

'Not long, not long at all.'

She watched as Henry singed off the skin by laying the goanna on the fire. When the flames died down, he spread out the ashes, lay the goanna on top and covered it with the glowing coals.

'This is my earth-oven missus. It works proper good.'

'So, I see. It smells ... well, it smells good ... just like chicken, I suppose.'

'I told ya, didn't I?'

After a short time, Henry poked the sizzling goanna with a stick, broke off the end of its tail and threw it away.

'Can't eat that bit missus ... it's the law for all us fellas here in the east.'

'Law?'

'Yeah missus, we got all kinds of laws. In olden times young boys weren't allowed to eat everythin' ... them young boys, they had to do that special dancing, that corroboree, and if the girl he wanted was a goanna totem, he couldn't eat this bloody good goanna until he had finished knowin' that law ... could be two, maybe three years ... not so much these days though ... some of them old laws have been forgotten.'

'That's a long time to go without goanna.' teased Lizzy.

'Too right! That's probably why I like it so much now missus.'

'We can't serve it like that Henry. Alex will know that it's a goanna straight off.'

'Don't worry, I'll chop it up and he'll never bloody know.'

She giggled. 'I'm going to love every second of this.'

Henry smiled to himself and used his stick to remove the goanna from the hot coals and put it on a long strip of tree bark, produced a knife, scraped off the excess skin and filleted out the goanna meat, dividing it into portions that would make its origins difficult to detect.

'Remember, it's bush chicken,' sniggered Lizzy, as they walked back into the shack.

Henry nodded, enjoying the conspiracy.

'Wake up sleepy head. Dinner is ready.'

'What are we having?' replied Lizzy's brother.

'Beer and chicken.'

She placed the plate of *bush chicken* on the table, opened the fridge and took out three bottles of Burns' beer, but her brother just yawned and buried his head in an anorexic pillow.

'It smells like chicken and that looks amazingly like a beer ... yep, I'm still asleep. I knew it.'

He yawned again, stretched and fell back onto the camp stretcher.

'Up you get ... dinner is ready.'

'Leave me alone. I was having a dream about some dinner ... beer and chicken. It was good.'

'Then wake up because that's what we're having.'

'Chicken?' said Henry, offering the platter.

'What kind of chicken?'

'Bush chicken. Them things run around wild out there.'

'And you caught it ... and cooked it?'

'No Alex. There's a KFC store just down the road,' teased Lizzy.

'Ya got to have the knack.' said Henry, '...they're tricky little buggers ... ya gotta hold ya mouth just right.'

'Hold your mouth ... ?'

'Yeah, like this.' replied Henry, contorting his face.

'How does that help?' asked Alex taking a bite. 'This is good.'

Lizzy grinned.

'Them bush chickens is short-sighted so if ya hold ya mouth the right way then they think you're a big one of them ... ya just gotta go, *cluck, cluck* a bit and they stand dead still all petrified ... then ya just pick 'em up and there's ya bloody good dinner.'

'Really?' asked Alex, tearing off another mouthful.

'Beer?' asked his sister.

'Yeah, sure, thanks. This isn't really what I expected.'

'Sure isn't,' Lizzy replied, trying to stifle a laugh.

'This place isn't all that bad I suppose. Is there any more of that chicken?' asked Alex, demolishing the last piece on his plate.

'Sure,' offered his sister. 'Take mine. I'm not very hungry.'

'Thanks.' replied her brother, taking the extra plate and his beer then sitting down at the battered table. 'Have you got those rocks you had before.'

'Rosie's rain stones? Sure.'

'Rosie gave them to you?' said Henry, surprised.

'Yes, she did.'

'Did she tell ya that there ain't no diamonds out here?'

'She said she found these over towards Mount Parker.'

Henry looked Lizzy up and down warily, like she knew something that she wasn't supposed to.

'It's all right Henry ... she told me a bit, but not too much, besides we're not going to tell anyone, are we Alex?'

'Not a word,' agreed Alex, licking his fingers.

'Do *you* think there are more diamonds out here Henry?'

'Not for me to say missus.'

'Why not?'

'Best we just say nothin' about all this. There are just a few of them rain stones. They're too hard to find.'

'Maybe if you held you mouth just right and went *cluck, cluck*? Maybe that would help?'

'What's that?'

Alex looked at his sister like she was crazier than he already thought.

'You could just go cluck, cluck and pick them up,' she explained.

'No that's ...'

Before Henry could finish his sentence, the joke dawned on him, and he slapped his knee and started to laugh so hard he almost fell off his chair. Lizzy joined in while Alex looked at them, dumbfounded.

'What on earth has gotten into you two?'

'Nothing.'

'Hee, hee, he ... bush chicken.' laughed Henry.

Alex looked at his empty plate, then back at them.

'Was that chicken I just ate? It was, wasn't it?'

That was enough for Henry and Lizzy to dissolve in gales of laughter, bending over to hold their bellies and point at Alex like they had played a great joke on him.

'It wasn't, was it? It was something else, wasn't it?'

Lizzy couldn't contain herself. 'It was ... it was goanna ... a big fat juicy goanna ... wasn't it Henry?'

'Yeah, it was a bloody good goanna alright, everyone knows that they go *cluck, cluck* ... pretty good huh?'

Alex swiped his empty plate off the table, but as he did, he pushed the three diamonds his sister had put next to it off as well. Two fell harmlessly onto the floor, but the largest rolled and disappeared into a crack in the wooden floorboards; the same hole they had seen a lizard dive into earlier in the day. Suddenly everyone stopped laughing and

Alex forgot the imagined bad taste in his mouth.

'Ah shit,' he grimaced, falling to his knees, and looking into the hole.

'Damn, we're going to need that when Andrew gets here if we want my plan to work,' added Lizzy.

'It can't have gone too far. It can't be more than a foot or so to the ground.'

'There's a crowbar outside boss. I'll go get it. We'll just lift some of them boards up ... no problem.'

'I'll give you *no problem*,' scolded Alex.

'It was just a joke.'

'Yeah, ha, ha, ha. Very funny,' continued Alex, chugging his beer.

'But you liked it,' laughed Lizzy.

'Here ya go,' said Henry, returning with a long steel pole.

Henry stuck the flat end into the crack the diamond had fallen though and levered up the floorboard.

'Can you see anything?' said Lizzy.

'Nah, not yet ... I'll have to get another one of them boards out of the way.'

He levered the second floorboard up and placed it to one side.

'What now?' she asked.

'Have ya got a torch?' said Henry, peering into the hole.

Lizzy and her brother looked at each other and shrugged.

'How about a candle?' replied Alex, spying one on a shelf.

'Yeah. Gimme that,' replied Henry, with his head and shoulders halfway into the hole. 'This hole is blacker than me.'

Alex lit the candle and passed it to Henry.

'Ah yes ... here it is.' said Henry. 'But there's somethin' else down here too.'

'What?' replied Lizzy.

'Looks like some kinda box. I can only see the handles. It's just pokin' out of the dirt, but it looks pretty big if ya ask me,' grunted Henry, pulling himself up out of the hole and handing Lizzy the lost rain stone.

'There's somethin' bloody big under there ... do ya want me ta have a look?'

'What kind of something big?'

'Some kinda steel box I'm thinkin' ... I can just see the handle pokin' out through the dirt.'

'Come on. Let's see what it is.' clamoured Alex.

Henry used the crowbar to remove another three floorboards and soon the hole was big enough for him to stand in, so he crouched down, and started brushing away the soil with his hands.

'You got a spoon or something?' he asked, making slow progress.

Slowly he could make out the top of a studded, steel box.

'Yep, it's a bloody box alright.'

It took another twenty minutes for him to free it and drag it up into the light of the shack.

'It's bloody locked missus.'

Henry put it on the table and Alex jumped up, grabbed the crowbar, rammed it into the u-shaped lock and prized it as hard as he could. With a clatter, a clunk and a *fuck* from Alex when he fell forward as the lock gave way, it snapped open. They stared at him, as if he was an expert safe cracker.

'City-boy stuff ... running with the wrong crowd when I was young,' grinned Alex, like that was a good thing.

His sister opened the lid cautiously.

'Oh my God,' she said. 'This is why he's coming back here.'

Alex's jaw dropped, and he reached into the box and peeled back the plastic on top.

'Where do you think it all came from?' he said.

'The women of course.' replied Lizzy.

'Women?'

'The women he conned. He told me that he hated banks. *This* is his bank.'

'There has to be at least half a million-dollars in here.' replied Alex.

'At least.'

'And what's this?' he said, pulling out a ledger book that had been shoved down beside the money, and opening it.

'Jesus Christ,' he said. 'Look, it's a list of all his women.'

'It's all here,' replied Lizzy, looking over his shoulder. 'Names, addresses, dates, amounts … all going back ten years. That arsehole has been busy for a long time.'

'And what's that?' asked her brother, indicating a column with a star-rating for each name.

'I'll leave that to your imagination.'

'I take back what I said,' he replied, shaking his head in amazement.

'About what?'

'He's coming here alright. Why would anyone leave all this?'

'He wouldn't, and I think we just got something better to bargain with.' smiled Lizzy.

'That could be true, but there's just one problem.'

'And what's that?'

'Your name isn't here. Nothing,' he said, running his finger down the page.'

'Why?'

'I don't know. Maybe your money isn't in here yet. You only noticed that it was missing a few days ago. He would have had to transfer it to an account, go to the bank, make a withdrawal, and bring it up here. Maybe you only get in the book, when your money is in the box.'

'It all seems pretty amateur hour,' replied Lizzy. 'Why not transfer it to an overseas account like they do in the movies?'

'Like you said. He doesn't trust banks. Besides, who the hell would look for his stash all the way out here?'

'So what about my money?'

'Maybe he's on his way here to make a deposit.'

'Or a withdrawal. He has to get the hell out of Dodge before the cops track him down.'

'You *kartiya*, you worry about money too much.' interrupted Henry. 'What do ya need money for? The land gives ya all ya need.'

'Like GOANNA?' teased Alex.

'Good that bloody goanna,' laughed Henry. 'Bloody good.'

'I think that this time the joke might be on Andrew Burns,' grinned Lizzy.

CHAPTER 28

Just before dawn Henry rubbed his eyes and looked over to where Lizzy should have been sleeping. For a second, he panicked, but then noticed the door was ajar. He saw her outside, wrapped in a blanket, staring out to the east.

As he approached, he made sure that he made enough noise, so he wouldn't surprise her, like he had done so many times before, but not too much to disturb her peace. A minute twitch of her ears was enough to tell him she had heard him, but she didn't turn. She just stood quietly, hypnotized.

'That's what we call the piccaninny dawn,' whispered Henry, as he stopped beside her.

'Piccaninny?'

'The baby dawn, it's that little bit of light just before the sunrise.'

'The light, before the light?'

'Yeah, that's it. Ya see it and ya know that big old sun is comin' soon. It's like it's sendin' some little light first so all them animals and all them people don't get too scared ... the sun comes up every day but imagine if it just popped up over there ... *BOO! Here I am*. All them animals and all them people they'd be jumpin' all over the place tryin' ta hide.'

'It's so peaceful.'

'Except for that generator out back, it's always peaceful out here. None of them big buildings, none of them electricity poles pokin' up everywhere, no cars and telephones drivin' ya crazy ... out here, it's just you and the bloody wind.'

'I wonder what's blowing our way today, Henry.'

'Rosie says some days you wake up and you just know the best part is gonna be goin' back to sleep again.'

'I think this is going to be one of those days Henry.'

'Do ya think Mr. Andrew is comin' for sure?'

'Now that I've seen the money and that book, I would bet on it. There's enough information in that ledger to put him away for a long time.'

'What are ya gonna do when he gets here?'

'I was just thinking about that.'

'That makes two of us,' said a drowsy voice behind them.

Alex joined them and as his eyes followed theirs out to the horizon, a small crescent of yellow rose in the white morning sky and shimmered like a portion of giant fried egg fresh from the pan. At first the new sun hung suspended in the distance but then sped towards them like a radiant dust storm with a cyclone at its back. Then, as if to signal another day had begun, the wake-up calls of the corellas and parrots squawked out across the morning sky followed by the black crows with an echoing arrrk, arrrk which seemed to linger forever.

'Do you ever get lonely out here Henry?' Lizzy finally said.

'Lonely is what's inside ya ... not what's out here.'

'Yes, I think I'm beginning to understand that.'

'You ask Rosie ... she'll tell ya ... when she was workin' at that cattle station, there were lots of people, plenty of people to talk to, a bloody big mob, but she had no one ... she could've been a lonely bugger in a crowd of people, but she understands Ngarrangkarni time real good ... she wasn't lonely ... nah ... she had her relatives all around her ... I told ya before, we're parta the sky, parta the land, the water ... we're all parta the life-giving forces. It's the law, the sacred law that gives all things their right place, their happy place ... where they belong ... it's the cycle of life. Rosie told ya about the seasons, but it's more than the seasons like you *kartiya* understand it. It's not about the weather. It's about bein' born and then how ya do ya growin' and then dyin'. Nah, it's never lonely out here. This is my land. I rest in it. I come from here.'

Alex and Lizzy stood silently, breathing in the scale of the alien landscape. In every direction there was beauty as far as the eye could see then it abruptly ended at a thin, black line marking the horizon. Usually between them and that line there would be no more than the air they breathed and the light of day, but on that day, a thin plume of dust was approaching. Only Henry saw it.

'What are you making for breakfast?' said Alex, putting his arm around Henry's shoulders, indicating he had been forgiven for serving bush chicken. 'Bush cornflakes?'

'Don't think there will be any time for breakfast,' replied Henry, pointing towards the dust.

'What is it?' said Lizzy.

'I'm thinkin' that might be Mr. Andrew. Do ya know anyone else comin' all the way out here today?'

'Now would be a good time for a plan,' suggested Alex.

'Surprise party,' smiled Lizzy. 'I say we just go inside and wait for him. He wasn't expecting us at Eagle Bay, and he won't be expecting us here ... he won't be expecting anyone here.'

'And that plan worked so well before, didn't it? What if he's got a gun this time?'

'We have a great big shield.'

'What are you talking about?'

'The money and the book. Until he has them, we're safe.'

'They're inside.'

'I know, but very soon they need to be somewhere else.'

'Down that mine, over there. There are a hundred places to hide that stuff.'

'Good idea Henry. Just the money. Leave the book. I may need some proof to show him. Now let's get moving.'

As the vehicle came closer, Henry and Alex manhandled the box to the mine, attached a rope they found hanging in the shack, lowered it into the blackness, hid it, climbed back to the surface, and went back inside to wait. At least, one of them did.

'Where's Henry?' said Lizzy, as her brother walked in.

'Right behind me ...' replied Alex turning. 'Well, I thought he was.'

'Shit! That man is like a bloody ghost.'

'Where's he gone?'

'Your guess is as good as mine.'

'Inside or outside?' said Alex.

'Pardon?'

'Will we wait to be killed inside or outside?'

'Inside. I'm in the mood for a little bit of payback.'

'Payback?'

'You'll see. Go around the back and turn off that generator.'

'Good point. What about Henry?'

'He'll be back.'

'When?'

'That's the question, isn't it?'

When Alex returned, his sister was sitting at the table with a lit candle, speaking on the satellite phone and punching keys on her laptop. All Alex heard was o*kay, good, fine.*

'What was that all about?'

'Weather report,' smiled Lizzy.

'Jesus Lizzy, I hope whatever disease you've got doesn't run in the family.'

She ignored him. 'He'll be here soon. Are you ready?'

'For what?'

'To see an old friend.'

Alex shook his head. 'Man, I don't know how you persuaded me to do this.'

'As I recall, you volunteered.'

'Not for all this.' he added, feeling his way to a camp stretcher, where he sat down and began mining red mud from under his fingernails.

CHAPTER 29

Ten minutes later they heard a vehicle pull up and a door slam. Alex and Lizzy sat in silence as they heard someone walk around the back of the shack, tinker with the generator and pull the cord to start it.

'Fucking thing decides to work first time just when I don't need it anymore.' grumbled a man's voice.

They heard footsteps on the front step, then the door creaked open. Alex and Lizzy braced themselves, and when the light went on, Burns jumped out of his skin.

'What the fuck?' he shouted, realizing who was there. 'You've got to be fucking kidding me. You're like a bloody bad smell that won't go away.'

'Welcome home,' said Lizzy calmly. 'We've been expecting you.'

Burns didn't answer but looked straight at the gaping hole where the floorboards had once been and walked over to inspect the gap.

'Fuck! Okay, waddya want?'

'I don't want much.' replied Lizzy. '$53,624.00 should do it.'

'What are you trying to prove Lizzy? I already told you once that you're delusional.'

'It won't work this time, Andrew. I've come for my money.'

'I've already told you that ...'

'Listen, if you want that buried treasure of yours back, then I better start seeing an account number and password for whatever bank you've ferreted it away in. BankWest if my guess is correct.'

'What the hell are you talking about?'

'More than you know Andrew. This isn't the first time I've been here. How do you think I knew about Ellen Hansen down at Margaret River? Email trail on that Noah's Ark computer of yours. Easy. And as you probably know from your wife Helena, we found Greg Wheeler's body down your mine after you killed him.'

'For fuck sake, you're out of your mind.'

'Am I? It was nice of your wife to try and pin that one on me.'

'You don't know anything!'

'I know how many women you've ripped off,' she replied, grabbing the ledger off the table. 'Names, dates and amounts, so Andrew, the fact is, I know more than you could possibly imagine, much more, so do yourself a favour and give me your account number before I get really pissed off.'

'You're out of your mind,' he replied, breaking into a sweat.

'I don't think he was expecting us?' smiled Alex, mimicking his sister's calmness.

'What the fuck is this all about Alex? Surely, you've got more sense than to make stupid accusations. Your sister is around the twist.'

Alex took a step towards him. 'Mate, I would hate this to get ugly, so you had better watch your mouth.'

'What about these?' said Lizzy, opening the palm of her hand to reveal Rosie's rain stones.

Burns' mouth gaped. 'Where did you get those?'

'Just out there.' she smiled, nodding towards the door. 'I saw some of your famous little blue flashes when we arrived yesterday ... and there they were. Bloody miracle ... the rain must have washed the dirt away.'

'There aren't any diamonds here.'

'Oh really? Why am I not surprised?'

'You're full of shit.'

'And maybe I'm not.'

'Listen, I'm warning you … just tell me where my fucking money is, and I'll be on my way.'

'*Your* money?

Burns was getting fidgety and his tone growing angrier.

'This is the last fucking time. If you don't tell me where my money is, I'll …'

'You'll what Andrew? Shoot my face off so no-one will recognize me? That'll be another murder you can add to your resume.'

'I didn't murder anyone. That idiot came here to kill *me*.'

'And why was that Andrew? Nice guy like you, why would anyone want to hurt you?'

'I don't know. It was an accident. We fought. The gun went off.'

'Then why not tell the police that?' said Lizzy, stepping towards him. 'It's over Andrew.'

Burns was ready to explode. 'It's over when I say it's fucking over.'

'Now would be a good time to say that.'

'Fucking smart arse bitch,' he replied, grabbing an empty beer bottle, smashing it over the back of a chair, grabbing Lizzy around her shoulders and holding the jagged glass to her throat.

'Give me my fucking money or so help me I'll …'

Alex took a determined step towards him, but knew discretion was the better part of valour. Panic flared in Lizzy's eyes. Burns had already killed one man. He had nothing to lose and everything to gain.

'Now, now Andrew, take it easy.' smoothed Alex. 'I'm sure that we can work something out.'

'The money. I want it now!'

The words were no sooner out of Burns' mouth than they heard an eerie chanting punctuated by clapping noises. Accompanying it was a rhythmic stomping that sent shockwaves through the ground.

'What the fuck is that?' said Alex, trying to distract Burns.

'Whatever it is, tell it to piss off,' snarled Burns, but the chanting grew louder.

'Please Andrew.' begged Lizzy. 'Let me go. This is only going to end badly for everyone.'

'Get outside!' yelled Burns, curling up his lip at Alex. 'Find out what the fuck it is.'

Burns pulled Lizzy back to let him past, but as he stepped outside, he walked into another world. It was an ancient time, a time before the *kartiya* arrived with their cattle and guns and diseases; before gold-hungry miners drove whole tribes off cliffs. It was a time before the men who owned the mines dug into the spine of Rosie's long-ago relatives, and it was a time of mythical creatures with legends to match.

'What is it?' yelled Burns.

'I'm not really sure,' replied Alex, dumbfounded. 'You had better come take a look.'

Burns dragged Lizzy towards the door and stepped into a time when the Rainbow Serpent created the land and all that was in it. The Dreamtime was suddenly alive.

CHAPTER 30

Under black storm clouds, dissected by slivers of silver lightening, ten aboriginal men spread out in a long line, chanted and stomped. Each was painted with the white mowuntum corroboree clay that Rosie had shown Lizzy. Most wore sprigs of gum-leaves in their hair. They had that look in their eyes; the look that said, *don't fuck with us*. Each man was slapping two boomerangs together and had two spears. Standing in the middle of them, Henry was stomping, clapping and chanting as loud as any of them.

While the surprised *kartiya* stood with their mouths open, Henry's men continued their slow rhythmic beat with the volume increasing by the second. .

'What the fuck?' sneered Burns, pushing Lizzy forward like a shield.

'Andrew, look, like my sister just said, this is only going to end badly,' cajoled Alex.

'Yeah, for you maybe.'

'What are you going to do? It's all a bit public now don't you think?'

'Where's my fucking money?'

'Leave her alone.'

'Jesus, you're really pissing me off now.'

'Andrew, please,' gasped Lizzy. 'Let me go.'

Burns pushed the bottle into her neck a little harder. A trickle of blood appeared.

'Stop it now! Leave her alone. I'll get your fucking money,' said Alex, taking a step forward. 'It's down the mine.'

'Go get it. Now!'

'I will, I will, but leave Lizzy alone.'

'Get the fucking money, and while you're at it, tell those clowns to fuck off.'

'A gold-plated dickhead right until the very end hey Andrew?' grunted Lizzy.

Burns pulled her tighter. 'Like you said, you're hard ...' but before he could finish his sentence, his grip broke, his legs gave way and he collapsed in agony with the *Kija* men, pointing their spears at him. Each of them still had two boomerangs, except for Henry. One of his was lying at Burns' feet.

'You've broken my fucking leg,' grimaced Burns, clutching the back of his knee.

'Nah boss. If I had wanted to break your bloody leg, I would have used this one.' replied Henry, waving his remaining boomerang. 'This is the leg breakin' one.'

'Are you okay Lizzy,' grimaced Alex, helping his sister up.

'Yes, fine. I think,' she stammered, feeling for blood on her throat.

'Arsehole,' said her brother, turning and stomping down hard in Burns' injured leg.

'Arrrrghhh.'

'What do you wanna do with him?' said Henry.

'A bank account and a password would be useful.'

'No fucking way,' bellowed Burns.

'I don't see that you've got much choice,' chided Lizzy.

'I'm not saying anything. You can't prove a thing.'

'We've got the ledger, so I think we can and *will* prove plenty.'

'Get stuffed! I'll take my chances with the coppers.'

'I don't like the odds,' laughed Alex, crouching next to his former friend. 'Why don't you just be a good boy and do what you're asked, or do I have to give your leg another reminder?'

'Go to hell. Bloody well call the police. I'll tell them how you broke into my mine and stole my money, then attacked me.'

'What about your old mate Wheeler?'

'That was an accident ... my wife was coming back to me. He must have found out. God's truth ... he jumped me ... I just did what I had to do.'

'Including shooting his face off?'

'There was a struggle ... it happened ... what can I do about it?'

'So why shoot him full of diamonds?'

'None of your bloody business.'

'Look Andrew, for all I care you can keep your bloody secrets about shooting diamonds into the wall of your mine. Don't worry, I know what that's all about. All I want is my money back, so if you don't mind, I would like the name of the bank, an account number, and a password.'

'Fuck off. You're getting nothing,' dribbled Burns.

'Excuse me,' said Henry. 'Can I talk to you over there for a bit?'

Lizzy looked at him quizzically but did as he asked.

While they talked, Alex watched. Henry did most of the talking. At first Lizzy shook her head like she disagreed, but then nodded and smiled. Henry returned and said something in his *Kija* language to the other men who laughed, lifted Burns to his feet and led him away.

'What the fuck do you think you're doing?' he growled. 'You can't do this.'

'What's going on?' said Alex.

'You'll see. I'll be back in a second. Wait here.' smiled his sister.

'Come on.' said Lizzy, returning with her laptop and satellite phone.

'What are *they* for?' said Alex.

'Patience is a virtue.'

'Don't tell me that you've finally got a plan?'

'Okay, I won't, but you might be surprised to know that I've always had one.' she replied striding off.

'Where the hell are we going now?'

'You'll see.'

'For Christ's sake what's all the secrecy about?'

'It's a surprise. I think you'll like it. It was Henry's idea. It's very inventive.'

They walked for ten minutes before they spotted the *Kija* men gathered in a tight circle.

'Sorry, we had to go a bit further than I thought to find one,' smiled Henry.

'Find what?' said Alex.

'Be patient.'

'What the hell is he up to?' replied Alex, wiping his brow.

Henry turned and when he did, the *Kija* men opened their circle forming a wide arc. In the middle of them, Burns was tied, face up, to a log, with his arms wrapped backwards around it and his legs hanging on, like he was riding a horse the wrong way.

'Alex. Alex help me ... please,' he yelled.

'Mate, after what you just did to my sister you've got no chance, so I suggest that you give her exactly what she wants.'

Lizzy walked over to where Burns' head was strapped to the log by a rope around his neck and forehead, so that he couldn't move. She knelt next to him.

'Hot day.'

'Fuck off.'

'You're pretty brave for someone about to get eaten alive.'

'You're full of shit.'

'We'll see,' she replied, opening the laptop and connecting the satellite phone. 'All I want to know is where my money is ... and then I want the account number and a password. When I get those, my friend Henry will untie you ... we're going to transfer the money back to my account right here ... easy.'

'It's not going to happen,' spluttered Burns.

'Full marks for stupidity Andrew.'

'Yeah well, I think you win that prize. All you women want to do is get laid.'

'You know, I feel sorry for you. Somebody, somewhere, really screwed with your head.'

'Piss off.'

'Last chance.'

Burns spat.

'You might need that spit. I don't think you'll be having a drink for a while.'

Lizzy looked up at the storm clouds and guessed she may be wrong, then waved at Henry who was carrying a small tin can towards her.

'He's all yours Henry. Do what you have to do.'

'This will get that *kartiya* jarrak, jarrak ... talkin' till dem cows come home ... like you white fellas say.'

Henry dipped his fingers into the can and scooped out a large dollop of sugar bag honey and spread it all over Burns' face.

'What the fuck do you think you're doing ... get the fuck away from me,' yelled Burns, shaking his head from side to side trying to escape the sticky glue.

'Sweet honey Mr. Andrew ... tastes bloody good.'

When he had finished, Henry called to another man who walked carefully towards him, knelt next to Burns' head, and put down a small tower of red earth resting on a large piece of paperbark.

'I think he'll be ready to talk in about one minute.' said Henry.

Lizzy knelt beside Burns again. 'Last chance tough guy.'

'Fuck off!'

The ant's nest on the bark sprang to life and thousands of tiny creatures picked up the scent of the honey and headed straight for it.

'You can't fucking-well do this,' screamed Burns.

'Bank, account number, password ... then it stops.'

At a distance, Alex squatted watching the proceedings. He had never seen his sister behave like this. It was a different version of her in the same body. A more forceful version. Someone who wasn't taking shit from anyone. Where had she come from? What switch had been flicked in her head?

'Bloody amazing,' he whispered, to no one in particular.

As the first ant touched Burns' face, he saw a mass of its friends following close behind.

'They're fucking ginger ants!' he yelled.

'Is that bad?' said Lizzy, innocently.

Henry smiled, 'They hurt like hell, but they're not as bad as them bloody fire ants.'

'Okay, okay, stop it!' spluttered Burns. 'I'll give you want you want.'

'Fire away.'

'Stop the ants!'

'Give me a reason.'

'BankWest,' he spluttered, urgently.

'Okay, good start.' said Lizzy, punching the website address into her laptop and finding the internet banking section.

'So far so good. What's the account number?'

'8-8-1-3-7-6-7-0-8'

'Password.'

'A.D.A.M.A.S.1 ... Stop the ants ... make them stop.'

'Let me just work out how their transfer system works ... ah yes.'

'Bitch.'

'Henry,' she called. 'Have you got any more of that honey?'

'Okay, okay, I'm sorry. Make him stop the ants.'

Lizzy nodded and Henry reluctantly dragged the bark tray away and with it, all but a few of the more determined ants.

'Untie me.'

'You're kidding me?' said Lizzy, looking at her laptop. 'This account is empty. Zero.

Henry, put them back,' she added, pointing at the ant's nest.

'No, no, don't,' squirmed Burns. 'I can explain.'

'Well I would be doing that sooner rather than later if I were you,' replied Lizzy, as the first ant crawled up Burn's cheek.

'Stop them. Please,' begged Burns.

'Listen Andrew, I don't have time for this shit, so if you want it to stop, tell me what I need to know.'

Burns growled as the first ant bit, then another and another.

'Alright, alright. It's in my truck. In the bag. Back seat.'

'Bullshit!'

'It is, I promise.'

'I've heard your promises before.'

'Get your brother to check, but while he's doing that, stop the ants. Aargh.'

Lizzy called Alex over, told him what to do and he ran off. A few minutes later, he appeared on a ridge, carrying a sports bag and gave the thumbs up.

'So, your mine is your bank hey Andrew. Personally, I think that's taking mistrust of banks just a little bit too far, but each to their own.'

'You've got what you want, now untie me.'

'I'm not quite finished with you yet.'

'What the fuck do you want now?' said Burns, as Lizzy punched more keys on her laptop.

'Say hello to Sergeant Manfredi.'

'...and who the hell is he?'

'Kununurra police. He wants to talk to you. Look into my little camera on top of the computer ... right there ... see?'

'Sergeant are you there?' said Lizzy.

'I sure am,' he replied. 'Is Mr Burns behaving himself?'

'Something like that.'

'Good. Thanks for your call yesterday. It was very useful. We had our boys in Perth go around to that address in Cottesloe and just as you said, Helena Burns was there. She tried to play hard-arse, but once she was

232

under arrest, she confirmed everything you told us. She wants a deal, but I'm sure if you and all those women that Burns ripped off are prepared to testify, that won't be necessary. My men are already on their way to get Mr Burns. Can you take care of him until they get there?'

'I'll see what I can do,' grinned Lizzy.

'Oh and just one more thing Ms. Lawson, do you have any idea why he went back to his mine?'

'No idea.' replied Lizzy with a straight face. 'No idea at all. Why would anyone want to come all the way out here to this pile of rubbish? I thought he may have left some diamonds here but, well, there aren't any.'

'Yeah I suppose you're right, so no sign of any money then.'

'None, but I have some bank account details that you might want to investigate. I'll text the details to you. Burns gave them to me, but they could be a dead end. He's not known for telling the truth, is he? My guess is that he has spent all the money.'

'Criminals aren't known for their financial management Ms. Lawson. Thanks for your help. We'll see you soon.'

As Manfredi finished his sentence the first rain drops fell on the laptop's screen and within seconds, the clouds parted. Before long, they were surrounded by a mass of slithering water-snakes on their way to the lowest point they could find. Lizzy ignored the rain, snapped the computer shut, removed the satellite phone, and started to walk away.

'Don't leave me here.' yelled Burns.

'Better untie him, Henry.' smiled Lizzy.

'Are ya sure?'

'Yes Henry. I'm sure. He's had enough, for now anyway.'

The *Kija* men laughed as they fiddled with the knots, but every so often, one of them would shout *yilkurruny jiyliny*, bad man, and wave a threatening finger. Soon Burns was free and stood not daring to move. His muddy clothes hung on him like limp rags that matched the newly acquired drop of his jowls.

'He's part of the land hey Henry?' laughed Lizzy.

'Not part of *my* land missus.' smiled Henry, licking the rain from his lips.

Burns was soon washed clean, and except for a morose look and a couple of ant bites, there was no evidence of what had happened to him.

'You'd better get back to the shack. Plenty more rain comin' ... these *Kija* fellas and me will make sure he gets back ... you get goin' now.'

'Come on,' yelled Lizzy to Alex

'What the hell was that all about?'

'True confessions,' replied Lizzy, as they ran.

'Where are they taking him?'

'Back to the mine. We've got to look after him until Manfredi's men get here.'

They put their heads down and ran, trying to avoid every muddy bog but it was impossible, so they stopped and walked, resigning themselves to becoming filthy, drowned rats. By the time they reached the shack, that's exactly what they were.

For a moment, Lizzy and Alex just looked at each other, dripping and listening to the rain on the tin roof.

'That could have gone very south very quickly,' said Alex, eventually. 'How's your neck?'

'Fine,' she replied, touching it. 'It's a scratch.'

'You were lucky. Your friend Henry is a good man. He and his men saved the day.'

'I've got a lot to thank him for ... and you too Alex. If you hadn't have come with me, I would never have done this alone, and I needed to, I really needed to. I needed to see Andrew squirm. I needed to stand up to him. I needed to do it for me.'

'Well you certainly did that Lizzy. What is it with this new you?'

'I don't know. I guess that I just feel better about myself.'

'It's a good look.' smiled her brother, hugging her.

'We better get out of these wet things,' replied Lizzy, shyly. 'So, if you don't mind, I would like some privacy to get changed. Why don't you go and get that box up from the mine? Add that money in the bag to it.'

'But it's pissing down out there.'

'Alex, you're not going to get any wetter.'

'It took two to get it down there so maybe more to get it back up. Let's wait until Henry gets back.'

'Alex, I want some privacy.'

He blushed. 'Oh yes, sorry, sorry. I'll wait outside.'

CHAPTER 31

The canvas awning over the front door leaked like a sieve, but with a bit of trial-and-error Alex found a spot where he was mostly under cover. An old car tyre leaning against the shack provided a makeshift seat.

'Mr. Alex, what are ya doin' out here?' asked Henry, as he approached, closely followed by four other *Kija* men with a sad looking Andrew Burns in tow. His hands were tied behind his back.

'Lizzy wants some privacy.'

'It's a bloody strange time for that.'

'I've given up trying to understand ...'

'Me too... a bloody long time ago.'

'What the fuck do you think you're up to Alex?' called Burns, standing just outside the cover of the awning.

'The police will be here soon. We'll let them handle it.'

'Can I at least get out of the rain?'

'Bring him in.' said Alex, to the *Kija* men.

'Some-kind-of friend you turned out to be,' said Burns, shaking his head like a wet dog.

'Yeah well, you know what they say about blood and water.'

'I'll give you half of everything I've got to get rid of these bastards.'

'Is that a bribe?'

236

'No, it's a bloody invitation to dinner, of course it fucking-well is.'

'Did you hear that Henry, Mr. Burns is offering the heir to a considerable fruit and vegetable fortune, a bribe.'

'Don't be a smart arse.'

'Sit down,' demanded Alex, getting up from his tyre seat.

Burns did as he was told, but only because he could see that Alex occupied the driest spot available.

'You've never seen this kind of rain have you Alex. It could go on for bloody days ... those coppers aren't getting anywhere near here until the roads dry out. You could be an old man by the time they get here ... don't you have to get back to Sydney and sell a banana or something?'

'I've got all the time in the world. Besides, I need some more of Henry's bush chicken before I go.'

'There's no such thing.'

'Oh yes there is, isn't there Henry?'

'Sure there is.'

They waited in silence as the rain continued to fall, but finally the door of the shack creaked open. Lizzy stood there with her long black hair slicked back off her face wearing the same pretty floral dress she wore to the beach dinner at Eagle Bay. It looked particularly out of place.

'Going to a party?' said her brother.

'There wasn't much to choose from.'

'Well, if it isn't Miss Easy Fucking Money,' sulked Burns.

Burns never saw the punch that hit him. Without even thinking, Alex smashed the heel of his open palm into Burns' lip, then the same blow continued up to break his nose. The impact drove his head back onto the wooden shack with a crack then it bounced off and Burns fell to the ground with blood exploding from his ruptured lips and nostrils which mixed with the rain giving his injury the appearance of a massive red flood.

'Shut your mouth ... and don't *ever* fuck with my sister again,' spat Alex.

'Too late for that,' sneered Burns, spitting out two teeth.

The comment earned Burns a kick in the ribs. The others watched without emotion. Even Lizzy found it hard to offer any sympathy. *You hit like a girl* was all Burns could say while his face contorted.

'Give me a few minutes with him,' suggested Lizzy.

'You've got to be kidding,' replied her brother. 'This asshole could do anything.'

'Henry, you and your men wait over there,' she instructed, pointing towards a tin roof held up by four weathered sapling posts. 'If this arsehole takes one step towards me, put one of those spears right through his heart ... oh, I'm sorry, you don't have one of those, do you? You had better stick one right between his legs instead. It might remind him to stop thinking with his ...'

'You wouldn't.'

'I wouldn't, but they might,' replied Lizzy. 'Strange shit happens out here Andrew, so who knows.'

'What am *I* supposed to do?' said Alex.

'Trust me.'

'Fuck,' he whispered, reluctantly turning towards the door. 'If you touch a hair on her fucking head, I'll ...'

'You'll what Alex?' slimed Burns. 'Flog me with a lettuce leaf ... you act tough, but you're a weak fuck. I always knew that.'

Alex took a step towards him, but Lizzy held out her arm to block her brother.

'I know how to shut this waste of space up ... go on, give me a moment.'

Henry and the *Kija* men retreated to the shelter and waited but never took their eyes off Burns.

'You've got a big mouth for a man who's about to go to jail,' said Lizzy, calmly, once they were alone.

'Yeah well, that remains to be seen, doesn't it?' replied Burns, struggling awkwardly to his feet, and returning to his car tyre seat.

'Never say die hey Andrew? Well, try this for size. Do you see this mine of yours ... the mine that you thought had no diamonds, well it does.' she smiled, unfolding her hand to reveal Rosie's rain stones.

'That doesn't prove a thing. They could be from any bloody where.'

'These *Kija* people have been laughing at you because they knew you were so near, yet so far. Henry showed me a place just near here ... just over that rise...we just picked these up off the ground ... nice aren't they ... big too.'

'Bullshit!'

'Well, that's the good news Andrew, the bad news is that very soon this lease, your tenement number 12967/99, which just so happens to include the area just over that rise, is going to belong to me.'

'You're full of shit.'

'You know, I took that geologist report of yours to a friend of mine who knows about these things. He said it was prepared by a pretty average geologist, well, it also seems that you're a pretty average businessman.'

'What the hell are you talking about?'

'You've probably forgotten that you need to pay the government $14.52 rent for every hectare of your tenement, every year and you've got what ... one thousand hectares ... oh no ... it turns out that you don't have that ... it's ten ... ten hectares ... so that's one hundred and forty-five dollars and twenty cents you owe the government ... for let me see ... oh yeah, the last fifteen years.'

'Yeah, so what? It's nothing. I'll pay it later.'

'It won't be here when you get out of jail, at least not for you anyway.'

'What's this, more of your bullshit?'

'You also seem to have forgotten that to hang onto your tenement, you have to pay that bill every so often. It also seems that you have to spend ten thousand dollars a year actually doing something with the land.'

'I have ...'

'Mmmm nice shack. Listen, it's quite simple, you've defaulted on the most basic requirements of your lease for a very long time, so I've applied for it to be forfeited to me. My new friends at the Department of Industry and Resources tell me it's all very straight-forward.'

'You can't ...'

'It's already underway, so it looks like I'll be rich from diamonds after all. Thanks for all the hard work, Andrew. I really appreciate it.'

'The government has to notify me first ...'

'... and what address should they use? Broome jail?'

'They might just fine me.'

'They could, but given your track record, the minister's department will also be *very* interested in what work you have planned for your site ... sorry *my* site ... *use it or lose it* so they say Andrew ... and once they find out you're going to jail, I don't think too much work is going to be done ... do you?

'I can still pay ... it'll all go away.'

'Pay with what?'

'My money, the money you hid in the mine.'

'What money is that, Andrew?'

'You know very well what money.'

'Oh, Andrew you're ... what did you call me back at Margaret River ... of yes, *delusional*. I've never seen any money.'

'That's *my* money.'

'No Andrew, it belongs to those women, and I intend to see they get it all back.'

'You can't prove anything.'

'I don't have to. Those women are going to do it for me and they're all going to tell the police how much you stole from them and because that bank account of yours is empty, it's going to look like you've spent it all. My guess is that once the police start looking into it, they'll discover that you made lots of big cash withdrawals to stick in that big box you had hidden under the floorboards...just like you did with the money you brought with you today. My money.'

'You're just making shit up as you go.'

'Maybe I am, and maybe I'm not, but when the police don't find any money, they're going to think that you spent it all and the lucky judge who hears your case is going to take that into account and give you an even longer sentence.'

'I'll tell the police you stole it.'

'Stole what Andrew? I came here looking for my money too. This weather must be getting to you ... washed away your sense of reason.'

'I'll be out on bail in no time.'

'Somehow I don't think so.'

'Why?'

'You seem to have conveniently forgotten about the murder charge.'

'It was an accident.'

'I don't think the police will see it that way ... let's think about it for a moment ... you, the jealous ex-husband, that never got divorced ... wife has moved on, but you keep asking her to come back ...her de facto gets wind of that ... you want him out of the way ... you flee the scene of his murder and try to disappear, you even plant your wallet on him to make it appear that it was you ... that's called trying to fake your own death ... then there are the big cash withdrawals that I reckon you've made ... Jesus Andrew, your partner-in-crime is already looking for a deal with the police to spill the beans ... I can hear her now ... I knew about it, but I wasn't involved ... he'd just brag about it to me ... what could I do? Who knows what she'll say? No, I don't think so Andrew. I would say that you're going away for a very long time and while some tattooed monster has you bent over in the showers, I'm going to see what I can do about raising some real money and then I'm going into the diamond business. So, thank you Andrew. I want you to think about that while you're rotting in jail. I want you to think about me every day and try to imagine just how filthy rich I'm getting from the diamonds that *you* led me to.'

Burns' face turned beetroot. He wanted to speak but his anger prevented him, so he stood and took a step towards Lizzy struggling to free his hands, but then he froze. Five *Kija* men had their spears up to their shoulders, ready to launch their missiles.

'Looks like the rain is clearing,' smiled Lizzy, as a small blanket of blue emerged from between the rain clouds.

'What's the matter lover-boy? Has the cat got your tongue?'

'This isn't over Lizzy.'

'Oh yes, it is, Andrew.'

Lizzy heard her satellite phone ring inside the shack so motioned to Henry and his men, 'Make sure our friend doesn't go anywhere will you please Henry.'

'Sure missus. No problem.'

Henry bounded up and jabbed Burns with the tip of his spear and he sat back down. After what Lizzy had said to him, somehow, he looked more hen-pecked than cocksure.

When she stepped back inside her brother was speaking on the satellite phone.

'Who is it?' she whispered.

'Sergeant Manfredi.'

'Yes Sergeant,' she said, taking the phone.

She listened while the policeman spoke. 'Okay, no problem.'

'What's happening?'

'The roads are all cut. They're sending a chopper from Turkey Creek for him. It won't be long.'

'What about us?'

'We're here for a while I'm afraid.'

'How long?'

'Well, that depends on the weather.'

Half an hour later they heard the distant dugger, dugger, dugger of a helicopter approaching so went outside.

'You'd better get your men out of here, Henry.' said Lizzy. 'I don't want those *coppers* knowing what went on here. Thank them for me will you.'

'Sure missus. They're as good as gone.'

While Henry spoke to his men, they listened then laughed and dispersed in different directions waving as they went and before long, they were *parta de land*.

'You better get yourself cleaned up too,' suggested Lizzy, wiping a large white spot of clay off Henry's arm.

The thud of the helicopter grew louder and before they knew it, it was above them, fanning the muddy puddles and spraying everything and everyone with a dirty red mist.

'What do they think we are? Bloody fish?' bellowed Alex, over the noise.

Finally, it settled, but the pilot stayed buckled in his seat while two uniformed officers emerged from the side, ducked under the spinning rotors, and ran towards the shack.

'Is this Burns?' asked the taller of the two uniformed men, eyeing the dishevelled mess in front of him.

'That's him.' replied Lizzy. 'In all his glory.'

'Give us a minute alone with him, will you?' asked the shorter policeman.

The constables asked Burns a few questions which he nodded the answers to then they removed the rope tying his hands and replaced it with handcuffs. After that there was an animated conversation with Burns doing a lot of nodding towards Lizzy and Alex then at Henry. Finally Burns nodded in the direction of the mine and then towards where they had taken him to visit the ants. Lizzy, Alex and Henry waited patiently for the interrogation to be completed and when Burns had finished his story, the shorter policeman stayed to guard him while the other constable walked towards where the others were waiting.

'He's got quite an imagination that fella.'

'What do you mean?' replied Lizzy.

'He says that you and some aboriginal men tied him to a log, covered his face with honey and set ginger ants loose on him and made him say a whole lot of things that weren't true. He also said something about half a million dollars in cash being down that mine over there ... he says ...

243

ah never mind ... this country does that to some people ... makes 'em go around the twist and ...'

'It's got a way a killing a person and it's got a way a saving a person, but that person has got to want to be saved in the first place,' interrupted Lizzy, speaking Rosie's words without thinking.

'Yeah, and some people are just bullshit artists and this fella takes the cake.'

'Sergeant Manfredi has my number if you need me,' smiled Lizzy.

'What about food?' asked Alex.

'No worries,' answered Henry, 'There's plenty more bush chicken where that other one came from ... might even find you some of that special bush spaghetti maybe.'

The policeman shook his head, shrugged and started to walk away. 'If you need anything, just call.'

'What about a pizza?' yelled Alex, but the policeman just waved his hand over his shoulder to indicate he had heard him but had absolutely no intention of obliging.

'Ya want a bush one?' laughed Henry.

'Bush pizza?'

The two policemen escorted Burns to the helicopter, buckled him in, and in swirl of muddy water, they disappeared north-west towards Kununurra.

'Your former boyfriend didn't look very happy.' said Alex, as they walked back to the shack.

'That's probably because I told him that I had found Rosie's rain stones just over that rise there. I also told him Henry and his people have known he was digging in the wrong place for years.'

'Are there really diamonds around here?'

'No. At least I don't think so.'

'So why did you tell him that?'

'Because I also told him that I have applied to have his tenement lease forfeited to me because he hasn't paid his bills.'

'Have you?'

'No. Who would want this pile of crap?'

'Then why?'

'Because he ripped the heart out of all those women and I wanted to take away the one thing that is going to be most important to him, now that he's on his way to jail.'

'The mine?'

'No, hope.'

'But you haven't done any of what you just said, have you?'

'No, of course not, but he thinks I have, and that's all that really matters. He's going to spend his time in jail thinking that his life was a waste of time and wondering what might have been. As far as he's concerned, there will be nothing for him to come back to. No hope.'

Alex shook his head. 'You're a hard woman Lizzy. Does this mean that you're going to make me suffer with some unbelievably awful fate for introducing him to you?'

'Witchetty grubs for dinner.'

'We call that *bush pasta*,' laughed Henry.

Once the echo of the helicopter had disappeared, a peaceful silence returned to Mistake Creek, and if not for the faint hum of the generator, it would have been the most perfect silence they had ever known. While the clouds still hurried by twenty thousand feet up, on the ground, nothing moved. Not a single creature stirred; not an ant, nor a lizard; even the snakes had found holes to slither into. The loudest noise any of them could hear was the drip, drip, drip of water as everything started to dry out.

'Come on let's get a drink. All that humiliation has made me thirsty.' smiled Lizzy, as she turned back toward the shack, but by the time she reached the door, Henry was nowhere to be seen.

'He does that a lot,' said Alex, looking around.

'Too often.'

'Maybe he's gone to get the money.'

'I'll go take-a-look.'

Lizzy was just getting comfortable when her brother burst through the door.

'The money. It's gone!'

CHAPTER 32

As if to put an exclamation mark after what he had just said, a lone lightning bolt cracked open the sky.

'What do you mean it's gone?' shuddered Lizzy.

'Well, it's not down the bloody mine where we put it.'

'Are you sure you looked in the right place? It can get a bit confusing down there.'

'Yes of course I'm bloody well sure.'

'Then where is it? Only we knew where it was. Where's Henry? Could he have taken it?'

'No, of course not. He hates money. He thinks its evil.'

'Evil or not, he's looking like a prime suspect right now.'

Suddenly, there was a thud on the ground outside.

'What's that?' said Lizzy, on full alert.

'Alex ... go on ... look.'

The door squeaked open. He peered outside.

'Gidday. Brung us some dinner,' smiled Henry. 'Bush cow, but us *Kija* people, we call it wallaby.'

Alex looked incredulously at the carcass next to Henry's feet.

'At least my bloody spear was good for something today after all.'

Lizzy appeared at the door shaking her head. 'Henry, can you please tell us when you're going to run off?'

'Sure, I'm gonna run off *right now*…gonna see if I can find some dry firewood. I'll be back soon.'

'Henry just a minute.'

'What?'

'The money, down the mine, it's gone.'

'How can it bloody be gone? There's no-one here but us lot.'

'You didn't move it like you moved Wheeler's body, did you?'

'That money we put down the mine?'

'Yes Henry. What other money is there?'

'Nah, no idea. Are you sure you looked in the right place … you keep losin' things down that hole, don't ya?'

'I looked exactly where you and I put it,' interrupted Alex, kicking the wallaby just to make sure it was dead.

'It can't just disappear. Come on let's go look again.'

'Do you see anything?' yelled Lizzy, from the top of the mine shaft.

'Still looking,' echoed the reply.

Henry and Alex finally emerged and the look on their faces and the shake of their heads said all Lizzy needed to know.

'Money in a big box doesn't just get up and walk away,' she said. 'Are you absolutely sure that you looked in the right place?'

'We looked everywhere. It's *not* down there,' grimaced Alex.

'Then who the hell could have taken it?'

'I'm buggered if I know.'

'Let's think about this for a moment. The only people who knew it was down there, were you and Henry and me, and the only time we left here was when we went to show Andrew those ants all up close and personal.'

'… and when we were inside, waiting for Andrew to arrive, Henry was out here somewhere,' said Alex, turning on the old aboriginal man.

'Now listen, just because I got ya with that bush chicken joke, there's no need to be sayin' that kinda stuff.'

'You've hidden it out there somewhere,' said Alex, pointing, '... and you're going to come back for it after we've gone ... aren't you?'

'No boss. That's not true. Somethin' goes missin' and you bloody *kartiya* always blame us black fellas. Then when ya find it somewhere else, ya don't say sorry or nothin'. I didn't take it. Honest.'

Lizzy stepped in. 'Take it easy Alex. Henry could have just run off with it ... no one would ever have found it ... besides he came back to help.'

'Yeah, that's right. I could have just run off, but I brung ya dinner instead.'

'Okay, so if none of us took it, who the bloody hell did?' said Lizzy.

They looked at each other confused.

'What are we going to do?' said Alex.

Lizzy shook her head. 'What *can* we do? It's a damned Bermuda Triangle down there.'

'Did you see anyone out there, Henry?' asked Lizzy. 'Did we miss something?'

'No missus, just me and them other *Kija* fellas.'

'Could they have taken it?'

'Nah missus, they didn't even know about it.'

'This is way too weird.'

'Gonna get that firewood now missus. I'm runnin' off now. Just thought I'd let ya know.'

'Thanks Henry. Thanks for telling me.'

As she watched Henry wander off into the distance, Lizzy scratched her head. This was way too weird, but she was getting used to Mistake Creek living up to its name.

'It can't just disappear,' said Alex, as the sky rumbled.

'Maybe we need to look again. Come on, let's go. It's got to be here somewhere.'

'So, Miss Brand New Person...' said Alex, turning to his sister. 'Where should we start looking?'

'We're in the middle of nowhere, right?'

'Yep, you got that right.'

'Well, if someone took it, then they had to get here some way or other.'

'Do you have any other keen insights?'

'No need for sarcasm,' she smiled. 'So, we need to be looking for car tracks, motor bike tracks ...'

' ... or maybe the outline of an alien spaceship?'

'Maybe even that.'

'But this morning's rain would have washed everything away.'

'Henry is getting firewood, right?'

'Yeah, so?'

'So, somewhere it's dry ... under trees maybe?'

'Have you had a look around? We're not exactly in a forest.'

'So, we start with what trees there are.'

'The only ones are back up over that ridge ... where Henry's Toyota is parked.'

'So, we'll start there I suppose.'

'Is that Henry down there?' said Lizzy, as they reached the top of a ridge.

Down in the gully Henry was walking around under the trees with an armful of wood but he was acting very strangely.

'What's he doing?'

'I have no idea.'

'It looks like he's got firewood though.'

They stumbled down the muddy ridge until they were within shouting distance.

'Hey Henry, Henry what are you doing?' called Alex.

The old aboriginal man looked up and beckoned them to come quickly.

'Look at this. There's been another truck here, four-wheel-drive, parked here for a bit and then backed out and headed in that direction.'

'How do you know?' said Alex, looking at the ground.

'Look here ... see them four bits there, there, there and there ...'

replied Henry, indicating four slight indentations in the soil under the biggest desert oak. 'That's where it parked. I know that it's a 4x4 'cause of the space between the holes and the depth of them holes ... and see that little sweep around there and that other one out there ... backing up and driving off ... made a little hole ... the rain just smoothed it off ... but somethin' was there all right.'

'Where does that go to?' said Alex, pointing to the direction the tracks went.

'That's the way to Jimmy Orion's place, but ya can get to Turkey Creek that way too if ya wanna, but look at this,' said Henry, pointing to the negligible remains of a long furrow which ran away from the trees into rain compacted soil then disappeared.

'What are you pointing at, there's nothing there.'

'You gotta look real careful like ta see it. Come this way.'

Henry guided them up the ridge still carrying his armful of firewood, and where the soil disappeared and the gritty stone clusters took over, a nuance of the long furrow re-emerged. As they followed it up the rise, every now and then, the line was punctuated with muddy footprints the same size as Alex's boot.

'You've been walking over it the whole time.' said Lizzy.

'How was I supposed to know what it was? What is it anyway?'

Henry was already several steps ahead of them and suddenly broke into a trot.

'Come on.' he called. 'I reckon I know exactly where this leads to.'

Sure enough, the faint furrow ran all the way back to the lip of the mine.

'Why didn't you see this before?' Alex asked Henry.

'I was too busy defending myself. Too busy lookin' into your angry eyes.'

Alex frowned. 'I'm sorry Henry.'

'Did you just say *sorry*?'

'Yes, Henry I did. I shouldn't have blamed you.'

'Well, I'll be buggered. First, that new big boss *kartiya* that runs the country says *Sorry* and now I've heard it the first time for meself … it's a bloody miracle.'

'Don't push your luck, Henry.'

'Sorry, I just didn't think it would ever happen while I was alive.'

Lizzy looked worried. 'Okay, so now we know that someone took the money, but we need to know who and why … and where the hell they're going with it, but what I really want to know is how they knew it was down the mine in the first place. We only put it there when Henry spotted Andrew coming.'

'But the tracks we saw over the ridge came from the other direction.' replied Alex.

'So, you're saying whoever was driving was here all along and they saw us put it down the mine?'

'Dunno, but it's a possibility.'

'And when we went off to get a few answers from Andrew, they took it. Andrew wasn't expecting us to be here and so nor would anyone else be. They were coming here anyway so they must have known about the money.'

'Well, they weren't just dropping in for afternoon tea, were they?'

'Who else knew?'

'Your guess is as good as mine. Burns could've told anyone.'

'Maybe his wife knew,' said Alex, apprehensively.

They looked at each other like they hadn't thought of the obvious.

'Of course,' said Lizzy.

'She must have known that Andrew was on his way here to get the money,' replied Alex, 'but Manfredi's boys in blue arrested her.'

'She's a piece of work so maybe she was going to double-cross him,' smiled Lizzy, 'Maybe she sent someone who was a bit closer to get it.'

'Her brother!' they yelled in unison.

'Henry even said those tyre tracks were going towards this Jimmy Orion guy's pub.' added Alex.

'So how far do you think he got?' replied Lizzy, with a Cheshire cat grin spread across her face.

'What do you mean?'

'The police had to send a chopper for Andrew because all the roads were closed ... too much rain ... so if Jimmy took the money out by four-wheel-drive and even the coppers couldn't get through, just how far do you think that little shit got?'

Alex grinned. 'I'm inclined to say not very far at all.'

'So, I'm thinking that he's out there somewhere stuck in a big pile of mud sitting on top of half million dollars.'

'And he can't go anywhere until we do and we're not going anywhere in a big hurry ... are we?'

'Not necessarily,' smiled Lizzy, suddenly pleased with herself, but her smile quickly disappeared when she was startled by an almighty thunderclap and rain splattering against the tin roof.

'What are you talking about?' asked her brother, following her eyes up to the heavens.

'The helicopter will be back for us in the morning.'

'So, we're here for the night?'

'Unless you've got a better idea.'

'Do I have to eat Henry's wallaby?'

'Are you hungry?'

'Starving.'

'Then I suggest you do. Cluck cluck.'

'Yeah, yeah, I know, I should be thankful for small mercies I suppose. What are we going to do about the cars?'

'I've already spoken to Manfredi about that. The chopper will bring Henry back for his as soon as it dries out and I'm sure the rental company will be very happy to find out where Andrew left their new LandCruiser.'

'If it ever dries out,' replied her brother, as another lightning bolt fractured the sky.

CHAPTER 33

While Alex and Lizzy headed back towards the shack, Henry strode off towards a corrugated iron shelter where he set about building a fire to roast his *bush cow*. Within a few minutes a small plume of smoke wandered out the open sides and up towards the grey sky, but it didn't have to go too far. By then the incoming rain clouds seemed to hug the ground, and even though it was only mid-afternoon, the sun had already disappeared, and the light had faded to a funereal grey. Henry followed the smoke up to the clouds and shook his head apprehensively. He had seen this kind of weather before.

An hour later, the storm barked like a junk-yard dog, the clouds puffed out their chests and then, as if by magic, day became night just as Henry stepped into the shack, carrying wallaby hocks on a dented hubcap. Straight after, a trillion ball-bearing sized globs of rain smashed into the tin roof, making so much noise that it was impossible to hear anyone speak.

'Real bad storm this one. Real bad.' yelled Henry, as he put the food on the table.

His usual giant smile had disappeared, and in its place, a worried look had taken up residence. It was contagious.

'Is everything alright Henry?' yelled Lizzy, over the din.

'We'll be okay here for a bit.'

'A bit?'

'We'll see how we go hey, but I wouldn't want to be that bloody Jimmy Orion right now,' replied Henry.

They didn't hear the generator cut out with the noise of the rain belting down, but the instant darkness told them that it had. The blackness was totally and utterly complete.

'What the ...?'

'Must have run out of fuel,' yelled Alex in the darkness.

'None left,' replied Henry.

'None?'

'All gone. Used the last little bit to get that fire of mine started ... the wood was still wet.'

'Where are those candles?' said Lizzy, groping in the darkness.

'Over on that shelf ... to your right.'

The candles were soon lit and everyone, except Henry, sat around the table listening to the rain, and the howl of a wind that had arrived with it. The old man preferred to stand in the doorway watching loose corrugated iron on the out-buildings flap about like a rusty rabbit caught in a snare. Above him, the awning covering the front door, filled like a spinnaker, and was attempting to lift the saplings, which supported it, out of the ground. The large puddles, left over from the morning storm, merged into a giant shallow sea which flowed off in a single torrent towards a small gully, then on to a larger ravine where it leapt over large rocks and filled up what was once probably a dry creek bed. In the other direction, the yawning opening to the Adamas mine shaft provided a perfect waterfall.

'That rain is comin' here for a long time,' worried Henry. 'That Kaleruny he's makin' sure that you got that river of yours to follow, no matter where ya are missus, that's for sure.'

'Is it bad Henry?'

'Pretty soon this whole part of the Kimberley is gonna be one big river. That's why this shack is off the ground a bit ... that Andrew fella, he knew about this kinda rain.' yelled Henry from the doorway, ' ... this rain ain't goin' away in no hurry, no, not this one.'

'What about the chopper?' yelled Alex. 'Is it still coming back for us?'

'Even them little birds is hidin' from this one Mr Alex. There's no chance that a big bird is gonna fly in this kind of weather. Maybe it'll all be gone by the morning, but I don't think so, not this one…this bloody big wet is here ta stay for while if ya ask me.'

More lightning jagged the sky, momentarily lighting their faces through a crack in the door. Lizzy and Alex exchanged glances. What did the old man really mean?

'Anyone hungry?' said Lizzy, trying to lighten the mood.

Henry turned from the door, joined them at the table and carved the wallaby meat into thick slices, but his regular chatter had dried up.

'What's going on,' asked Lizzy. 'What aren't you telling us?'

Henry sighed. 'It's okay. Nothin' ta worry about.'

But there was, and she knew it. 'You can tell us, Henry.'

'Just worrying about my mother, Rosie. Last time we had rain like this, all bloody Turkey Creek got washed away. The weather is changin' alright.'

'I'm sure she'll be fine Henry.' replied Lizzy, rubbing his shoulder. 'Dig in.' she added, giving Alex a tight smile. 'It's been quite a day one way or another.'

The intensity of the rain continued unabated for the next two hours, and while they tried to ignore it, each of them found themselves drifting back to the door or a window to look outside.

'I'm going to see if I can get some sleep,' said Lizzy, yawning.

It wasn't long before they all found stretchers.

'This is very, um, *cosy*,' said Alex, in the darkness.

'Not so crowded. When I was a kid, sometimes when the wet comes, we got twelve ... sometimes fifteen of my relations in a shed this size.

'Ah shit,' exclaimed Alex.

'No, that's true story.'

'Not that, Henry. The roof, it's leaking right on my head.'

No one slept much that night. Between the thunder and lightning, and the equally loud snoring coming from Henry's bunk, they mostly just lay there wondering if they would be washed away and end up on some modern-day Mount Ararat. Towards dawn the rain eased a little, but it was just to tease them and before long, another wave came rolling over them.

CHAPTER 34

As the grey day emerged from its sodden night-time cocoon, Henry found Lizzy standing in the doorway watching meteorite-sized rain drops crashing to the ground. She felt him behind her.

'Where did your men go Henry? Are they out there in this?'

'Nah, that lot will be high and dry somewhere … in a cave just like you were.'

'Who were they Henry?'

'They're all my relations ... nephews, cousins, grandchildren and what not ... all family. They work on a cattle station not too far from here ... but this is their holiday time, so they go walkabout a bit and find them caves.'

'Families come in handy sometimes don't they.'

'Sure. Family is a good idea.'

'Did you ever get married Henry,' she asked, dreamily.

Henry scratched his ear and thought for a second. 'A lot of years ago I married my Nampin, she was a good woman.'

'What happened to her?'

'Ah, she got took by a croc over there at Geikie Gorge on the Fitzroy River ... bloody sad that.'

Lizzy turned. 'A crocodile? Really?'

'Yeah. She was over there visitin' them Bunaba women and she was just gettin' a drink and old Lalangkarrany he poked his head out of the water and took her away.'

'Henry that's terrible!'

'She's part of the land, part of the water now ... it's the right way ... we're all goin' there some day. We're all goin' somewhere. How's that river of yours anyway?'

'What do you mean?'

'Did it go where you were expectin' it to?'

'When?'

'I saw the look on ya face when that helicopter took Mr. Andrew away.'

'My face?'

'It was kind of confused ... like you thought you would be happy that them coppers got him, but you weren't.'

She took half a step away pulling her blanket further up over her shoulders, then looked at the old man like he was reading her mind.

'What do you mean?' she said, buying time to think.

'Never mind old Henry, he says too much sometimes.'

'No ... no, please ... tell me.'

'Ah sometimes you think you're gonna feel a certain way about something and it don't turn out that way.'

'But I was glad the police took Andrew.'

'So why ya standin' here with that same look on ya face?'

'What look?'

'The look that says I thought that would be enough ... that would be the end of it ... but it's not.'

'How can you tell?' she replied, shyly.

'Because you're standin' here watchin' that river of yours in ya mind and wonderin' where it's goin' next. That problem ya had with Mr. Andrew, well I think ya just worked out that it wasn't the real problem. Now ya know that there *is* a river of life to follow, but the only trouble is, you want to know where it's goin' to and where it ends ... and ya wanna know right now ... you want to know the end when you're only halfway there, maybe quarter of the way ... who knows?'

'But I...'

'Thing is ya see, ya don't know if either end of the river is the beginning or the end. That's because where it starts and where it finishes, sometimes they're the same bloody place ... it's what happens along that river as ya go that matters. Like Rosie told ya, sometimes sittin' down and takin' ya time is good ... take a proper good look, but right now you're too busy wantin' to be somewhere to see that there's good tucker in the river right in front of ya. Sometimes that river, it wanders off and makes nice little billabongs. It's a good place for them frogs and turtles, place for them fish to breed ... and then when they get bigger and stronger, they can swim out into that river and go where-ever they want ... but even then, the likes of them barramundi fish, they'll find a proper good hole and stick by it. Their home could be the whole bloody river, but they're choosin' the good spot. You gotta be choosin' a good spot too.'

'Here in the middle of nowhere?'

'Nah, here.' said Henry, putting his hand over his heart.

'I thought I would be okay if I could ...'

'What?'

She swallowed hard, 'If I could feel alive again.'

'Right now, you're livin' more than you know.'

'Out here, outside of my body, maybe you're right, but inside ... I don't know, maybe I'm just being too ...'

'What ya bein'?'

'Maybe I'm just being too sorry for myself.'

'Rosie told me about that husband of yours what died.'

'She did?'

'We're the same ya know. That croc took Nampin away from me and somethin' took that husband of yours away. That God up top he's got a plan for all of us ya know. When Nampin died my heart got eaten by that croc too, but God, he told me *no use bein' a silly old bugger Henry.*

260

Ya got to get on with livin'. You're a long time dead. Ya got to follow that river of yours to a livin' place, a smilin' place. Ya gotta look in that water and see ya happiness and that's inside ya ... bugger all that stuff ya gotta carry around ... life gives ya too much guilt and worry to carry, so ya just got to pack it up and send it away.'

'It's not guilt or worry Henry ... its love.'

'Love for what?'

'Love for my husband.'

'If that husband of yours was smart enough to marry a woman like you, I reckon he'd be smart enough to give ya some good advice too.'

'What do you mean?'

'He'd be tellin' ya first things first. First ya got to love yourself and then maybe you've got some left over for someone else. He'd be tellin' ya to get on with livin' rather than keepin' one foot on the other side with him. He'd be tellin' ya that you got a good heart and that a good heart like yours should never go to waste.'

'Like mother, like son, hey Henry?'

'Don't know what ya mean.' replied Henry, embarrassed. 'Anyway, that's for later. First, we got to get you lot back to where it ain't so wet.'

Lizzy kissed Henry on the cheek and when she did, the rain stopped as quickly as it had started. Off in the distance a small speck of blue sky poked its head through the grey clouds.

'About bloody time,' yawned Alex, behind them. 'Bloody hell,' he added, as he looked out the door at the sheets of water covering the ground. 'Are we floating?'

'Lots of water, but not very deep.' laughed Henry. 'That land out there will eat that water in no time ... it's very bloody thirsty.'

'Why don't you get on that phone of yours and see when that chopper can get in here?' suggested Alex.

'Good idea.'

On the way past Henry, Lizzy mouthed *thank you*. Henry nodded a polite acknowledgement.

'Thanks for what?' whispered Alex, as he walked with her.

'Never mind. It's secret business.'

She picked up her phone. 'Bloody hell! I hope this doesn't mean what I think it does?' she said, trying to turn it on.

Alex saw the look on her face.

'You're not serious?'

'I was charging it. I used all the power out there with Andrew when I had the laptop connected ...'

'And the generator died.'

'Exactly.'

'What are we going to do now?'

'Hope that they don't forget to send the chopper.'

'Does anyone want some cold bush cow?' asked Alex, carving himself a slice.

'Did you sleep?' said Lizzy, sitting down to eat.

'About as well as you by the looks of your eyes,' replied Alex, ripping at the meat.

'I've been thinking.' she replied. 'What if there really are diamonds over there at Mount Parker. What if ...'

'Oh, come on Lizzy. Don't *you* bloody start on about all that stuff.'

'Start what?'

'Behaving like Andrew. Haven't you had enough of all of this *where are the diamonds* shit yet?'

'Do *you* think there is Henry?' said Lizzy.

'Not for me to say. I saw what those fellas did up at Argyle. Rosie and them women, they got pretty upset ... and ya know what happens when women get upset don't ya?'

'No Henry, I don't,' smiled Lizzy. 'What happens?'

'Ah, that's not for this old fella to say anythin' about either.'

'But what if there was a way? What if we could ...'

'No use even talkin' about it,' interrupted Henry. 'Them *kartiya* killed the Barramundi Dreaming without askin' and that Lake Argyle took all the land from the Miriwoong people over there near Kununurra. They just told us that they were buildin' that lake and that's all there is to it.

No askin' or talkin'. They didn't care about all of them aboriginal people. Them *kartiya*, they come in and got all worried about the animals and some old buildings left over from them early cattle stations. They were all worried about that, but no-one asked them people that owned the land, they just took it and gave 'em nothin' … so ya see, us blackfellas we're not too happy … so it's no use talkin' about no more mines like you've got on your mind … no use at all.'

'But isn't that the problem Henry? No-one ever asks you. What if *you* did it? What if you and your people owned the mine or at least most of it anyway?'

'Ah what do we know about doin' that? Nah, too many relatives and important places from the Dreamtime to be lookin' after to go diggin' around with them great big bulldozers. Nah, too sad ta even think about that. Too sad.'

CHAPTER 35

By late morning, the small speck of blue sky had become an expanse of cobalt, but a dank humidity hung in the air. It was another hour before their ears picked up the sound of the chopper approaching. Suddenly it leapt over the ridge behind them and dropped onto the ground not far from the shack. The pilot didn't bother to turn off the engine, he just waved at them to get their heads down and get on board. Within seconds, they were strapped into their seats and above the shack, looking out over an expanse of sodden soil.

Heading west, they could make out a herd of wild bullocks wading through chest deep water, and on higher ground, mobs of wallabies preened themselves and tended to their young. Overhead, flocks of corellas squawked off into the blue sky looking for a meal, and as the helicopter followed the flow of a revitalized river, it startled a flock of long-legged brolgas that swarmed into the sky. Not far from where they had taken flight, a dozen freshwater crocodiles slithered into the muddy river water looking to surprise hungry wallabies that had come to feed on the fresh grass shoots sprouting along the fertile river plains. The Kimberley was undergoing an astounding metamorphosis; out of what looked like death, life had prevailed yet again. There was a season for everything.

With the sun in their eyes forcing them to squint, they weren't sure if what they saw next was real or not. Alex saw it first and jabbed his sister in the ribs, pointing towards the ground. She tapped the pilot on the shoulder. Below them, there was a man on top of a Toyota frantically waving his muddy shirt towards the sky.

'We better get down there and take a look. Poor bugger,' said the pilot.

As the ground came closer, Lizzy knew the vehicle wore the indelible stink of Wheeler's dead body. She smiled knowingly to herself.

The pilot put the helicopter down on a rocky ridge that jutted out over a small gully leading down to what a few days before had probably been a dirt road. The Toyota was hopelessly bogged, and if not for the large boulder it had ended up leaning against, probably would've floated off in a sea of mud sometime during the previous night.

'Stay here,' said the pilot, removing his headphones and opening his door.

'No, let me do this,' said Lizzy. 'I know this guy. We're old friends. He trusts me.'

'It's pretty bloody messy down there ... wouldn't you prefer ...?'

'No, no I'm absolutely looking forward to getting as dirty as possible. I'm going to be happy as a pig in mud as they say.'

'Are you sure you know what you're doing?' said Alex.

'Do you want to come?'

'Sure. I would like to meet this dipstick I've heard so much about.'

They clambered out of the helicopter and over to the edge of the ridge, slid down the gully turning their clothes ochre red as they went, and finally stopped about ten meters from Jimmy Orion's grim face.

'Have you got a problem Jimmy?' smiled Lizzy, flicking mud from her hands.

Suddenly he was still. His hands dropped to his side and his shoulders sank.

'Boy, I'm glad to see you,' he lied. 'Can ya give me a ride?'

'Sure Jimmy, but can you pay the fare?'

'What are ya talkin' about?'

'Come on Jimmy, I didn't come down in the last bloody shower.'

'Is that meant to be a joke?' whispered Alex.

'I don't know what you're talking about,' yelled Orion.

'Half a million ... the meter is ticking.'

'A ride back to my pub is the least you could do for me after I lent you my bloody truck.'

'Still smelly, is it? Mind you, you probably don't smell anything over the stink of your own greed.'

'Don't know what you're talking about.'

'Let's cut to the chase Jimmy. You give me what you took from the mine, and we'll give you a ride ... or we can just go back up there and tell our pilot that you were just waving your arms for a bit of exercise. I'll tell him you're very happy to be out here for quite a bit longer.'

'You can't just leave me here.'

'Where have I heard that before?' asked Lizzy, turning to her brother. 'Oh yes. Andrew. The ants.'

'What did you do with him?' replied Orion.

'Why do you think we did anything?'

'Listen, I might be a country hick, but I ain't stupid, so cut the crap.'

'I suggest we make that a two-way street Jimmy.'

'We can share it.'

'It's not ours to share Jimmy. It belongs to some very nice ladies, and I intend to see they all get it back.'

'Did you leave Burns out there tied to that log?'

'You saw that did you Jimmy? That's unfortunate.'

'What the fuck do you mean *unfortunate?*'

'Well, we don't want you telling the police we made Andrew say things he may not want to.'

'Yeah, well you fucking well did ... so piss off.'

'Okay Jimmy ... see you around.' yelled Lizzy, turning to go. 'Oh, and by the way, your sister Helena has been arrested in Perth. She's

Andrew's accomplice in all this shit, as it turns out. She's asking for a deal; immunity, so she can drop everyone else in it, and that probably includes you.'

'So, what? I got nothin' to do with this.'

'And just exactly what is *this*? I haven't said a thing ... so what are *you* talking about Jimmy?'

'If you're so fucking smart, you tell me.'

'I only have one question for you.'

'What's that?'

'What are you doing all the way out here in the middle of a storm?'

'Mindin' me own business. I suggest that you do the same.'

'Come on Alex, he wants to be alone. Let's go.'

'No, no wait. Them clouds over there, they're headin' this way,' squealed Orion.

'Then you had better put on your raincoat.'

'You think you're so fucking clever, don't ya?'

'No Jimmy, I just want those women to get their money back, so here are your options. You can get out the box in your truck and bring it over here or you can wait until the roads dry out. As you know, that might take some time and it's not as though another helicopter is going to be along anytime soon; at least not a friendly one like us. It might be a police force one.'

'And then what happens?'

'All I want to do is get that money back to the women. If you play along and do the right thing, I might forget this ever happened.'

'So, if I give it to ya you'll just forget about all this?'

'Maybe ... whatever *this* is.'

'How do I know ya will?'

'You don't, but I don't see that you've got much of a choice.'

'Jesus Christ ... ya tellin' me I'll just have ta trust ya to shut ya gob?'

'We're leaving in two minutes Jimmy, so I suggest you make a decision.'

'Ah fuck ya!'

Jimmy clambered down from the roof, onto the bonnet, over the bull bar and squelched through the treacle mud to the back where he opened the tailgate, tossed aside a blanket and pulled out the metal box, but miscalculated its weight, and as it slid out the back, Orion fell flat on his bum.

'It's no use to me down there, Jimmy. Bring it up here or the deal is off.'

'Shut ya face. I know you ain't goin' anywhere without this bloody money.'

'Two minutes Jimmy.'

Orion huffed and puffed and swore under his breath, but eventually he lifted the metal box out of the mud and up onto the ridge.

'Are ya fucking happy now?' he glared.

'Let's get it over to the helicopter. My brother Alex will give you a hand. Get some of that mud off it will you Jimmy ... it's messy.'

'Have ya had a look in the mirror lately?'

Alex shot him a look that said one more word out of place and he might regret it.

'No Jimmy I haven't. As it turns out, I've been a little bit busy lately.'

'Grab the other end.' commanded Alex, reaching for a handle.

They trudged the twenty meters to the helicopter where the pilot's scornful look greeted them.

'And just where do you suppose we're going to put him and that thing?' he asked, pointing at the box. 'It's a bloody Jet Ranger, not a jumbo jet. We're already over-loaded,' added the pilot. 'Look, we can get the box in the storage compartment in the back, but one of you has to stay here until I can come back and get you, otherwise ... well never mind about that ... it's up to you people to decide who stays.'

They all looked at each other wondering who would draw the short straw.

'I'm not fucking staying out here,' snapped Jimmy, pushing Lizzy out of the way, but he didn't get far before Alex clamped down hard on his shoulder.

'You know Jimmy, or whatever the fuck your name is ... I'm not having a good day, so why don't you just fucking behave? Have you got that?'

'If I don't get a ride out of here then the money stays with me.'

Lizzy stepped forward and glared at Orion nose to nose.

'Jimmy I would really love to play your macho bullshit games but let me tell *you* what's going to happen. We're leaving now, with the money, and you're going to get back to your truck to wait for the helicopter to come back. If you don't like that then my brother here is going to slug you and then we're going to forget we ever saw you out here. Am I clear?'

'No fucking way! Bloody Henry can stay. He knows how to survive out here in this shit.'

'Can't swim boss.' called Henry, already walking toward the Jet Ranger. 'Besides, it's my shift at the roadhouse tomorrow. If I don't work, I don't get no money to buy your bloody beer.'

In the distance a fresh sheaf of lightening daggers dissected the sky and the rumble of thunder rolled over the plain, momentarily startling them. The pilot took off his sunglasses and wiped his brow.

'Look, you can all bloody stay here for all I care. I'm leavin' now, so whoever is comin', get onboard because I don't want to fly into all that shit.'

'You're gonna bloody leave me out here aren't ya?'

'Think of it as a slight delay in departure Jimmy ... it happens at airports all the time.'

'I'm not gonna forget this.'

'That's funny because I can feel my memory coming back too,' smiled Lizzy, holding her fingers up to her temples.

'Fuck off ... just make sure Captain Dickhead there doesn't forget to come back for me.'

'How could we forget someone so sweet and loveable like *you* Jimmy?'

The pilot shook his head and walked away. 'Bloody tourists. Not worth the bloody trouble.'

He climbed into his seat, strapped himself in, put on his headphones, flicked the ignition switch, the turbine engine bit, the rotors sprang to life and the blades started to spin. He was leaving with or without them, so Alex and Henry loaded the box into the back while Lizzy tried to placate Orion.

'Look at it this way Jimmy ...' she yelled, over the noise of the helicopter. 'It's either a few more hours in your truck or ten years in jail. I know which one I'd pick.'

Jimmy rolled his eyes. 'Get hold of Helena when you get back. Tell her what happened. She won't believe me. She'll think I knocked all the money off for meself.'

'Why would she think that Jimmy?'

'There's no fucking trust in the world anymore.'

'Gotta go. See you around.'

'Call her.'

'It's the least that I could do Jimmy. Not.'

They travelled in silence with only the occasional crackle of radio noise to interrupt the thud of the rotors above them. Henry let his head fall against the window while Lizzy watched him out the corner of her eye. The look on his face was the same one he had the first time they drove towards The Bungle Bungles, a faraway dreaming, that at one time she couldn't have hoped to understand, but now she had a good idea what was going on inside the old man's head, at least she thought she did, because while it was the same, it was different. This time it had a tinge of regret about it, and around the edges, a softness, a kind of loving look, a look that she had often caught herself having when she thought about Tony. She put her hand on his knee. He turned and gave her a half-smile then looked back out to his Dreamtime. Half an hour later they landed.

'Waddya gonna do with this money?' whispered Henry to Lizzy, as he

270

and Alex lugged it towards a small building.

'I was kind of hoping you had somewhere we could stash it until we could get it back to the women.'

'Yeah sure missus, old Henry, he's got plenty of places…only you might never see it again.'

'Don't worry Henry. Even if my brother doesn't trust you, I do.'

'I'll call the roadhouse and get someone to bring your car down.'

'You look like you've been swimming in that river of yours.' laughed Alex.

Lizzy was still wearing the floral dress she wore to the Eagle Bay beach dinner, except it was a soaked, muddy mess that looked more like a dirty dishcloth. Her hair was so tussled that she wouldn't have been surprised to find a stray bug roosting amongst it and any make-up was a smudge in the past.

'It's my new look.' smiled Lizzy. 'I kind of like it.'

'There's a lot of new things about you.' he replied, flatly. 'A lot. What did you do with my sister?'

Lizzy smirked. 'Maybe the real one came back.'

CHAPTER 36

They were about to leave the roadhouse but, as usual, there was no sign of Henry, so Lizzy went looking for him and found him at the back of the restaurant, raking leaves.

'Aren't you going to say good-bye?'

'Hate good-byes. No use jarrak jarrak ... just got to bloody get on with it.'

'Were you just going to let us leave without saying anything?'

'Nah, I said plenty already.'

'Is there anything else you want to say Henry?'

'Nah, I'm done talkin'.'

'You seem upset?'

'Nah, not upset, no use gettin' upset about nothin' at my age.'

'Then what is it Henry?' she said, holding him by both arms so he would stop raking.

Henry took a deep breath.

'I was just thinkin' about my Nampin ... while we're comin' here in that helicopter, I was lookin' down on all them mountains and land ... all of them trees and every one of them new rivers ... the whole time I was wonderin' which one was Nampin ... wonderin' which one she was part of now ... just dreamin' about yesterday ... that's all ... an old man alone with his thoughts.'

'You still miss her don't you Henry?'

'Every bloody day missus ... every night when I'm lookin' up at those stars ... but when you're up there in that helicopter, ya lookin' out over everything like that Kaleruny, the Rainbow Serpent could do ... he's lookin' over all the things he made ... lookin' down, I can see the land just like in them paintings that them fellas are doin' here at Turkey Creek. How do they know what the ground looks like from up in the sky when they've never been up in no helicopter? How do they know what Ngapuny, that God up top, sees?'

'I don't know Henry.'

'I'll tell ya, it's because them people that do the paintings, they're not people, they're rocks and mountains and dirt and trees and rivers and all of them things talk to each other.'

'Maybe they can tell you where Nampin is?'

'She is anywhere I want her to be ... that's what ya gotta feel inside ya. Sure I'm lookin' and wonderin' but I'm also knowin' ... knowin' in my heart and in my head.'

'You're a good man Henry.'

'I was thinkin' what a good woman Nampin was and how much you remind me of her ... you're both strong, but you, you still got that sad bit that sits in ya eyes ... like I told ya back at the mine, it's not over for you yet ... I just don't want ya to wander too far from that river of yours and never be able to find your way back. That mother of mine she gave you her name ...'

'Nangari'

'That's makin' you ma aunty, so you're my relation too ... it's always sad when a relative goes away.'

'Who said I'm going anywhere?'

'What do ya meanin'?'

'Thanks to you and Rosie I think I know exactly where that river of my life is flowing. Besides, I think Rosie has got a plan that she might need a little help with.'

Henry's smile returned, but the whites of his paling-sized teeth stood in sharp contrast to the new sky above them. While they were talking, it had turned a deep purple mixed with a dirty green and an eerie wind had sprung up from the west.

'You're not goin' nowhere ... at least not for a while,' said Henry, looking up.

CHAPTER 37

Under a blanket of blue sky and a sweltering mid-afternoon sun, Lizzy and Rosie sat on a low ridge watching the hive of activity below them. Lizzy's hair was tied back in a sensible ponytail, her skin was well-tanned and there wasn't a skerrick of make-up on her face. She wore dirty moleskin trousers, a rust-coloured shirt, and a pair of well-worn riding boots. Rosie wore the same yellow smock dress which had served her well for years, and even though it was a little faded, like Rosie herself, it was her favourite and she knew that an important day such as the one ahead was not the day to wear anything but that.

'Did you ever think this would actually happen?' said Lizzy.

'Took some good talkin' to them bloody elders.'

'Yes it did Rosie. I'm glad you wanted my help. I feel very happy here.'

'Ya part of the land now, just like us.'

'I'm wearing half of it anyway,' she smiled, slapping dust off her sleeve.

'You've been a good friend to us *Kija* mob. We got a lot to thank our sister Nangari for.'

'It's you that's done it all Rosie, you. I just helped a little, that's all.'

'Nah, sometimes it's not about what ya do, but how ya been doin' it.

275

Like I told ya a couple of years ago … when those mining fellas dug up that barramundi hill, only some of us knew what was happening, but you, you helped us all to sit down and talk about it. You showed us the way and ya even got that grumpy old bugger Possum Jack to say his bit.'

'He was a hard one.'

'Silly old bugger,' laughed Rosie, plaiting grass.

'Do you remember what he said when everyone had agreed?'

Rosie smiled and started to mimic the old man.

'You're an old woman Rosie and you're sitting here on the ground drawing pictures in the dirt and making us think that us mob can have all kind of things … but what ya got to remember is that they are all just things … not like remembering where ya come from … but that's the place where we start and finish.'

'Then you said …'

'Ahh, no use remembering the silly stuff.'

'You looked him right in the eye and said, the things we are talking about here today are not stoves and cars and books, we are talking about our survival. Ngarrangkarni … our Dreamtime, it's about tomorrow as well as yesterday. That's when old Jack knew you were serious, and he knew you were right. I saw it in his eyes. I even saw them go a little bit red. I thought I was going to cry. In that moment Rosie, I knew you had done it. I knew you had convinced them.'

'But it is about survival. It's about that long walk towards the horizon. It's going to be a lot easier for everyone if we can do something about unemployment and health and education. That's why it's all been written into the agreement … but not just your *kartiya* education, the Dreamtime too. The Dreamtime stories might be spiritual and mystical, but they're also practical. Old people like me. we're not going to be around much longer, so we got to find a way to make yesterday into tomorrow … and it won't happen doing it the same way we've always been. No use hoping that things will get better if ya don't do something about it.'

Lizzy smiled and took the old woman's hand in hers and stroked it like it was the most precious thing in the whole world.

'Yes, you needed to do something different, but you did that Rosie. You knew. You know what they say, doing the same thing again and again and expecting a different result is just plain crazy.'

'Amen to that. I been praying to that God up top. Asking for his help.'

'I think he might have smiled on you Rosie but for it to really work, us white fellas, we have to show a genuine respect for the land and the culture that's so much a part of who you *Kija* and other tribes are ... but no matter how much you and I want that to be the case, it's going to take time ... that's time you lot ... don't have ... so while the rest of the world is catching up, it's up to you and your friends down there, to make sure it happens.'

'I couldn't have done it without you sister, but this, all this, is because of you. You made me realize that it had to be done. It was always strange to me that the land can hold so much wealth, but the people who have always lived here could be so poor. It just didn't seem right. If the conditions my people are forced to live in stay the same, then we'll always have issues that hold us back.'

'You're fixing all that and today is just the first day.'

'We've got to make it good for our kids to stay here. They got to be healthy and have jobs and houses. They got to get an education. We've got to keep as many of them here for as long as we can. It's no use them running off to somewhere else. Our culture won't survive that way. There has got to be something here for them, they have to learn to love their culture all over again and then they have to pass it on to their kids and their kids after them. Part of the story is now about the kartiya girl what brung the rain,' smiled Rosie, remembering the first time they had met.

'No Rosie, I'll soon be forgotten.'

'Nah misses. Not true. Just you wait and see.'

'Like you been telling me, if we get this plan right, there's no telling what will happen next.'

'If it all works out, then all kinds of jobs will be opening up ... tourism, agriculture, retail, government services ... you've just got to get a healthy, educated lot who turn up for work ... that's not so much to ask ... is it?' smiled Lizzy.

'Them kids at school, they need to know there are good jobs out there for 'em when they done finished. They got to see their relations working and making that money to support their families.'

'It's going to work out just fine.' added Lizzy, putting her arm around the old woman's shoulders, and resting her cheek on her.

'And maybe there might even be something for the women's side, hey…might get us a bus ... maybe ... aah never bloody mind. Don't listen ta old Rosie she's just flapping her gums.'

Below them, a swarm of people sweated as they put the finishing touches to the celebrations for the official opening of Kanany Mine, the diamond mine owned and run by the *Kija* people. It had been financed with a little help from their new sister Nangari, when she sold Rosie's rain stones, and Peter O'Leary at Black Peak Mining, along with some of his mining friends. It had taken two years, a good deal of patience, but Rosie finally managed to persuade the *Kija* elders that no scared sites would be harmed and that if everything went to plan, the future of the Dreaming and their children was assured. Before Lizzy left Turkey Creek, after the wet season storm, two years before, Rosie had told Lizzy her idea. What grew below them were the buds of that conversation. Lizzy never did tell Rosie that she was thinking the same thing.

When the wet season had passed Lizzy returned to Turkey Creek and Rosie and Henry had taken her to sit down under the shade of a scribbly desert oak not far from Mount Parker. Rosie hardly said a word on the drive out and that made Lizzy worry that the old woman's plan for *Kija* self-sufficiency may never see the light of day, but after a long moment staring at her sister, the old woman finally smiled and said, *the elders have agreed, but that old Possum Jack he said that there is one condition.*

'Condition?'

'That bugger, he can still surprise this old woman. He said, *you must remember that all things are temporary if your name is eternity*. This is the place,' Rosie told her. 'this is where we'll dig, but no further than the three hills over there and the bend in the land over there, this will be Kanany.'

'It means *digging stick,* doesn't it?'

Rosie smiled and patted Lizzy's hand. 'You been doin' ya homework.'

Soon after that, Peter O'Leary showed the old woman how to file an exploration lease and arranged for JORC compliant core samples to be drilled. The whole deal was then wrapped in an agreement they called The Kanany Trust, that would ensure all profits flowed back to the *Kija* people in a managed and orderly way and that investors were properly compensated. The trust would be responsible for investing any profits for future generations of *Kija*, as well as investing in health, education, housing and employment programs…and maybe even something for the women's side.

'Come on. We better get down there. I think they're expecting me ta say something.' said Rosie with a cheeky grin. 'Buggered if I know what.'

Lizzy smiled and dusted herself off. 'Yes, I suppose we should, besides there are some very special people I would like you to meet. They should be here by now.'

'Ma new leg … it works bloody good.' replied Rosie, getting to her feet. 'This titanium stuff is so light … it feels like there's nothing there at all.'

Soon they were among a crowd of people gathered to celebrate the opening. Old Possum Jack sat under a canvas awning teaching a group of children to paint. To his right a huddle of *Kija* women were busy putting the finishing touches to the celebration feast of wallaby, lizard and bush turkey. Behind them, a slightly annoyed teacher was busy finishing off rehearsals for a children's choir. Henry and two other men were building a fire for the smoking ceremony that would happen later in the afternoon and under a large red and white striped tent with no sides, a small group of men, who looked like they were important, ran their fingers around their buttoned-up collars trying to keep cool.

Off to Lizzy's left she saw her brother Alex with his arm around a woman's waist. Natalie. She had met her the night before. They were talking to John Murphy, the lawyer, showing off their new engagement ring. To her right, a small group of white women stood under umbrellas and wide-brimmed hats chattering away like they had known each other forever. They were all the women that Andrew Burns had stolen money from. Lizzy had given their money back and Rosie had offered them the opportunity to invest in a real mine. They had taken some time to think about it but once they were convinced that the old woman was genuine, they all agreed to be part of it. Even Ellen Hansen, the woman who had the close shave with Andrew Burns at Margaret River, had joined in. They waved as Lizzy and Rosie walked by and they waved back and pointed to the drinks tent where trestle tables yawned under the weight of soft drinks and ice. Sergeant Manfredi and his offsider stood to one side with unnecessary stern looks painted on their faces, but it was none of these people that Lizzy and Rosie were headed for.

Seated on two deck chairs, in the shade of a giant boab tree, were an elderly man and woman. The woman was dressed in a neat white cotton dress and white shoes with a small heel. She held a green umbrella over her head. The man wore a camel-coloured linen suit, a white shirt, and a striped tie. While he waited for the ceremony to begin, he took turns alternately fanning himself and swatting flies with a newspaper.

'Mamaka, Babaka, mother, father,' Lizzy called, holding out her hands and breaking into a jog.

Smiles spread across her parent's faces and Constantine helped his frail wife, Eleni, to her feet, so by the time their daughter reached them, they fell into a huddle of arms and kisses where they stayed, each breathing in the other knowing that whatever had gone before had been forgiven during the previous two years while they had got to know each other all over again.

'Mama, Pappa,' said Lizzy, finally taking a step back. 'I would like you to meet my very good friend, Rosie.'

Constantine pumped Rosie's old hand. 'We all heara so mucha about you. It'sa like we know you already.'

But Eleni was not so forthcoming. She stood stiffly with her handbag over her arm pursing her lips and staring at Rosie. Rosie met her stare with a wizened softness and just as Constantine was about to chide her, Eleni stepped towards Rosie and held her by the forearms.

'We are the mother of the same daughter,' she said, just loud enough for her daughter and husband to hear. Then she hugged Rosie. 'She a tell me ... that you are her river ... it'sa you that she looks at to see herself ...'

'I don't think ...' started Rosie, acutely aware that another mother's feelings were being hurt.

'No, no, it'sa okay. Long time ago my mother she died, she was a very brave woman ... but I was just a small girl and no have anybody ... my father he tried to protect her, but he was killed too ... my aunty, she wiped away my tears and helped me. She showed me how to be a woman. She told me the things that my mother never could ... I looked at her and saw my mother ... I know she's not my mother, but I love her just like she was ... our daughter she loves you just like you are her mother ... I no die, but I not there for a very long time ... stubborn these other two are ... now she has two mothers ... it's good ... no?'

'It's good. Very good,' smiled Rosie,

Before they could say anymore, a small aboriginal child ran breathlessly up to Rosie and yanked at her dress.

'Quick, come quick. That Governor General man he's here ... comin' up the new road now.'

Rosie looked at her new sister then Lizzy's mother with a look that asked them what she should do.

'Shoo,' they both said, in unison.

Eleni and Lizzy laughed, and Rosie hurried off to meet the King's man.

'She bought a new dress for this, but she's been so busy I've been too afraid to remind her to get changed.' smiled Lizzy. 'She'll just have to meet that Governor General like she is.'

'Like she is … is very good.' nodded Eleni, as a tear ran down her cheek.

A few minutes later Eleni, Constantine and Lizzy saw smoke rising above the assembled crowd.

'That's the manthe, it's a welcome ceremony,' explained Lizzy. 'It gives safe passage to everyone that comes here today … it means that all of Rosie's ancestors … all of her relations, they'll look after us.'

'Can they do anything about the heat?' asked Constantine, running his finger around the inside of his collar.

'It's a cool day today. Wait till you see a hot one.'

When the Governor General had completed his speech and turned the first sod of soil with an elaborately painted digging stick, the Master of Ceremonies introduced Rosie.

The old woman hobbled up onto the stage and stood behind a microphone. She looked uncomfortable but after a little shuffling, began to speak softly.

'When I was a young girl, my children, they got taken away from me. My son Henry over there, he came back, but my daughter, well, she is gone for good. Maybe she's lookin' for her mother and maybe one day I'll find her, but today, well today, I have a new daughter. The second one is Nangari, that pretty lady over there, who lots of ya know now as Lizzy Lawson, but that isn't her real name.'

The crowd hushed and cast sideways looks at each other. Sergeant Manfredi looked up as if he might be needed at any moment.

'Sometimes she is known as Nangari, sister of Rosie and therefore aunty of my son Henry, but she is also the sister of Alex and daughter of Constantine and Eleni, but her real name, her proper good name is Anastasia Dimitriades … it is where she comes from.'

To one side of the crowd Eleni squeezed her husband's arm and they looked at each other knowing that while their daughter had gone away all those years before, she had finally returned. Next to them Lizzy stood silently with tears running down her cheeks, realizing that her season of knowing had arrived and that her river, as she had hoped it would one day, had doubled back on itself. She turned and hugged her parents. Her mother cried. Her father cried. Alex smirked a knowing smile.

'So why am I talking about Nangari today?' continued Rosie. 'Well, we got a lot of important people here today and that's good, but the idea for this mine, this way to help us *Kija* people was born because her love for us *Kija* people was greater than the pain what she had inside herself when she came to this place, and for that, we all need to say thank you. All this is because of my proper good new sister and Kanany, with your help, will be a proper good mine. That's all I wanna say. Enjoy ya selves today because tomorrow, lots of us have got work to do.'

As Rosie left the stage, the eerie wail of didgeridoos and the slow rhythmic clap of music sticks filled the air. The crowd stepped back to form a large circle and forty *Kija* men dressed in loin cloths and covered in patterns made from white mowuntum clay, weaved their way into the middle of the circle in two long, parallel lines. They moved slowly around the circle like a long snake before they finally stopped along with the didgeridoo music. From the back of the crowd the clack clack, clack clack of two music sticks parted the crowd and a *Kija* man, wearing a rope wig of long dark hair, danced his way along the snake of men stopping every so often and looking in between them.

'This is for you,' said Henry, walking up to Lizzy with Rosie beside him. 'This is our proper thank you.'

'Thank you? For what?'

'It was you what planted the seed for all this sister.'

'But I only...' protested Lizzy.

'Sometimes it's what ya don't say that's important,' replied the old woman. 'Henry, he told me that ya wanted ta see a corroboree ... now you've got one named after ya.'

'Me?'

'Yes.' said Henry. 'This corroboree, in English, it's called Nangari's River.'

'But why?'

Henry looked at Lizzy like she had *a few kangaroos loose in her top paddock* but when her face showed that she was none-the-wiser why there would be a corroboree to honor her, he simply replied, 'Respect missus.'

'I don't understand.'

'You watch missus ... that long line of men ... two rows ... see ... that's your river ... windin' in and out ... that single person, that's you ... see your long black hair ...'

The single dancer stopped and jerked his head from left to right and then back again.

'That's you findin' out which way to go ... not knowin' ... and look ... look now ... that face from the river is lookin' back at you ... that's you lookin' at yourself ... see, he's got the black hair too.'

With that, the river men moved forward winding their way around the circle while the single dancer stopped and peered into the distance. He was wondering where they had gone but then the river men returned and flowed in and out of the people. While the didgeridoos and the clack, clack of the music sticks ebbed and flowed, the river moved slowly along either side of the single dancer.

'That's you now, goin' with the river ... see that thing with the wings comin' in there now ... that's your plane landin' at Turkey Creek when you dropped me off...and now ... it's flyin' away ... see that river ... now it's all dried up.'

Just as Henry said it, the forty dancers evaporated into the crowd, but a single didgeridoo kept playing, and as its long mournful notes drifted off into the blue winter sky, the paper mâché plane returned.

'Look now.' said Henry. 'That circle they're makin' is Rosie meetin' with all us *Kija* and see there, that black haired person watchin' from the side, that's you ... that fella throwin' his hands in the air, that's Possum Jack ... he wanted to be himself in your corroboree.'

'But why Henry? Why are they doing this for *me*?'

There was a tear in her eye.

'Like I told ya … respect … see that now … that's you, and all them men, they're not the river no more … they're the rainbow serpent takin' you away to be with him so your memory can live forever.'

'I don't know what to say,' sobbed Lizzy.

'Like Rosie said, sometimes nothin' is good,' smiled Henry, holding his hat to his chest.

As the music died down and the dancers slowly made their exits, applause broke out and the feast began. While some people lined up for food, others joined small groups where men played guitars and sang songs. On the stage, where the Governor General had made his speech, the choir from Rosie's Ngalangangpum School in Turkey Creek sang. The grumpy teacher seemed happy with their performance. In another large tent a long board had been set up and a line had formed for people to put their handprints on it as a permanent reminder of this great day. Above the handprints were the words, *we own our future.*

The celebrations continued long into the afternoon and as night fell, small fires and tents of all description sprang up all around the main area. Children laughed, dogs yapped, and music drifted on the evening breeze up to the ridge above the celebrations where Lizzy had gone to be alone. She sat staring up at the full moon that hung in the sky like a dinner plate, fondling the diamond pendant she always wore around her neck, deep in thought, wondering what Tony might make of all this, when Rosie sat down beside her. For a while the old woman said nothing, but then she took Lizzy's hand in hers, black on white, and followed her gaze up towards the moon.

'You know, I reckon there might be more than one fella who will live forever.'

ACKNOWLEDGEMENTS

I would particularly like to acknowledge the permission given by the late Sister Veronica Ryan, to use her book, From Digging Sticks to Writing Sticks to paint the colour of Rosie's life. While the name is different, everything about her life is based on real events; events that perhaps one day, history will judge white Australia harshly for.

I would also like to thank Greg Barron at Stories of Oz Publishing for his confidence in my story and all the hard work to get it out there.
Writing is a solitary profession so without the help and continual feedback from friends this story would not be possible. I would particularly like to say thank you to my 'brother' Murray McInnes and his wife Susan.

Chris Muir worked in advertising for many years and has travelled widely. His adventurous spirit has seen him trekking the Kokoda Track, being kidnapped by orang-utans in Borneo, driving herds of brumbies across the Australian Alps, living with the Masai in Tanzania, spending months on end in the Congo (the setting for his first novel, A Savage Garden), living with gorillas on the top of mountains and climbing Mount Kilimanjaro. He has seen the worst of humanity in the prelude to the Rwandan genocide, canoed down the Zambezi River, hot air ballooned across the Serengeti, sailed a dhow across Lake Victoria and lived in New York, London, and Singapore.

These days he writes full time. Season of the River is his second novel and he's working on three more.